# Insinuendo

## Murder in the Museum

Miriam Clavir

BAYEUX

INSINUENDO: MURDER IN THE MUSEUM
© Copyright 2012 Bayeux Arts, Inc. and Miriam Clavir

Published by
Bayeux Arts, Inc.
119 Stratton Crescent SW,
Calgary, Canada T3H 1T7

**www.bayeux.com**
First printing: October 2012

Cover and Book design: PreMediaGlobal
Cover image courtesy The Corning Museum of Glass
Plaque (half) with satyr head
Roman Empire, Alexandria or Rome possibly, late 1st century B.C. – mid
1st century A.D.
Translucent blue and multicolored glass; molded and inlaid
    H. 2.7 cm
Collection of The Corning Museum of Glass, Corning, New York (59.1.95)

Library and Archives Canada Cataloguing in Publication

Clavir, Miriam, 1948-
    Insinuendo : murder in the museum / Miriam Clavir.

ISBN 978-1-897411-38-4
    I. Title.

PS8605.L378I58 2012       C813'.6       C2012-903024-4

Printed in Canada

Books published by Bayeux Arts are available at special quantity discounts
to use in premiums and sales promotions, or for use in corporate training
programs. For more information, please write to Special Sales, Bayeux Arts,
Inc., 119 Stratton Crescent SW, Calgary, Canada T3H 1T7.

The ongoing publishing activities of Bayeux Arts, under its "Bayeux" and
"Gondolier" imprints, are supported by the Canada Council for the Arts,
the Government of Alberta, Alberta Multimedia Development Fund,
and the Government of Canada through the Book Publishing Industry
Development Program.

Canada Council for the Arts    Conseil des Arts du Canada

**Government of Alberta** ■

LIVRES CANADA BOOKS

For friends,
and family,
especially John.

# Contents

# *Acknowledgements*

My sincere thanks to Dr. James Russell, Professor Emeritus, and Prof. Hector Williams, both from the Department of Classical, Near Eastern and Religious Studies at the University of British Columbia, for their absolutely invaluable help with the Classical antiquities in this novel. My appreciation and great thanks to The Corning Museum of Glass, N.Y., for the perfect cover image. Enormous thanks also to my friends and colleagues who advised on elements in the story or who read drafts of the manuscript. I am particularly indebted to those who are writers and/or editors: Cynthia Flood, Nancy Richler, Cheryl and Elaine Freedman, Susan Gillis, Tom Wayman and John Donlan. If I have not followed well enough all the excellent advice I received, it is entirely my own fault. Special thanks as well to Ashis Gupta and everyone at Bayeux Arts.

I am indebted as well to MOA, the Museum of Anthropology at the University of British Columbia, for providing both the setting for this fictional mystery story and the setting for a non-fictional, real-life and virtual, unsurpassed museum experience.

# Author's Note

This book is a work of fiction set in a genuine place, MOA, the Museum of Anthropology at the University of British Columbia, Vancouver, Canada. The real MOA, however, has never been the site of murder or scandalous breaches of museum ethics such as forgery. In this novel, the incidents in the plot and the characters who speak are the products of the author's imagination. Based in reality, however, are the descriptions of British Columbia, and the information about museum collections, preservation and restoration. In addition, Norval Morrisseau, the Anishnaabe painter who is mentioned, was an important Canadian artist but never painted the work described, "The Big Creation". The painter Graham Bells is fictional. The reader is encouraged to visit MOA in Vancouver or at < http://www.moa.ubc.ca > but to remember that the elements of the plot in this novel never occurred and that the characters and what they say have no connection with any person past or present, living or dead.

# Chapter

# 1

∞

## My Work Week Begins Sunday, June 8, 2008

"You'll see a sumo wrestler dressed up like an antiques dealer. Or the other way around. You'll find him. Here," Reiko said, cradling the VIP parking pass the man had demanded, as if she held a precious illuminated manuscript. "He's not a big fan of Conservation. Give this to him gently."

I took the pass from Reiko's gloved hands and pushed open the doors of the Museum of Anthropology. Stepping outside, inhaling the forest scents of fresh cedar and hemlock, I was struck again by how much I already loved this place and my new job.

Not ten yards away stood a distinguished-looking man, briefcase open on the hood of a sleek black sedan. The back of his leather coat stretched taut against his shoulders as he rearranged his papers. He could qualify as a sumo wrestler in every dimension except clothing.

"Mr. Foley?"

"Just Cuyler, please," he turned, smiling at my voice. "And you are . . . ?"

"Berenice Cates. The museum's new intern in the Conservation Department. Call me Berry."

"New intern?" Most people, Cuyler Foley included, couldn't help commenting when they saw my grayish hair and southbound face.

"My secret to staying young." I pushed two fingers through my thinning hair as if primping in front of a mirror. "Never leave school."

Foley chuckled, unconsciously for an instant smoothing his own remaining strands, and said. "Well, as a student, then, are you coming to my lecture? New discoveries." The big man beamed. "The media are here. Or aren't you interested in the Classical world?"

"In fact I'm the one looking after the artifacts for you."

The smile collapsed. "Oh yes, here we go again in this museum. Reiko's rules. We can't be trusted, only the Conservation Department handles the kinds of antiquities I've worked with all my life."

He stared down for my response. Stepping back automatically, I held the parking pass out at arm's length and wished I'd written "Courtesy of Conservation" on its envelope. Foley shoved it in the car and snapped his briefcase shut.

"During the lecture you'll answer to my instructions?" His eyes dared me to talk back.

"My supervisor is Reiko Smithson, the Head of Conservation," I said, and folded my arms. Mature students have some advantages over the young. I added, "And she's not going to be there."

Foley's grin reappeared, and with a gentlemanly mock bow he said, "Thank you very much for the pass. Rather insulting to pay top dollar for a day's parking when you're the one giving the lecture, don't you think? Now I've time for the library." He glanced towards the museum entrance. "First, though, Berry, there's a special present I need to buy for my grandson. May I be so bold as to ask if you get a staff discount at the giftshop?"

We reached the museum's glass doors just as more West Coast rain started. Foley headed straight for the stuffed animals and I waited by the cash where I could see the coastal First Nations silver jewelry gleaming in its closely-monitored cabinets. The inch-wide bracelets had struck me as ostentatious when I first arrived three months ago, but now I had my heart set on one with its curving, elegant designs. Foley purchased a furry Haida bear that was no commonplace toy but a miniature replica in plush of one of the museum's signature pieces.

"You've got a brave grandson not to be frightened by that bear. What a fierce face."

"The boy's special, all right. He'll like this, he loves the carvings here. I'm rather proud he's developing this aesthetic." Foley surveyed the nearby shelves with a professional eye. "MOA hasn't given in to the market demand for cuddly cuteness and I applaud that. They're first-class with their reproductions. Not to mention the originals."

I could be classy too. "I've got my eye on one of the silver bracelets."

"Buy it. I keep a watch on the market for Native art as well as Classical antiquities. You'll love it, and it'll maintain its value even though you wear it." His smile warmed and I thought he might be about to ask for a commission, but he finished with, "Trust me, you can't lose."

Except the money I was putting aside to pay off my midlife-crisis student debts. I headed empty-handed down into the stuffiness of the museum basement. I needed to know from Reiko in her own words what she'd expect me to do if someone like Foley, or anyone else not MOA personnel, tried to touch or move one of the antiquities. Or do anything else forbidden by museum rules.

⁓◦⟨♡⟩◦⁓

The door to the Collections workroom was propped open. This breach of museum safety shook me, even if it was only the drab staff corridor I was in now that the door opened onto. In the workroom I saw no one, not one person to monitor the open door, a huge security lapse. Especially today. The lab table in the centre, its beige surface usually no different from any of the others, held the museum's newest treasures. The antiquities selected for Foley's lecture were breathtaking: two Greek and Roman bronze statues, more fine metalwork examples from knife blades to hairpins, and several exquisite ancient ceramics depicting men on galloping horses and processions of robed women with head wreaths. The museum's Classics collection was known as the best in western Canada.

The Conservation lab and workrooms were side-by-side in the basement, and the air was more stagnant down here than upstairs. Today the atmosphere was worse than usual; the climate control system had gone on the fritz late last week and had not been fixed in time for the weekend. The auditorium where Foley's lecture would take place had a high ceiling, but Foley had better be interesting or the hundred or so people in there would be comatose from lack of oxygen. This might work in my favour, though, if no one moved out of their seats. Reiko would be gone from the museum by lunchtime, and despite my newness, I was the one in charge of the security of the new antiquities.

"No Foley?" Reiko's voice piped up from the far end of the forty-foot workroom. She appeared around the corner of a supplies shelf carrying a tissue-sized box of surgical gloves, the form-fitting blue nitrile ones we all wore to handle precious objects.

"Shit *de merde*, you scared me. I didn't think anyone was here."

"Scared you more than the Colossus? Where is he?"

"Off to the library. He didn't like it that I'll be handling the antiquities for him."

"Heartbreak Hotel for that big boy. Look, I found more gloves." She stopped in front of me. "So, what'd you tell him about touching the antiquities?" Reiko seized every "teaching moment" for her staff and students.

"I told him I answered to you."

She gave me a thumbs up. "And? How'd he react?"

"Fine once I said you wouldn't be there."

Reiko threw back her head and hooted. Her energy was infectious even while her petite figure played the role of demure demoiselle. Reiko was a good four inches shorter than me, her long dark hair tied back in a trademark ponytail, lab coat covering all but the hem of one of the simple black dresses she often wore. She could slip easily from the dirty work of moving old boxes of artifacts, to the delicacy of conservation treatments on rare works of art, and on afterwards to the elegant receptions for donors. But Reiko's body and heart lived for jiving to fifties rock 'n' roll.

My first week on the job had been awful, me pretending to be both the humble new intern and still act with the confidence of life experience. Reiko, fifteen years younger, joked and challenged and made sure to end each session with a boss-like serious discussion. Now me the newbie wasn't afraid to ask stupid questions, and Reiko wasn't hiding her good spirits behind her position of being in charge.

I said, "What do you want me to do if Mr. Foley starts to handle the artifacts? He knows I'm only an intern."

"What do you think you should do?"

"I'd be uncomfortable shaming a famous expert. What about letting him go ahead but having my hands out so it's obvious I'm trying to prevent accidents?"

"Run around with a net to catch the falling vase? Berry, tell it to him like it is. Before the lecture. Reiterate your instructions, go over the rules. Signed, 'From Reiko with love.'"

I cringed, and Reiko started singing an Elvis song about being evil.

"Reiko, I don't get it." I sat down on one of the metal stools used for the high lab tables. "You're adamant about the handling rules but the door to the Workroom was left open."

"Use the active voice. Own your issues. 'But Reiko, you left the door open.'"

I grunted. This was starting to be a difficult day. "How exactly do I tell my supervisor she committed a breach of security?"

"You're telling Reiko, the person you lunch and joke with, not just your supervisor." She spoke softly but firmly. "Try it out."

Reddening, I began. "Reiko, the door was open to the corridor, and when I walked in, I couldn't see you."

She nodded.

"If I couldn't see you, you couldn't see the open door. Isn't that a breach of security?"

"You're absolutely right. Before I answer, tell me what *you* did then."

"The truth? I just stood there." She'd asked for it. "You aren't careless. You're very principled with your work. This wasn't like you. So either someone new like the Collections Assistants had left the door open, or something was wrong. Then you showed up with the box of gloves."

"My fault for not closing the door when I went for supplies. You're right. I have to remember next time." Reiko began pulling on her blue surgical gloves, the signal to get back to work. "I appreciate the compliment about being principled. Thanks."

"But that's just it. Reiko, you've got enough seniority to decide policy." My voice was strained. "But enforcing some rules like 'handling,' and breaking others? I came here because your specialty is conservation ethics."

"I admit I got too engrossed ferreting out the gloves we'd ordered. Good for you for pointing out the situation. Thank you. It took too much time and the door was left open because it's so stuffy down here. The fault was mine."

"Use the active voice," I murmured.

Reiko grinned. "Only if you admit you didn't come here because of my supposed sterling reputation. You came 'cause it was a job offer."

Reiko had a reputation for pure honesty, damn her. And mischievousness. She was right. After my first internship ended early, after returning home to Toronto from my humiliation at the Seattle museum, still needing to work a full year to graduate as a professional conservator, after subsequent months of wrenching open dozens of form letter rejections—the prize being two "you were shortlisted; what more do you want?" insinuations—after I'd needed money and almost wrecked my spine shelving stock at a box store, I'd found myself back on Heaven's "A" list. Finally, I'd had a real job offer, and a fabulous one. I had beaten, bounced, and trounced the other applicants for the coveted internship at MOA, the Museum of Anthropology on the campus of the University of British Columbia. I would move to a great city: snowcapped mountains beside the ocean. I would work in a landmark museum, in a job environment that followed the university model; staff kept an open-office policy, so colleagues and students could knock on anyone's door and ask questions. The perfect placement. Until today, when I'd already had to correct my supervisor, and soon would be telling a renowned antiquities expert he couldn't touch the artifacts that were the stars of his lecture.

"Why'd you hire *me* anyway?"

"You were good in the phone interview. And I wanted something new. I'd never had someone older in a junior position."

Too true. Berry Cates had graduated from conservation school with hot flashes.

---

Fifteen minutes later the morning was shot. Professor Theo Younge, MOA's noted expert in Greek and Roman and organizer of today's lecture, had marched into the workroom straight to the dazzling antiquities and picked up a large amphora with his bare hands.

Reiko, with the sharpness of a schoolmarm, commanded him to put it down.

"What could possibly happen if I touch it? The body's hard." The chief curator's voice mirrored his statement.

"Berry?" Reiko said. "How would you respond?"

I already had the unenviable task of telling the invited guest lecturer he couldn't touch the material he was lecturing about, and now, in this windowless workroom downstairs, Reiko had neatly dumped me with a worse job: an intern making a senior curator comply with conservation guidelines.

"Well?" said Reiko. There was no edge to her teaching voice now, just a stillness like the practiced moves of a Kabuki actor. Reiko's diminutive body leaned in towards the table.

"I've only been in Conservation here for three months . . ." I murmured, desperate for a quick strategic answer.

"Could you refer to the handling rules, Berry?" Reiko prompted.

Rolling his eyes, Professor Theo Younge glanced in my direction to see if I too thought Reiko was being condescending. He looked his role, the stereotype of a professor of Classical Studies, slack tweedy jacket hiding rumpled shirt, paunchy grey slacks and a desk-fat build. Baldness kept his hair from being unkempt. But even though he was a full university professor and the Chief Curator of Greek and Roman, he had once shattered a rare vase in his eagerness to clean it himself. Dunked into a bowl of water, the artifact exploded into tiny fragments as the air rushed too quickly out of the porous earthenware. The sherds were sitting in our lab.

Right now, unfortunately, the big preservation problem was mine. The self-preservation problem. This time I agreed with the chief curator, not my supervisor in Conservation.

"Reiko," I said, "the body of the amphora Theo wants to handle is strong, well-fired pottery. If he washes his hands or puts on gloves, is there a problem?"

"Sure the ceramic's hard." Reiko's square glasses honed in on me. "It's also thin and brittle. Point number two: are you in agreement with lifting it off the table in a way that puts it over our concrete floor?"

She dug into a near-empty box that proffered the bright blue synthetic gloves. "Even a Chief . . . ," Reiko noticed a circled 'small' on the box and pivoted towards the large ones she had recently rescued from the supply shelf. But whatever she was saying was lost to me because Theo's round face had darkened to red-purple. School had given me no "people preservation" training.

Her back briefly to us, Reiko continued, ". . . Chief Curator, everyone, is required to follow MOA guidelines for collections' safety." She placed two large blue gloves on the table and seemed unconcerned about Theo's health. I guessed she'd met this reaction before.

"Give me those stupid plastic gloves your rules call for." Theo snapped out the words. "It's much easier to lose my grip that way than if I handle the pots with my bare hands, but you told me to do it."

My own experience with slippery gloves agreed. I'd washed enough dishes in my life.

———— ❦ ————

Today, even though it was a Sunday, I had volunteered to work the museum visitors program because I'd wanted to see this public aspect of MOA, and the job would be easy enough: wheeling out the artifacts and moving them under the microscope when the lecturer asked. Now the day was accelerating into disaster like a ship towards rocks in a storm. By the time the audience and media had assembled, Reiko would have gone, leaving me, the new intern, in charge of the safety of unique treasures while enforcing nit-picking rules whose inflexibility denigrated two senior experts in their field. At least with the public there was the chance the rules for the care of collections could be enforced with authority, and I had already donned the weighty symbols of white lab coat and blue nitrile surgical gloves. But behind the scenes in this workroom, and later out on the auditorium's stage, I was the newest staff caught between the expectations of my supervisor and the museum's senior hierarchy. Job suicide. Another internship hits the bug light.

In the silence following Theo's outburst, we heard a key scraping in the doorlock. A museum guard walked in. An interruption, thank God.

"In the lobby . . ." the guard growled. Reiko stiffened.

"Yes?" Theo was already pulling his gloves off.

"A situation."

# Chapter
# 2

### Sunday Morning Continues

H er chin pointed at the workroom door, the guard marched out. Theo and Reiko scurried after her, while I switched off the lights, checked the locks, and ran as fast as my fifty-three-year-old professional behaviour would allow.

The only museum disturbance I could see was the one wrecking the architect's design of austere concrete and calm wood. The lobby upstairs boomeranged squealing voices and garish colours. To a museum director it would have signalled an excellent "situation." Over the lobby's clamor, a listener with the sensibilities of a birder would have discerned a continuous musical k'ching k'ching from the admissions desk and the museum shop. Whenever Vancouver's "wet coast" weather began to dissolve the landscape, the humans sought refuge in its indoor beauty. MOA sang in the rain and prayed for what the Director called her "Deus ex Mackinaw" phenomenon. A tremendous tizzy of visitors surrounded me. In the humidity of boots and umbrellas, an ancient scent rose from the totem poles. At the security desk, Reiko, Theo, and the guard, backs to the visitors crowding towards the galleries, had circled a young woman.

The woman stood, one hand folded over the Northwest Coast eagle design on her red shirt, the other clutching a squirming toddler. I could hear Theo say, "On Sunday?"

"What do you think I'm here for? Pay to get in to see the stuff you stole?"

Theo groaned, audible even through the din. "Stole? You know that's untrue. Let's discuss this without the smear campaign."

Reiko interrupted, "Which weaving do you want to borrow?"

The woman answered, "The Salish one, by my auntie Wilma."

"I'll need to look that up. We have lots of Salish weavings."

"You've got lots of everything. What time is it? The ceremony's at four."

"Look," Theo said. "Please understand. Requests need to be made in advance so they can be reviewed by the Director. Today's Sunday, she's not here, and," he squinted at his old watch, "We're due to have artifacts out for a public lecture in less than half an hour. I can't imagine . . ."

The woman pulled her little girl closer. "I need my auntie's blanket. Now. For a funeral." The "don't you get it?" continued in staccato. "Wilma said okay. I don't have one. Kids were sick last week. I'm here now."

I noticed that our guard stood a little apart, closer to the woman and the security desk than to Reiko and Theo. I hardly knew Mama, a quiet guard of indeterminate age. Her name was Rose Mam, but everyone called her 'Mama', happy she wasn't theirs. She rarely went to the coffee lounge, didn't smile in the morning when you signed in, and would turn away silently if you so much as commented on the rain. Short, squat, and beak-nosed, Mama was a formidable old raven, but much more wary of being heard.

Mama's mouth had tightened into a thin line. It struck me for the first time, seeing the woman and the guard together, that Mama might be aboriginal. The likeness seemed real, but what riveted me, and maybe this was my imagination, was the resemblance of Theo's half-turned profile to the woman, too. For an instant I was holding one of those family photos where the children take after one parent but a pentimento, a shadowy impression, of the other side of the family has surfaced in a feature or a gesture.

A rising heat blasted over my face. Only my time of life, I knew, aided by my nerves. I began to wriggle out of my lab coat. As I extricated an arm from my white sleeve, the young woman stepped right in front of me.

"My name is Uta Vickers." Her hand jerked forward. "I'm here to borrow my auntie's blanket for a funeral at four."

How could she know that the person in front of her with greying hair and white lab coat was the least important? For the second time in less than an hour, I was supposed to act with an authority I didn't have. I smiled. "I'm Berenice . . . 'Berry' Cates. I'm a Conservation intern." I held out a hand to shake hers and saw instead my lurid blue-gloved fingers.

Vickers yanked her hand back. "Won't even touch my skin, is that it? Afraid you'll catch something? Afraid somebody'll die, doctor?"

My "No!" came out as a hoarse whisper.

"You guys got barriers for everything," Vickers said. "Well, your so-called protection won't work. My auntie said I could get her blanket." Then she said in a voice loud enough for any visitors to hear, "You think this museum's great, but it's one big disappointment."

Theo turned crimson, but he came to my rescue with, "Now, see here, Ms. Vickers, the museum bought that blanket. We paid your aunt's asking price." The situation wasn't improving, he knew it, and shut up. I glanced at Mama. Her features had set into a mask, impassive. Theo and I shifted to stare at Reiko.

She was trying to make a funny face and engage the little girl. Dark eyes flared at Theo as Reiko looked up, extending her ungloved hand to Vickers. "I'm Reiko, the senior conservator. I'm so sorry for your loss, and your family's," she said. "I'll get the weaving for you. I just have to phone your aunt first to double-check it's okay, hear it directly so I'm not in any trouble."

"Aren't you calling the Director too?" Theo's voice rose in a squawk. "You're going to loan out a museum object without Sally Luykes knowing? And you, the head of Conservation. Imagine! Let it be touched, Reiko? Worn?"

The lobby was no place for intimate museum squabbles, but I heard Reiko take Theo's bait.

"Loan-backs to aboriginal owners for ceremonies are museum policy. I'm aware you don't get these requests in Greek and Roman."

"Loans are on a case-by case basis, my dear Reiko Smithson, as one well knows."

"It's a contemporary piece, and it's urgent." Reiko's voice remained steady. "You and Berry go downstairs and finish prepping the lecture objects."

Theo's face had hardened in concentration as if he were processing detailed notes of what he would report to the Director. Planted in my spot, I wasn't going to miss any of this. Reiko turned to Mama. "I'm going downstairs with Berry and Theo to make sure they settle everything for the lecture. Do you have time to show our guests the staff lounge and get Ms. Vickers a coffee?" Mama nodded, and Reiko shot out the door, uprooting us.

———— ∞⊙⊙⊙∞ ————

Reiko's fifties-style ponytail flew behind her as she blazed down the corridor outside the labs and workrooms. Theo, who carried twice Reiko's bulk, acted with a voice and agility I hadn't imagined. He started yelling as soon as we were in the staff-only area, and when Reiko didn't turn around, caught up before she had her key in the lock. Gripping Reiko's elbow, trying to catch his breath, Theo gasped, "What the . . . doing? . . . Double bloody standard your rules . . . I can't touch . . . you give this girl . . . a $4,000 weaving to wear? Quote the handling rules, will she?"

"Theo," Reiko spoke slowly. "It's our policy. Native people have rights to their pieces even when they're in a museum."

"Don't lecture me."

"Oh for God's sake. Wilma Vicker's still weaving blankets, MOA can purchase more, and her niece gets to pay respect at a funeral in a more ceremonial way." Reiko jammed her key into the lock and sprinted to the computer with the museum's catalogue.

The files and computer stations were at the far end of the long workroom, next to the rack of supplies. Most of the white metal shelving was on the walls, though, housing the backlog burden of museum collections work, hundreds of artifacts from all over the world awaiting cataloguing, condition reporting, and loan documentation. Under the objects' silent gaze Reiko clicked away, murmuring, as Theo and I exchanged quiet shrugs, then looked over the remaining lecture pieces to be placed on a padded trolley cart.

We finished quickly and I rolled the trolley carefully out into the galleries towards the lecture theatre. In the protection of a back wall, Theo placed a large hand on the cart's edge, stopping it gently. "I hope I'm not putting you on the spot, but I'd like to hear what you think of Reiko."

"I don't always agree with her." Neutral enough.

"So you like working for her?"

"Yes," I said. "Definitely."

"Well, I don't. Curatorial does not work for Conservation, but she acts like it. She doesn't get it that she's going to be fired."

"Fired?" I swallowed the "international standards for museum rules" argument I'd been preparing and leaned against the blank wall. His words had hit like a blow to the gut.

"I'm afraid so," he said. "One individual just can't take it upon herself to lend out pieces from the permanent collection." He paused, and looked at me slowly. "I apologize for letting my irritation show like this. I've had it with Reiko's rules."

"Oh," I replied, eloquently. My mind was telling me to shut up when my lips blurted, "Are you really going to the Director about the loan of the weaving? I'm sure Reiko'll leave a message so Sally Luykes knows."

"Tomorrow."

I pushed the trolley forward, concentrating on doing and not thinking. Reiko, my mentor, fired—and this internship abruptly over.

<hr>

In the lecture hall, the speaker was pressing buttons on the podium. Theo strode up and he and Foley clasped shoulders. Theo was large, but Foley could have waltzed him around the stage. I wheeled the trolley over to the microscope we had positioned earlier, but for the big guys I no longer existed. Eyes devouring the antiquities, Theo jabbed in the air excitedly and Foley fussed almost in rhythm, bobbing on one side of the cart and then the other. The audience craned in their seats. The artifacts were so newly acquired they had never before been seen in public.

The lecture began with slides of ancient ceramics painted with portraits of athletes and competitions. Foley's subject was sports in Greek and Roman times, and the audience oohed and aahed at each depiction. I played robot. After a group of images, Foley would call out from the podium for me to move one of the antiquities under the microscope, position it this way, that way, and I carefully did the mechanics, refocusing the microscope for each object, and moving another one when required. The microscope's camera attachment projected the image onto a screen so the whole audience could see the details. I was gratified by the noises of appreciation. They helped me focus on the positive of conservation work and not that it might be over for me, that Reiko might get fired.

As I paused by the microscope, looking up at the screen and then out at the rapt faces, listening to Foley's enthusiasm, I was catapulted into the other half of my life in Vancouver. In the second row, dead centre, sat Daniel, my Québécois upstairs neighbour, *"Le beau* Daniel" as I called him to myself. No taller than me, lean and vivid, blue eyes and black hair announcing his Breton ancestry, large white patches in the dark hair disclosing his age, Daniel had been the unexpected in my move to Vancouver. In three short months he had made me feel more than welcome. He had shown me, through smiles and laughter and taking me here and there, that he genuinely enjoyed my company. Not since the Jurassic had I felt fresh and pursued in this way.

We were becoming good friends, and maybe, the thought had come to me more than once, at least before last Friday, we would end up as more than friends. That day, I'd found out he was leaving town, reassigned back to Quebec by his journalist's job with *Radio-Canada*. Goddammit. Shit *de merde*. So Saturday had been our first and now final big date. And there he was grinning up at me. I looked back at the screen, wishing he hadn't seen me staring.

"Ms. Cates? Ms. Cates?" Foley's voice filtered into my consciousness. I slammed to attention. "The amphora, please," Foley enunciated for what could have been the fourth or fifth time. "Please do turn it so we can see the horse's head near the handle." Concentrating now, I rotated the fine red and black ware in small stages, checking each time until the image was just right.

Foley drew everyone's attention to how the artist had represented speed with the flaring nostrils and wild mane, the deliberation of each delicate stroke. I became transfixed. Not by the horse. Not by the explanation. Not by Daniel out there. The microscope light raked across the vase at an angle that revealed tiny ridges. The hard ceramic body, fired into immobility in ancient times, held unmistakable evidence of its birth.

I left the artifacts. It would only take a minute. Theo wouldn't rat me out to Reiko.

I sidled across to him in the first row, and whispered and pointed.

"Cuyler!" shouted Theo, and waved his arms. "Wait! Under the handle!"

Foley's face did not welcome the interruption. I wondered if there was an element of professional competition between these two, despite the friendly bear-hug at the start. Scampering back to the microscope, I moved the amphora the way I wanted it. The light played over the surface, and there it was, the potter's thumbprint pressed into the soft clay over two thousand years ago. Theo trumpeted the find. The audience applauded, even Foley joining in.

⚬◦⦾◦⚬

After the lecture, Theo joined Foley on stage to share the deluge of questions. By the time they finished I had the microscope hooded and the artifacts safely returned to their supports on the trolley before members of the public came for a closer look. What they might do here to the antiquities, too many people crowding around, sticking out oily bare hands to touch the ancient thumbprint, a shove jostling the amphora, a handle cracking off.

Someone tapped my shoulder. "Here we go," I muttered, turning around with a kind explanation and gentle warning. Instead, there was a beaming Daniel air-kissing his "Bravo!" on both my cheeks. "*Un moment!*" he added, then raced around and came back to tell me he was going to interview both Foley and Theo, and would I wait.

Sure I'd wait for Daniel, even after the disappointing weekend, because there wasn't much time before he left Vancouver for good. Besides, despite everything, Daniel was the kind of man who lifted my spirits; he was charming and outgoing. Outgoing, I ruminated, in both senses.

With the artifacts stowed and my white coat giving the authoritative signal to back off, members of the audience milled instead around the speaker. Left alone, my hands tested that the trolley movement wouldn't disturb the re-mounted objects, and I started to thread the cart back to the workroom. Theo burst out of the crowd, held up one hand until he could reach me, and said, "Berry, I just wanted to give you my congratulations. I'll make sure to put in a good word for you tomorrow."

"You're still seeing the Director?"

"Most museums don't have Conservation departments. They hire people in private practice, on contract."

"But . . ." Would he consider this an intern talking back? It didn't matter. I had everything to lose if Reiko was thought to be a maverick who picked fights and gave away collections. "But the Conservation department's been here for decades."

"Yes, it has." Theo ran his hand over his baldness. "But the museum's been here longer. Universities close departments that are too small or can't make it financially. Besides, do you really think the Dean will countenance someone traipsing around in the rain draped in one of the museum's artifacts?"

He had it all plotted. I shrugged and pointed over to Foley and the crowd, making as if Theo had to go back and answer questions. He shook my hand and trotted off. I headed the heavy trolley back behind the scenes.

⁕◦◦⊙◦◦⁕

Daniel was on his way to the radio studio to mix and pre-pare his *reportage*, and I accepted the lift downtown. I was still off-balance, but he'd been a bright spot today, glad to see me and exuberant at my discovery of the thumbprint. Daniel exuded warmth and delight; I never did understand these 24/7 cheery people. But I hung out with them when I could. More than anything right now, I needed happy.

In the car, Daniel chattered about his report, planning it out loud, asking me this and that, but eventually picking up that I was only half there. I confessed that the guillotine might be about to drop on my internship, and if that wasn't bad enough, the person I'd come half way across the country to work with would end up chopped into bits too. Fired on an issue of ethics, she'd never get hired again by any museum.

"Can they really fire someone like that at a university?" I asked Daniel. "I thought they had tenure."

"Even for the faculty, close the department, they can do that."

"Are they reassigned, or fired?"

"Don't know." Daniel's eyes narrowed in concentration. "But I can find out. Easy for a journalist."

"Don't bother yourself. You leave in a few days."

"Leaving, town, yes, but I'm not dying! I'm the one they reassign, eh?" he chirped. Daniel smiled with those blue eyes of his. In the emotion of the day I stifled tears.

"Berry," Daniel said, giving it a French pronunciation, "Don't look so sad. They won't fire, and if they do, maybe they reassign you too, eh? Another museum, close to Québec?"

What the hell was going on? We'd had excursions together to sightsee and the one ridiculous Saturday night club date, and he was saying what? Was there the chance he had the kind of feelings for me that I'd developed for him in three ridiculously short months, a teenage-appropriate foolishness I'd blamed on loneliness in a new city?

"I'll miss Faux Paws," I lied. Daniel's annoying dowager cat was his only female attachment, as far as I knew.

"Of course."

"Are you always so cheerful?" I demanded.

"*Non, non, non.* You don't know me yet. I pretend. *La vie est belle, n'est-ce pas*? Why waste her?"

"So this is all an act?"

"*Non*, Berry, you miss the point. I am for sure sometimes sad—a lot—but I don't like it. So I make myself happy. Have fun, make a joke, it's more pleasant to live like that."

. "You lie to yourself?"

"It's like an actor. You dress up, you try out how you should walk and talk, and soon you are being a happy personage. It makes you that happy personage. Try it."

"Well, it certainly works for you." A thin *Bonhomme Carnaval*, the relentlessly jovial mascot of the Quebec Winter Carnival, was beside me at the wheel.

"For everyone. *La psychologie.* Change the behaviour, your mood change too."

"What do you know about psychology?"

"Ah, someday I tell you."

"You're so upbeat, have you even been to a therapist ever?" My hand hit the dashboard. "Sorry, it's none of my business." In the cramped car I couldn't mime pulling my foot out of my mouth, but in any case Daniel was staring out at the traffic.

I slumped in the seat, figuring the botched day had ended perfectly. Daniel drove in silence downtown. When I started to get out, he opened his mouth as if hesitating to speak what he'd been thinking, and said, "Therapy? In fact, yes, when I was in Montréal. The best in Canadian therapy. Paid out by the medicare and tried out in both official languages." His eyes crinkled into a smile when I burst out laughing.

"See," he said. "I don't lie about myself, I tell the truth but I make it funny. Now you laugh and now your mood changes."

"*Merci,* Daniel."

"*De rien.* You can count on me, Berry. I am here for you even when I leave." I got out of the car and waved excessively.

Following the guidelines, all I had to do now was figure out what to wear and how to talk so tomorrow I'd survive, happily.

# Chapter

# 3

## My Week Continues

Monday I had a hollow where my stomach should have been. I hadn't slept and couldn't even handle a cup of tea. After an hour in Conservation's lab dusting artifacts inch by inch, I had to spend the rest of the day in textile storage, a dim room too small for its collections. The clothing that filled the centre of the room looked like three-dimensional, ghostly outlines of people shadowed under dust covers, or lying on stacked shelves with their long arms folded in. The flat textiles—blankets, coverings, and small tapestries—were rolled, the racks climbing the walls to the ceiling with their rounds of pale sheeting. Hats and shoes were on side shelves, boxed in white, and my job was to put away the items Reiko had finished analyzing for any chemical residues from past insect control. Then lay out the next items for her project.

Usually the room felt no different from other museum storage, but today touching this intimate past made me uneasy. The finicky nature of the work grated as well, matching box to hat and wrappings to costume, and double-checking that the labels were correct. All the time my mind was with Reiko in the lab. She was the most forthright, candid person I had met in my three months at the museum. Her professionalism accepted few compromises, and today would be the result of her not shying away.

It was late in the afternoon when Reiko came to get me, gulping stale museum air. Dr. Sally Luykes, MOA's Director, was in our lab.

The Director sat perched on one of our lab stools, abstract tints in her silk blouse playing against the green of her linen suit and her dark hair. She motioned us to sit opposite.

"I'll make this short. There appears to be a very serious problem. I need to emphasize that you must trust your colleagues as professionals. Do not, in any way, block their legitimate access to their collections. They are perfectly capable of handling the artifacts. This goes for outside experts like Cuyler Foley too."

Luykes paused to point through our glass door towards the adjacent collections workroom. "When Theo and Cuyler come in this evening to evaluate the antiquities on that table, should either of you be here, they are to be left entirely on their own to do their work. Theo and Cuyler are the top specialists in western Canada. Do not act as if they aren't. Ever."

Luykes stood, surveyed our faces, and left.

That was all? She didn't even mention yesterday's loan of the weaving. When I questioned Reiko, she said Luykes had called her into her office right after Theo's appointment. The loan of the weaving to Uta Vickers was fine. As Director of the museum she was glad to demonstrate MOA's desire to make the collections more accessible to their originators. For a funeral, a contemporary piece, and the artist had wanted the loan—no question. Luykes had closed with, "Towards the end of the day I'll be free to see you and your intern Berenice about standing in the way of staff handling their collections."

For me Monday had ended well. My internship would continue. Reiko was chastised but not fired. Conservation would not be held responsible if anything happened to the antiquities while the two experts were going over the evaluations this evening. Or so I thought at the time. I'd gone home and slept well.

---

Tuesday morning, my thoughts on *le beau* Daniel, I drove to work humming "Heartbreak Hotel" and "Bye, Bye, Love". Tonight was our farewell dinner at one of Vancouver's few true French restaurants. I would at least enjoy the cuisine, although not the occasion. So it would be good to get lost in my work for the next eight hours.

Jen, the Collections Manager, signed in the same time as me, and I could tell something was wrong. Her face slouched and her voice was low and tired. Her polo shirt might be a clear bright pink but her slacks looked as if she'd grabbed them from the laundry basket. She usually wore no make-up, and this time she'd even left off earrings.

"Are you feeling okay?" I asked.

"I was called in last night. Couldn't get back to sleep."

My throat closed.

Jen glanced toward the entrance to the galleries and stairs, and I noticed several large uniformed men cordoning them off. "They wanted to know if anything was missing in the collections workroom. The rest I'm not allowed to say."

I remembered Sunday's confrontation about the weaving and how Uta Vickers saw museums—full of locked doors and smug custodians. But maybe Jen was just taking care to obey the rules, to re-order a work world where she had been hauled in for God-knows-what in the middle of the night.

Jen continued, "Because the Director will tell staff this morning. So what was Sunday like with Cuyler Foley?"

I stared at the police officers. "Fine really," I mumbled. "I have a real surprise to show you on the amphora. And Foley is such a good speaker."

"Was," Jen said.

⁊⟨◎⟩⁊

"No access to the work areas," a red-haired security guard informed us. "Only the staff lounge. Go there now, please. The Director's waiting." In the shabby, cosy lounge, Jen emptied the coffeemaker into her enormous mug, ignoring my silent questions.

The Director wasn't waiting. At 8:40 she entered the lounge looking like hell if that is the right way to describe someone who could probably never look like hell, only sleepless and unkempt: Sally Luykes, with still-chestnut hair to my grey, half-glasses to my full, poised on her Italian heels. One month younger than me, and the director of an internationally renowned museum.

"Last night a death occurred here at the Museum of Anthropology," she announced. "It is unutterably sad. Dr. Cuyler Foley, our friend and colleague, collapsed and died, probably from a massive heart attack. His knowledge of Greek and Roman antiquities and First Nations collections made him one of the most sought-after private curators in this country. We will all miss his expertise and generous support of culture and scholarship."

The room hummed. "A politician's speech," Jen whispered to me. "Yadda yadda, and a lot not said. Except," she continued, "now I understand why some people call museums and their collections 'dead.'"

I had to laugh, but I felt sick. I'd met him only two short days ago. Now he was gone. Cuyler Foley, superb speaker, excited connoisseur, renowned specialist. A few people covered their mouths in shock. But others didn't quite make it, and their grimaces held a hint of wry surprise.

"Our heartfelt condolences to his family." Luykes' voice was firm but compassionate. "Anyone who wishes to attend the funeral service will of course have leave to do so. Meanwhile the police are completing their routines and I ask you to give them any and all assistance." Luykes surveyed her numb listeners.

"Berenice," Dr. Luykes sought me out, "I'm afraid you're going to have the toughest job of all."

She paused, and the room's noise diminished as the curiosity rose. "Please come to my office and we'll discuss the details."

I raised my chin confidently as I followed her out, enduring my first fifteen seconds of fame in a museum staffroom.

--------------------⚬⟨⊙⟩⚬--------------------

Luykes reached for a half-finished coffee near her phone, her gold-ringed finger pointing me towards a thermos with cups and saucers on an inlaid tray. Every wall of her office was covered with filled bookshelves. There were only two empty spaces, one for the coffee service and another showing off an elegant arrangement of dried flowers and a photograph of a girl when she was small. Luykes' office was the image of "Director": a cherrywood desk with adjacent high-end computer station, file cabinets, bookshelves, and, taking up the rest of the space, a dark wood table with eight chairs for meetings. Above the computer, near the wall where a skylight curved down to become a large window overlooking MOA's roof patio, hung a signed Northwest Coast print of a pod of whales.

I helped myself to coffee, slowly stirring cream into a drink I rarely take, but it gave Luykes a few minutes. She had seated herself at her desk, head momentarily bowed. I lowered my dinner-with-Daniel outfit into the chair opposite, careful not to spill the delicate china cup.

Luykes started by talking about Cuyler Foley. She had known him for ages and couldn't believe he was gone. Luykes ended in a strong voice with, "I broke the news to his family, you know," drinking from her cup as if she were also warming her hands. "With the police. It was the least I could do."

I nodded. Tense in anticipation of "the toughest job of all," I almost blurted out how much Luykes impressed me. A sycophantic comment even if true. We were the same age, but I would be described as "mature," and she as "in the prime of life." On top of being a director and full university professor, Luykes possessed boundless energy under her calm exterior. She had a great marriage, I'd heard, and, to add to the unfairness of it all, she managed to be thin, striking, and inspiring. Even the tragedy that had struck her life had not diminished her character. She had lost her only child in a car accident early on. Apparently, in personal conversations at least, she occasionally spoke about her daughter, openly and always with enthusiasm and love. Sally Luykes was strong—the kind of person who could surface after the harshest of tragedies and go on to live to the core her ambitions and her delights. And now here was a museum director talking to the newest intern as one human to another. A boss who wasn't afraid of being a person. Impressive.

Me, at night, when I took my glasses off, I could see myself in the mirror as I wanted to be and once was. With eyes blurred, my skin became smooth, my smile relaxed. I'd had strength and dreams and who knew what could happen? Now I understood—about debtload, about emotional exhaustion, about a husband who had walked out the door. Norm hightailed it seven years ago: no kids, no grand old age, no now untainted memories. I'd been left instead with a sense of vulnerability and an absurd not-meeting-expectations feeling that I hadn't known since grade school.

I'd needed to obliterate this legacy from my past, or at least compost it into something better able to sustain life. I'd gone back to school and trained in a career I knew little about, studying art conservation and restoration. The old saying tells you not to put all your eggs in one basket, and God knows my eggshells were fragile enough at the time, but I longed to work, hidden away in a museum back room, on something old that had endured. And make it last forever.

---

Luykes was saying, "If Cuyler hadn't died from the heart attack, it would kill him now to know what happened." Soft joking to relieve distress.

I was hurting as well, but my laugh in response sounded forced. This discussion had loosened the still-raw trauma of the death. Luykes' words had amplified the memories of Sunday and the brilliant lecturer, and I almost missed her saying, "This is where you come in. Cuyler collapsed onto the worktable holding the antiquities from his Sunday lecture. These are prized acquisitions. The ceramics are crushed."

I knew their beauty intimately: the exquisite amphora, three delicate drinking cups, and a painted earthenware lecythos. She went on to say that there was also damage to two early bronze sculptures, but the other artifacts were flat metal in good condition and had only minor abrasions. A nearby tray of lab glassware had been shattered as well, unimportant except the shards of glass had contributed to his injuries.

"But all of them . . ." Luykes winced, "the hairpins and knife edges, the broken ceramics, these bear traces of our colleague." She suggested that it might be better to clean the artifacts sooner rather than later—would I agree? Forensics normally handled post-mortem disruption to materials, but they weren't going to be responsible for any damage to museum value. Luykes had offered Conservation's services.

"Aren't the sherds evidence?" I said.

"Not evidence that's going to be used as proof. The police say it's impossible the broken pieces would show something the body doesn't. Certainly they were reluctant at this early stage to allow anyone to touch the fragments, but if cleaning was important from a professional point of view. . . "

I had to agree that it was easier to clean almost anything when the dirt or stain was fresh.

"You'll do your work in the collections area, then, where there'll be an officer watching the room."

I grabbed a soothing tea in the hum of the lounge and sat with Jen on the hard chairs in the corner. "I'm just going to be cleaning some of what was broken last night," I replied to her curiosity about what Luykes had wanted. My few questions for Jen remained unsaid. I hardly wanted to speak Foley's name, and got up to go outside and breathe fresh air.

As I left the lounge I almost collided with Lorna Johnson, a young curator from an aboriginal community, responsible at MOA for artifacts and textiles in her Northwest Coast research area. Would she want the details on the loan of the weaving? Preoccupied, probably like me with this morning's events, she smiled a faint greeting and went past. Seeing her in the hallway in her slim navy slacks and vest with its Thunderbird design in pearly buttons, I was thinking, she'd been one of those at the meeting who hadn't looked upset.

"Lorna, wait," I called after her. "Can I ask you something delicate?" Her eyebrows rose. "Some people didn't like Cuyler Foley," I continued. "Why?"

"Oh?"

"I'm caught," I confessed, "between Dr. Luykes who told me he was wonderful, and a few, well, smiles I saw in the coffee room this morning."

"What did she want you for?" Lorna was as direct as I had been, and as curious. We traded our wares.

"I'm cleaning the pottery Foley broke when he fell. The antiquities."

Lorna shrugged. "Greek and Roman is Theo's department. In my world, Foley was a scumbag. He'd sniff around and get people to sell their heirlooms. He'd offer what seemed like a lot of money, but was way below market price, and he knew it. Then he'd sell high to museums and private collectors."

So Cuyler Foley had been more than a great lecturer and a specialist consultant. According to Lorna, he was the worst kind of shady art and artifacts dealer. I hurried outside.

Ten minutes later a policeman ushered me into the Conservation laboratory to pick up my equipment: Conservation's kit of small tweezers and jeweller's picks, dental tools, swabs and brushes, as well as a few possible solvent mixtures for lifting stains. The police escorted me to a newly cleaned table in the collections workroom, Jen's microscope and the fume evacuation apparatus already set up. At the far end of my table sat the one officer needed to monitor whatever museum activity was still necessary downstairs, now concentrated in this room. From the dark drips and hardened pools on the floor near a roped-off adjacent table, and on the potsherds in front of me, I guessed that the broken glassware and antiquities had cut Foley badly. My belly was near to puking.

Why does the Director want me to clean up the artifacts so immediately? Would she ask me to restore them after the cleaning, erase the awful memories by making the objects whole again? Okay, Reiko had called in sick this Tuesday morning, so I was the only staff in our lab. Me, though, I wasn't far from having graduated with my Masters in Art Conservation. These artifacts were treasures! Was I put to work in the hope that somebody mature, with life experience, would be able to handle death in bits and gobs magnified three times and ten inches from her nose?

As my gloved hand moved the first sherd under the microscope, I heard a few people assembling next to where police tape cordoned off the stained floor. Not fifteen feet back from my table, Cuyler Foley had kept his appointment in the quiet evening hours to evaluate the magnificent pieces in a basement museum workroom.

I heard someone in the group say "Reiko" and my head whipped around but the burly policemen accompanying this special group blocked my view of the speaker. One blue uniform, though, caught the motion and gave me a "this is a private conversation" glare. He signalled wordlessly to the cop sitting at the far end of my table to keep an eye on me. I redoubled my attempt to eavesdrop. Bending over my work looked good but I was now having trouble picking up my small tools. My fingers had curled, rigid like the 500-year-old Iceman's in the glacier, and I couldn't afford to make some clumsy mistake.

Have us staff been told the whole story? I wanted that man behind me to speak up. A low voice was saying, " . . .we're questioning her later . . ." and then more loudly something that began with, "I'd like to ask you all . . .". There was a lull, and then a yelp.

"Not ours? Are you absolutely sure?" I didn't need to strain to recognize Luykes. Her voice rose. "Show me exactly which pieces we've never seen before. Theo, this is your department."

The same man's voice I didn't recognize broke in quietly, "You don't have to look right now. Your conservationist is cleaning everything up. You can wait." Across my table, the policeman sitting monitoring my work smiled his approval.

What the hell? The "your conservationist" in question, me, Berry Cates—my lab stool was practically behind them, and they were talking as if I didn't exist. The last museum considered me expendable and I was damned if it was going to happen a second time. "That's conservator, by the way, not conservationist," I wanted to shout, "I have had specialized graduate training in the preservation of art and museum collections. Not trees."

The murmur again. Barely audible. "Theo Younge has identified the silver brooch pin as something he's never seen before. Not part of the Museum of Anthropology's collection."

"First century cloak pin," came a hoarse voice. I glimpsed a shadow rising from a stool nearer the supplies storage. A different, energetic male voice cut in. "Cuyler Foley might've brought it in with him. Theo, did Cuyler mention this to you? Want you to look at anything special?"

I caught myself as I almost turned around again, but re-hunched. Max Turpin's clear voice behind me was a practically irresistible force. The Curator of Contemporary Art raised the whole museum's pulse to an exciting level—nervy, amusing, committed to the young artists he worked with.

I heard Theo start to speak, his voice breaking as he said, "No, Cuyler didn't hint at anything, he didn't show it to me, it was only when the police . . . it's a perfect Roman fibula, silver and niello. Imagine. I don't know where it came from."

"It came from the breast pocket of Mr. Foley's shirt, gentlemen. Ladies. To be more precise . . ." I strained my ears to pick up the man's inaudible voice. "It came from Mr. Foley's body, the heart area in fact. The thing . . . squeezed between his ribs when he hit the table." There was a pause and a shudder of furniture.

Luykes cried, "Theo! Here, Jen, help him onto a better stool." I jumped up, too, but Jen and the burly policemen were already settling Theo in a different spot, murmuring competent, solicitous phrases.

"Sergeant, that was unnecessary," Max said sharply. "They were friends and colleagues." Slowly I sat down, able to catch a glimpse of the man standing beside Luykes and Max. Dark-haired, official-looking. Of course—the calm low voice had been a police officer's. A sergeant. The investigation.

The sergeant murmured, "I apologize, Dr. Turpin. A Roman brooch pin or whatever it is could just as easily belong to your antiquities curator, you know."

"We don't have personal artifacts!" snapped Luykes. She paused, softening her voice, and continued. "I apologize, Sergeant. I didn't mean to be short. I just meant that it would be a conflict of interest."

Max Turpin, a step behind the Director in this conversation, asked loudly, "What is this, gothic? Pierced by a pin in his breast pocket? Come off it, Sergeant. What are you talking about here? A heart attack? An accident? A ghoulish murder?"

I couldn't catch the murmured reply.

Exercising my fingers, I concentrated on the cleaning. If my wooden pick could pry up an edge of this dry fragment of flesh, I could lift it cleanly off the fragile ceramic. Pushing the magnifying light into a better position, I saw clearly that everywhere on my workbench were minuscule blotches of beige-grey and brownish-red, fragments of death assembled by my tools. Behind me the conversation ebbed and flowed in suitably muted tones. My hand steadied a pair of surgical tweezers against the edge of the table.

"Here, Theo, Sergeant Daley." The Director and her group had come to hover right around my worktable. I didn't need to look up to picture them: Theo Younge in crumpled shirt, baggy pants and old tweed jacket or vest, the quintessential professor of ancient history; Max Turpin the complete opposite, a going concern of contemporary style in his brilliant T-shirts and fitted jackets; Sally Luykes conservatively business-like but stunning in a suit and blouse I'd die for. Jen, the Collections Manager, would be standing a little behind the others and wearing the clothes of the downstairs staff: whatever you could put in the washer after moving heavy boxes.

I saw Luykes's hand stretch towards my box of blue surgical gloves, and I fixed on her agate ring, suppressing a deadly sin. Too quickly the ring and her manicured hand disappeared into one of the lab's blue nitrile gloves. More hands and arms reached in front of me. I just drew back, hunched, and waited it out. Pointing at the sherds, Luykes said, "See the pottery? Conservators are so patient. The cleaning will go very well."

Good about the word "conservator", but how much patience would I need to hear what was really going on? Or to be acknowledged now by name, as a person, not just a staff position? Was this Dr. Jekyll and Sally Luykes? What other habits were acquired—or discarded—even by the best at the top? The Director was chattering on, reprising her line about how Foley would have a heart attack if he knew what he'd broken. I willed her to acknowledge me sitting here. Did she even remember my name at this point?

I said, "May I ask a question?" a little too loudly, and my voice echoed through the workroom. Smiling as sweetly as my teeth could manage, I continued, "Are you testing the brooch for fingerprints?"

The sergeant repeated my question, curiosity in his voice.

Berry the student intern asked a second innocent question. "Would being in the body have wiped the brooch clean of any fingerprints?"

"I don't know absolutely," replied the sergeant. "Forensics would have to answer that."

"Mightn't fingerprints tell you something about who handled the brooch?"

"Here?" The sergeant asked. "In the museum?" He pointed at Luykes' blue hands. "You all wear gloves."

"Not necessarily," I said.

<hr/>

The sergeant was writing something in a notebook. Luykes had rolled off her gloves and left them in a heap on my table. The group was breaking up, but a soft flow of air tickled the left side of my neck as someone's hand reached around me towards the sherds. Except no hand appeared. I felt the light brush of air near my neck again. There was a little skin exposed, as I'd pulled my irrevocably nondescript hair back so it wouldn't fall in front of my eyes as I worked. There the disturbance was a third time, moving towards my cheek. I've lost some of my peripheral vision since I've had to wear glasses, but something was moving on my left side. There couldn't be an insect here; no buzzing allowed in a museum. But I pretended there was a mosquito and slapped my face. I slapped something else into my cheek at the same time.

Keeping control, even if I wasn't breathing very well, my arm quickly flipped the offending object onto the floor as I would any noxious bug. It turned out to be a hand. Safely attached to an arm. Attached to a tight black T-shirt worn by Max Turpin. I noticed that the Curator of Contemporary Art, without a jacket on, was more buff than a fortyish "let's go to another wild artist's party" kind of guy deserved to be. I tried to glare at the face attached to the T-shirt.

"Dr. Turpin!" my intern-deference exclaimed, and with faultless ingenuity, "I was worried that too many hands reaching across the worktable might damage the objects."

"Certainly, Ms. Cates," he replied equally formally. "You can't be too careful." Lowering his face so only I could see, he gave me a theatrical wink. In an instant he straightened up. "Let's leave Ms. Cates to her work," he gestured to the others. As they turned towards the exit, he bent down again and whispered, "Just checking to see if you'd shaved yet."

I chuckled into the workbench, remembering the riotous scene in the lunchroom that occurred on my first day, a clean-shaven Max dashing in and the ensuing uproar about a beard being gone. Today Max Turpin had relieved the gloom for a moment, and he had more than remembered my name. God, was I blushing? I put my head further down towards my work to hide my cheeks from the cop across the table. So . . . Max Turpin. A senior curator who also happened to be the life of the museum. He was—what—flirting with me? But he was ten years younger, far better looking, and more popular than I've ever been. Was he one of those amazing people born to love his life, freed from enough neuroses and social convention to be happy, energetic, and able to be, as the contemporary homilies recite, in the moment? In fact, enjoy the moment to the max? Oh, groan, Berry Cates, enough. Max seemed entirely comfortable, *"bien dans son peau"* as my grandmother used to say. Comfortable in his own skin. Or was he just a grown-up brat, getting what he wanted: attention—no—admiration. Was I a person he wanted to joke with, or was he a ladies' man, and I just happened to be the new woman?

Shit de *merde!* My tweezers skidded across one of the largest pottery fragments, cutting right into the robed figures in the design. Metal tools against old earthenware: no contest. Kill me now. The fresh ochre colour of the unweathered ceramic showed through the deep scratch. Okay, Cates, it doesn't exactly matter to the artifact, compared to the breakage, and it certainly doesn't matter compared to yesterday's death. But my belly, heart, and brain knew that it mattered to me.

Calamity Cates. My eyes couldn't leave that damned rift valley cutting across the face and bodies of two beautiful figures on the vase. The damage would always be there, a witness to my competence—in the potsherd, in what I'd have to write in the treatment report, and what ethically I'd have to tell Reiko.

"A conservator's job is to protect the artifacts, Berry, not ruin them further," her sharp schoolmistress voice would say. She'd have grounds to dismiss me then and there.

Would I ever land a real job, a woman my age starting a new career? Why did I even enter museum work, with its cupboards full of other people's belongings and the potential for disaster when you got near them? I gritted my teeth. I had chosen this basket of eggs. It was mine now. No more slip-ups. What would happen to the rest of my life if I flunked this internship? I was well on my way to finding out.

# Chapter

# 4

## Tuesday Morning Gets Worse

No chatter filtering through the workroom: the two Collections Assistants must have finished their work for the urgent loan. Zoe and Heather were two newly-minted graduates like myself, but the comparison ended there. They were all uplift bras, uplift camisoles and low jeans, talking the same and to the older me, looking enough alike despite Zoe, true to her unusual name, often dressing in bohemian black with outrageous earrings. Like other lucky young graduates they were having the time of their lives in new career jobs. While intern Berry Cates, fanning herself out of a hot flash, had just multiplied the reasons why conservation would be ditched in this museum. The policeman across my table had nowhere else to look now but at my work, and seemed mildly curious that I'd ripped off my blue gloves and stuffed my hands in my lab coat.

Maybe this sherd I've just gouged came from one of the artifacts Luykes and the others said they'd never seen before. But whoever the ceramics belonged to, whatever their value, my job was to clean them faultlessly. A young new graduate like Zoe or Heather, just past her age of majority, could make a mistake and be forgiven her lack of experience. A new graduate just past the onset of menopause would not be.

The pervading smell of newly unwrapped plastics and disinfectant still damped the air. Behind me were the stains and yellow tape on the floor. This museum had more to worry about than the condition of their antiquities in the hands of an intern. Who here knew the real details of how Cuyler Foley had died last night in this secure museum workroom? Shivering, I made myself rest by looking up at the shelves filled with baskets so finely made they could be silk rather than native grasses, tiny African village scenes, painted shadow puppets, ancient carvings in walrus ivory, transparent Chinese fans.

My post-divorce therapist asked me once why I liked museums. "Like?" I'd said then, "I love museums. Don't you?"

She replied, "My grandparents spent hours staring at displays of dusty antiques." My eyes swept across the pure angles of her office walls and the cream leather chairs we sat in. Reaching up, I'd hit the light switch and blacked out the room.

"Can you tan leather or generate the light for this office? I sure can't. Ordinary people used to be able to transform anything into what they needed. The evidence is in museums. To me they're humbling." Did she nod in the dark, or smile at my being still so earnest, at my age?

Maybe I did have something in common with Zoe and Heather.

———⚬⦵⦵⚬°———

A voice in the collections workroom catapulted me off my stool.

"You need a break."

I'd thought the room was empty except for the bored policeman sitting across the table.

"Did I startle you?" said Jen, the Collections Manager. "Sorry. Must be my new sneakers." She wiggled her foot but I wasn't keeping up with the niceties of the conversation and didn't bother to look.

"I'll have to try the sneaks on Zoe and Heather when they're gabbing instead of working. I was going for coffee and saw you looking pretty depressed. C'mon, let's go upstairs. Enough of this disaster area."

"You got that right." We headed for the corridor.

The policeman stopped us. His buzz cut and uniform emphasized an authority his youth could not. Would we please sign out? How long would we be gone? The room would now be off limits for one half-hour. The closest exit was the one into the galleries and we took it.

It meant we walked through the museum's most anti-traditional gallery, its artifact storage. MOA had placed on public view not just exhibits but half of its behind-the-scenes housing of collections. The famous innovation of 'Visible Storage' had now, though, become transformed into a Visible Nightmare by the on-going renovations. Jen and I scrambled through monstrosities of cabling, wall fragments, and construction dust curtaining off not-yet-emptied artifact cases. The whole area and the adjacent exhibition gallery were being reworked to make space for Native necessities such as a sound studio for oral history and rooms for private ritual maintenance of sacred pieces.

"I hate this reno!" coughed Jen as we picked our way through the debris. "The building committee wants the collection packed up yesterday, but they don't give me any money. Then Admin bitches about delays costing us, but they know we have to keep track of where each object gets stored. I wish our beloved . . ."

Jen ended with a squeak, clamping her lips. Visible Storage was originally built as one big room, but not as an open space. The collections were housed in their culture areas, designed as small bays and nooks created by the positioning of high glass-fronted cases. As we rounded a corner of the Haida area, Sally Luykes and Max Turpin were staring at us, their own conversation frozen.

"Were you going to say something about your beloved . . . Director?" Max inquired, mischief written all over his face. Jen opened her mouth and couldn't speak.

I said, "I wish our beloved university had given MOA more money." But Max wasn't going to be easily diverted. In a voice more chiding than harsh, he asked, "Do you know anything about poison arrows?"

I couldn't follow this segue and must have looked baffled because he explained, "The ones that were out where Cuyler Foley was working?"

"Poisoned arrows?" Luykes spoke, sounding as confused as I felt. "In the Classics collection?"

"No, the Bolivian donation. The old arrows are all poison-tipped with curare. Apparently they were on the table beside the Classics artifacts last night, pushed aside to make space for Cuyler. Seems there was blood on one of them and the police are sampling it to see if it's his. Maybe he was warding off a blow."

Jen found her voice. "The Bolivian donation is going out on loan. It's past due. That's why the arrows were out."

"Warding off a blow, Max?" Luykes was shaking her head. "That's crazy. Theo was with him. And they're colleagues." She picked up the conversation in a stronger voice. "You know, now that you mention it, Reiko was telling me months ago about some research she was doing on that Bolivian donation. To see if the curare was still active.

Whether the arrows needed any special Hazardous Materials storage." She turned towards me. "The details you conservators think of."

"Do *you* know if the poison's active, Ms. Cates?" Max looked serious. "Don't you conservators learn all about materials and how they deteriorate?"

Before I could come up with an answer that would be both truthful and shut him up, Luykes interjected, "Reiko was in the museum last night. My God, I hope she doesn't have the answer to her research question now."

Max was speaking faster. "Who else but Collections and Conservation would know? Okay, Sally, you remembered her research, but you had to search your memory. Would Theo know those arrows were poison tipped?"

Luykes shook her head and looked more relaxed. She had remembered the details of what Reiko was doing, and as Director had a legitimate explanation for what might have become deadly dangerous research.

Or murder?

Max Turpin might like to joke, but he was practically pointing a poison arrow at Collections and Conservation, and implicating Reiko. Jen and Reiko knew the details of the Bolivian donation, but that was part of their work.

Jen muttered an "Excuse me" and strode out. I nodded and followed, but she was soon far ahead, steaming up the main ramp past the galleries and towards the coffee room. My legs were barely able to carry me forward, the museum galleries now endlessly long, their walls too close. I stopped, gasping. I had to go back, evade the policemen, and phone Reiko. She called in sick this morning and I didn't think anything of it.

---

I picked my way back through Visible Storage to the behind-the-scenes corridor where I could see into the labs and workrooms. My role in the tragedy surrounding Foley's death should have been straightforward: clean the objects professionally before the stains set and anything hardened irreversibly. Maintain the dignity of the Conservation lab. But I had already scratched one piece, and it had been insinuated that Reiko, whose reputation was so good in conservation circles that students were advised to read her papers on professional ethics, might be related to the death last night. Is she being scapegoated by the powerful people she's had run-ins with? I couldn't let this happen to her. What if the ill will is aimed at all of Conservation, in which case, where do I and my new career fit in? If this internship ends—no qualifying as a full conservator, no new life, not even a reason to muse further about Daniel in the upstairs apartment. Daniel was a journalist. How would he follow up a story like this? How would he uncover the truth?

"Jen," I practised sotto voce, "What if Foley's death had occurred from the poison on an arrow? Reiko was doing curare research. Any reason she'd wanted him dead?"

———— ⚬⊙⚬ ————

The glass doors to the collections workroom were still locked, and I could see the yellow tape barring the adjacent Conservation lab. Without putting on the lights, I turned into Jen's office and, figuring she would be taking a longish coffee break, punched in Reiko's home number. I got her voice mail. Slamming the phone down, I worked out the phrases for what I was going to say, in case anyone came in and overheard, and dialled again.

"I hope you're feeling all right," I began, "have you heard the news at MOA? Cuyler Foley died last night in the Collections workroom, but you might know this already. The Director said you were here last night. Max Turpin said you knew all about curare, and blood was found on one of the South American arrows near Mr. Foley. I'm worried. I'll try again later."

Reiko picked up the phone. She must have been screening. "Hi Berry," she croaked. "I really am sick. Don't worry about anything Max Turpin says. He's a guy who's used to getting his own way, and when he doesn't, he carries the grudge until something comes through for him. I outed him about a painting once, and he's disliked me ever since. Turning down his manly charms eons ago didn't endear me to him either. If I'd screwed him physically rather than metaphorically, life'd be a breeze."

"He came on to you?" I asked. First things first.

"He comes on to everyone, let me tell you all about it. And for his own reasons, too, as well as being a guy who just enjoys the hell out of life. But I really can't talk now. My throat burns worse than my car engine and the police are coming any minute to question me. Damn, I think that's them. Bye now." She hung up.

⁘⦿⦿⁘

Standing in Jen's dark office, I peered through the glass of her door into the collections workroom. Still no activity. I glimpsed the adjacent Conservation lab, and there they were—blue jackets huddled around the safety cabinet where we kept flammable chemicals. I put together one Reiko conservator who happened to be at MOA the night Cuyler Foley died, plus one rumour of poison, all undoubtedly repeated to police by a guy whom I now knew held a grudge, and got "Conservation's chemical storage".

That meant I was suspect, too. I did fit in. I leaned against the door and hugged myself, and my heart hammered for the two of us.

Hold it. Berry Cates would fight this dissing and suspicion. Unlike some ex-husbands, I don't sneak out the back door quietly. I pushed my shoulders back. This intern would carry on the responsibilities of the lab until Reiko was in the clear, and do it brilliantly. I am good. Ramping up the self-talk a few degrees—Celsius: they're bigger and they're scientific—I almost grinned, but my smile hid a large measure of self-disgust. The smug thought was inescapable. I might be a beneficiary of Reiko's troubles. If I did well, a permanent job might be my reward, whatever Reiko's fate.

Then it hit me. There might be no use displaying to the world that I could have a high level of skill and professionalism. Nor should I worry about that tinge of schadenfreude over Reiko's troubles, or whether I'd ever have a career in my new profession of conservation. Useless to worry about these things if I can't clear the insinuation of Conservation's—a department composed of Reiko and her intern— involvement in murder.

# Chapter

# 5

## And Worse

As I stood gaping into the workroom and lab, my table-cop strode over and undid the door's upgraded lock. Before I was even into the room he was resetting it. I guess I was supposed to strut in, salute, and march over to my work. Irritated, I shuffled; it was way past coffee time, and I'd missed my break. It is amazing how quickly a person goes from thinking as a free student to thinking as an employee. I sat down and willed my mind to concentrate on the minutiae of cleaning—for fifteen minutes anyway and then I'll break, I told myself. I am going to do this right.

Instead, my failed first internship flashed by in uncontrollable replay. I heard the alarm shrieking through the grey Seattle corridor, saw my museum keys smacking a hard floor. I must have pushed against the staff-only door too soon, setting off emergency alarms that would only end with a counter-turn of the right key. I scrambled on the floor to recoup my keys, and then without warning the signal stopped.

"It's not a good idea," said a voice behind me in the sudden silence, "To set off the alarms on your way to an appointment with your boss. Which was at ten."

"I'm sorry." I turned to face the museum Director as he pocketed his set of keys. "I was at an emergency. A leaking pipe." He took this news by continuing to root around in his pockets.

"Water damage," I enunciated, "In the exhibit with the Tibetan robes and the old Maori cloaks."

"You want emergency, I've got emergency," he replied. "Be in my office at two." His oxfords squeaked down the inner corridor, and I was left with not quite four lousy hours.

By 2:30 I was out of a job at the Seattle museum. Fiscal year-end shortfall. Non-essential museum programs cut. "Berenice, I couldn't justify keeping on a Canadian in a state-funded position which ends in five months."

"I won this internship. Competitively."

"Yes, you did. There were two applicants." He took off his glasses and wiped them with a pocket handkerchief. It was a good excuse not to look me in the eye. "You also just about killed a schoolchild when he swallowed lead shot from one of your conservation weights."

"That's not true! The student broke open the weights and the teacher did nothing. I was showing the class the microscope, and when I lifted my head, the boy was popping the lead shot like pills."

"You're old enough to be the teacher's mother," he muttered. The Director held his glasses to his mouth and huffed twice. "March 31 is two weeks Friday. There'll be a little send-off Thursday afternoon."

He added by way of apology, "You're not the only one."

I replied, "I want a letter."

"Do you, now."

"I want a letter stating that my position was terminated due to a funding shortfall."

He wiped at his glasses some more. His computer beeped that he had incoming mail, and the Director turned his back to me and began to click and read.

I sat. A good fifteen minutes later he swung around to phone, and fumbled the handpiece as I gazed back. His fingers inched up towards his glasses, and then a grin disrupted his face. Leaning across some papers, he punched two buttons on a small dusty machine, and started dictating my letter. Before he threw me out, the Director came around the desk and shook my hand.

I shrugged and said. "To a sharp knife comes a tough steak", and had to live on that old saying for close to a year.

⚬◦⟨⚈⟩◦⚬

Looking up from my slow cleaning of the remains of the pottery antiquities, I met full on the eyes of Dr. Sally Luykes, and the constable now paying a great deal of attention. How had the Director entered the workroom without me hearing anything? Damn aging. Crappy things that happen much earlier than you're ever told they would. Hard enough to eavesdrop when your hearing isn't what it used to be, let alone be alert to other noise.

"Berenice, you're looking a little stressed. Take a break. I've told the police that we'd be finished by the end of today, but I don't want you to risk your health on it. We're all in shock. Take the time you need. How much longer, do you think?" asked Dr. Luykes.

"It's hard to estimate this early on," I replied, hoping this didn't sound like inexperience speaking, but I didn't want to get boxed in.

"We insisted on having museum artifacts cleaned by a professional, but we can't hold up what the police might need in their investigation."

"Investigation? Of staff?" I had to know. Then my heart started pounding. "The sherds aren't really evidence, though," I said. My whole body tensed with the memory of the scratch.

"No, but this has turned out to be more important than I thought. There's been some mix-up of the artifacts, and we have to sort them out." What I'd heard earlier—at least one of the objects didn't belong. Without giving much explanation, Luykes continued, "Which sherds fit which pot. The police need Theo to do this ASAP."

"If I can assist in any way . . ." I mouthed the formula.

"Thank you, Berenice, I'll let Theo know." And she was gone.

She had ignored me completely in front of the group this morning, and now here was my name and this mixed message about "take a break, but get the work done on time, and that's my time, by the way".

Maybe I've misjudged my future as a museum employee, the more I'm familiar with the games and the rules. Stumbling off the lab stool to head upstairs for my sanctioned workers' break, I detoured to the Ladies as Mama the grouch of a guard turned towards the staff-only area.

---

I never made it to the coffee room. The museum's receptionist called my name as she saw me coming up the stairs. A policeman intercepted: Was I Ms. Cates? Would I mind stepping inside this classroom for a few questions? Yes, now would be the most convenient. I was led in and seated at the small teacher's table in front of the whiteboard. The table was the only unscarred furniture in an otherwise worn down, over-lit, very school-looking room.

My right hand ran appreciatively over the smooth gloss of the new teacher's table while my mind wandered to the major renovations happening at MOA, for which, thankfully, money had been raised. In a few years Visible Storage would be much improved, even if it was chaotic and inconvenient now. The expanded facility might mean more jobs. I smiled to myself, that half of my brain escaping what was in front of me. The other half, connected to my eyes, was focused on the dark-haired man opposite with the middle-aged desk paunch who introduced himself as Sergeant Daley, and a fit young woman beside him, Constable Frick. The Sergeant was the soft-spoken man downstairs. I figured he knew what he was doing when the first question he murmured was what did I take in my coffee, and he waved away the other constable, the man who had intercepted me, to get it.

Normally I drink tea but especially here I didn't want to come across as the stereotype of the grey-haired, purple-wearing, tea-drinking fusspot, and any caffeine would do right now. Besides, occasionally I did enjoy coffee; I was bi that way.

First came the background; the police in front of me were RCMP, not Vancouver City Police. Not because the investigation had national importance, but simply because the RCMP had jurisdiction over the University Endowment Lands, as they did the suburbs of Vancouver and the rural areas of BC.

The Sergeant started in with the easy questions in a friendly tone.

"My full name is Berenice Cates," I responded. "My friends and close acquaintances call me 'Berry.'" Yes, I agreed with the sergeant, BC were my initials, just like British Columbia. Ha ha. Before here? I was in Kingston, Ontario, to do a Master's degree (no, not the Kingston Penitentiary, ha ha), and then I got this placement. Well no, it would depend on where I get a permanent job.

Did we use a lot of toxic substances in museum conservation work? Apart from the normal ones found in a university chemistry lab? Perhaps unusual mixtures used in what must be such specialized work? "Specifically, Ms. Cates, what would you use arsenic for?"

I gulped. Why was he asking about arsenic? The poison I'd heard mentioned was the curare on the South American arrows. He was staring at me, and my over-50 brain couldn't multitask the way it used to. It would have to be content with serial task monogamy. I said, "Arsenic?"

"We found a bottle in Conservation."

"That's for research. A project on pesticides to see if they left toxic residues on the artifacts." I was glad to have expertise to contribute. "Arsenic compounds used to be common pesticides for farms, city houses, anywhere there might be roaches or rats. Over the last hundred years museums used it too, as well as other chemicals, to protect collections from insect attack. Today we don't use poisons; museums kill bugs by freezing or inert gases. No chemicals, no residues."

The sergeant and constable both opened their mouths, probably to ask why then would arsenic still be in the lab cupboard. I ignored their body language. I don't do sound bites. Despite being a recent grad, I was not that linguistically up-to-date. Anyway, my voice was louder than his.

"Museums are now studying how toxic the residues of this past pesticide practice are," I continued. "In order to tell how harmful any arsenic still on the objects might be, we do a control sample with a measured amount of the arsenic.

We "salt" a pretend object with a given amount, and then use x-ray fluorescence to take readings. These are compared with the readings the instrument is giving us on the real objects. You see, the new portable XRF machines are designed for other purposes, for industry, for assessing toxic waste dumps, and we don't know how accurately they read out on things like woollen cloth, feathers, or a drumhead."

"So you keep arsenic to "salt" your objects for these experiments, is that correct?"

I nodded, "Arsenic trioxide." Constable Frick was taking notes, after all.

"How long has this been going on?"

"A few years, I think. I'm new. Ask Reiko Smithson. Or the Director. She'd know about the research."

"We already have asked Dr. Luykes, thank you," replied Sergeant Daley with an edge to his voice. "She was well aware of the arsenic project, but not the details. She suggested your name to fill us in." He leaned towards me. "Where did you get your arsenic?"

"I think the university's chemistry stores got it for us. I'm sure we have the requisition. You used to be able to get it as rat poison from any hardware or pharmacy." Did I sound dismissive? I had better bottle it.

"Where do you keep your arsenic, Ms. Cates?" A simple question to which he already knew the answer.

"It's kept, as you saw, in the flammable cabinet in the Conservation lab, the safety storage for solvents."

"Why in the flammable cabinet, Ms. Cates? It's not flammable, I believe, nor a solvent."

"No. But it seemed the best place to keep something dangerous, you know, with the other dangerous chemicals. I'm new here," I repeated, and shrugged in a way intended to be disarming.

"We aren't saying this was your decision," Constable Frick intervened. "We're just looking for information."

Sergeant Daley asked, "If the flammable cabinet contained dangerous chemicals, as you describe them, did you have any procedures for securing them?"

"Yes, the cabinet and its contents are all earthquake-proofed."

"I mean," said Sergeant Daley, authority sounding in every word, "did you use the lock in the cabinet's handle?"

I could see that the Sergeant had a keen eye for detail. He would make a good conservator. I answered that Reiko operated the lab to the highest professional standards under the circumstances.

"And what does that mean?"

"We label all our chemicals, for example. Reiko made a point of sending me for health and safety training."

"Is that it?"

"We follow the conservation code of ethics."

"I'm sure you do. What else?"

The else was that I needed him to believe me. Reiko's future, my future, might depend on it.

"I repeat, was the flammable cabinet kept locked?" His voice was grave.

I had to admit no. It was the only properly vented solvent cabinet in the whole building, although the renovation would rectify that. The cabinet was used by staff in other departments, and it was in fairly constant use. The Display department stored their plexi adhesive there, the guards on the midnight shift borrowed alcohol to clean their ancient tape deck, and even Sally Luykes once rushed into the lab to grab the bottle we'd labelled "computer mouse cleaner". Anyway, who else had keys to the lab's locked doors except those same staff and MOA's 24-hour security?

"Who keeps the record of the chemicals, then?" It was Constable Frick now.

"Each department knows what they bought."

"Can you show me how much arsenic was purchased and how much has been used so far in your "salting"?"

"I'll calculate those figures for you as soon as I clean the Greek antiquities." I deserved a dog biscuit for this "good employee, now sit" act. I would live with finding out later if it was possible to produce accurate numbers. If not, I'd blame cutbacks and having too much to do with too few resources. Cutbacks in many sectors had been in the news, but it had only really hit me when I first arrived at MOA and there was no desk as part of the job, only a kneehole under a recently cleared lab counter. The mute evidence of the ravages of cutbacks could be seen in MOA's behind-the-scenes areas, all showing the wear and tear of operations and growth far beyond what they were designed for. The renovation had been needed years ago.

Sergeant Daley stood. "We require the files on the pesticide research. Constable Frick will accompany you downstairs."

"I need the files too. The records are museum procedure."

"You're allowed to keep photocopies. Note the ones you want to have." Turning to Constable Frick he said, "Give me the files as soon as possible."

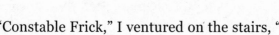

"Constable Frick," I ventured on the stairs, "I heard there was a problem with some arrows from South America. Some blood on them, I believe. Do you want me to clean those, too?"

"You don't want to clean them," she answered.

"Why not?"

"Don't you know?"

"Because they're evidence? Was there foul play?"

My too-obvious curiosity brought the answer, "You work for Reiko Smithson. You must know the research she's done on those arrowheads."

She might have been talking about how cleaning an artifact can alter its authenticity and museum value. But I heard it as Frick insinuating that Reiko was a suspect in Foley's death. I said, "That research was before my time." Frick was astute enough to see through my amateur "new-bie" acting. I shut up.

We continued downstairs towards the labs and work-rooms. In the corridor, the constable's face turned towards three posters of past exhibits that hung along the walls. One had photographs of people in ceremonial regalia coming to a potlatch in both canoes and modern fishing boats. Another celebrated the revitalization of Salish weaving with the image of a woman warping wool on an old-style loom as her child played with his plastic truck on a broadloomed floor. Nearby hung the third poster. It showed a man weaving, a complete gender break with tradition, and yet on his loom was a complicated blanket with its colours and figures; on his loom, then, was his deep respect for his heritage.

"Nothing is simple, is it?" I commented. "Nothing's black and white. It's always layered, always changing. Look at these posters. Native communities change, and yet they remain the same."

Frick turned towards me. "Like crime. Same old motives no matter who did it. Or when they lived. I wonder how many thousands of years people have been killing each other with sharp pointed objects."

"Too many," I replied. Then I asked outright, "Was Mr. Foley killed with those arrows?"

Frick paused, then relented. "No," she said. "He grabbed an arrow or hit it. We doubt if it killed him, but we're doing tests for poisons."

"They said this morning it was a heart attack."

"Possibly."

"Constable Frick," I stopped at the glass doors to the workroom. "I don't know how to ask this except directly. You just said "poisons". Why was Sergeant Daley asking me all those questions about arsenic? Why is the Conservation lab behind police tape?"

"Ms. Cates." Constable Frick said it as a fact rather than as an introductory remark.

"Berenice," I replied.

"Berenice," Constable Frick gave a quick nod of her head. "It's okay to ask." She grinned. "It *is* your workspace." She put her hand on the door handle to go into the workroom. "The coroner's report takes a bit longer. I can't say anything definite until then. It appears Mr. Foley had some kind of attack. He also died clutching his throat. The heart is not in the throat." She opened the door and held it for me to go through.

"At least the coroner's report," I said, "will confirm whether he had a heart."

"What's that?" Constable Frick stopped my progress. "Here!" she grasped my elbow and pulled me back out into the deserted corridor. "So you think Foley was heartless? Who did he hurt? Who hated him?"

"It's just something I heard. Second-hand."

"Tell me." With her tight grip on my elbow, did I have a choice?

"I don't want to incriminate anyone."

"You aren't incriminating anyone. You're telling me a rumour. Now what is it?" This woman could be a museum director, another cool-hand Luykes.

I said, "After staff knew what had happened to Mr. Foley, Jen told me that people in a lot of museums were disgusted by him." Constable Frick whipped out a notebook and jotted details as I continued. "She told me about an old First Nations mask that museums knew existed but the family never wanted to sell. The chief got sick and had to come down from the north to a hospital here. Foley arranged accommodation for his wife, and made sure the nurses treated the old man well. When the chief passed away, the family thanked Foley. He said, "It was my privilege", but made sure they knew what a valuable mask they had. How someone might steal it from the widow now that Chief Joe—I forget his last name—was gone. Sure enough, within the year, Foley had the mask for safekeeping in his vault, and then when he told the family that he could get a hundred thousand dollars for it, that one mask—who can resist that kind of money?"

"Difficult," Frick nodded. "But don't you think, Berenice, that Mr. Foley was doing some good deeds for that family, too?"

"But he was lying, on top of everything. Even if the mask sold for that, the price included his hefty commission. His crowning reward probably was he'd outwitted all the other dealers."

"So? Cuyler Foley was in business as an art dealer."

"A wheeler-dealer. He'd said he'd found a European buyer who would pay a hundred and fifty thousand. That means the only way the mask would stay in its home territory was for someone here to match the price. Even together, the museums couldn't do it. Not in this day and age of cutbacks. So the mask's somewhere now in a private collection, in a way that made Foley even more money. That's what I heard," I finished.

"Thanks, Berenice," Frick said. "I appreciate your help. It's not easy being the new person on the block, I know. I'll ask Jen to go over the details." She opened the workroom door again and we proceeded in silence through police tape into the Conservation lab.

The files on the arsenic research were, thank God, easy to locate. Conservators rely a great deal on keeping excellent records to know what was original and what was a later repair. I explained all this to Constable Frick. If these same records had been kept in the early days of museums, we would know exactly what pesticides had been used on each object.

"Good records weren't kept?"

"In some departments. But conservation as a profession didn't even exist then."

"So how were artifacts preserved?"

"Through housekeeping. And tarting up any damage." Did this make museums sound negligent? I bit my tongue and collected the files while Constable Frick waited.

Marking the reports I would need, I leafed briefly through the folders to make sure they were the pertinent ones. Losing the original documentation of our research, even if it was into police custody, was not helping my professionalism. Then Constable Frick took not only the files I handed her but also, politely, all the others I had laid aside.

"They will be kept secure," she reassured me. "You'll get copies, but it'll take a week or two."

"Yes."

"If you need any information before then, just contact me."

"Fine."

"Is there anything else right now you need?"

"No."

"Then let's go back upstairs."

We retraced our steps in silence, up the stairs, and then thankfully the police left me alone. Shit *de merde!* In my brief glances at the files, I could see that Reiko had indeed been working late in the lab these last few nights, writing down her results on arsenic and the other toxic pesticide residues. Reiko had been there when Foley had his attack. If that wasn't awful enough, something was wrong with her, too. No wonder she'd called in sick. Why did her reports show in the arsenic column what were obviously readings from mercuric chloride pesticides?

---

In the coffee room I steeped my tea, the hot cup a talisman in my hands. It was already 11:30, well past break time, too early for lunch, the morning gone, and with the cleaning deadline advancing. The only other person in the lounge was Theo, very much the dispirited curator of a now-diminished collection. A reupholstered couch sagged under his weight. Theo looked like a sad, drooping old animal. Maybe a sea lion, I thought, glancing at his badly shaven whiskers, small eyes, and bald head. The sea lion sat without speaking, sipping occasionally from an Italian faience mug, staring at the wall with its lively posters announcing current events, as if the wall were blank.

I began to feel awkward in the silence and said, "I'm sorry so much was broken. It's not irreparable, though,

Theo, the damage to your artifacts. You saw they're cleaning up well."

"Yes," he sighed, "So it all comes to what, in the end? A life, gone. A life. So much more valuable than an artifact. It gives one some perspective, doesn't it? I know what people thought of Cuyler but they never saw him like I did. He had an enormous range of knowledge—Greek and Roman and New World. Imagine."

"Unusual for one curator, isn't it, both Native American and Classical?"

"There's nothing wrong with that." But he barked the words. I wish I knew what I'd said to upset him.

My humiliation must have shown because Theo, like a good professor being delicate with a student who has asked a foolish question, explained, "Cuyler dealt in Native artifacts because that's what's sought after around here on the Northwest Coast. The Classics were his passion, though. We relied on Cuyler." Then he paused. "Maybe I never understood whether he was a curator first or a businessman first. But you know, once we were at an auction preview together and we saw this exquisite Roman lamp, and we both wanted it, and he said, "Theo, it's yours, for the museum. It's too beautiful not to be on public view." There was a long sigh as Theo sank back, staring down at his mug and wiping his forehead. I drank from my warm tea.

With a jerk of his head he roused again, facing me, no longer a sea lion diorama. "We used him for the entire Classics collection. Can you imagine his knowledge? Coins to marble statues. You probably know the law forbids us to evaluate acquisitions ourselves. Over a thousand dollars in value, it has to be arm's length."

Was I his audience for a practice lecture for the police?

Theo paused, looked at the floor, then raised his head. "Eventually you'll restore my broken pieces, and they'll always be restorations and not rare whole beauties, but the museum world has lost a great deal more with this tragedy."

Was this speech a little too forced? The praise a little too magnanimous for a colleague who might have rivalled him in some ways? Theo's life's work was devoted to ancient Greece and Rome. That was clear, although there was something having to do with knowing world cultures as well, or at least North American Native cultures, that Theo had reacted to; maybe Foley had bested or embarrassed him somehow. The Classics were Theo's sure ground. But he was clearly disturbed about Foley's death. Theo's upset made me curious not only about what had happened last night and what he might know about it, but made me think again of Sunday's lecture, wondering what the relationship between the two men had been.

"I hear the tragedy might be murder," I said. To me there is an obvious answer to "poison plus dead body equals. . . ."

"Yes," said Theo vaguely. He had sunk back again, gazing at the wall.

I asked the question I had wanted to all morning. "Theo, how did Mr. Foley die?"

He turned to face me. "Horribly."

I gasped. "How awful. I'm so sorry."

"I've heard he was . . ." Theo stammered, "poisoned. They think now by arsenic."

"Arsenic?" I said loudly, coughing to disguise the tremor in my voice. "How?"

"Apparently he had coffee with the Director before he came downstairs to evaluate the acquisitions, and this might have been the source."

"Apparently, Theo?" Dr. Sally Luykes stood in the coffee room doorway, china cup in hand. I knew immediately how she had appeared so suddenly and quietly. The staff lounge with its ever-open door was opposite the main office. The Director's office connected, naturally enough, to the main one, but also had another exit onto the hall, directly opposite the lounge. Luykes must have surprised coffee room conversations on a regular basis.

"Apparently arsenic might have been in the coffee," she continued, "and that will be determined by the police soon enough. It's interesting that when you and Cuyler came back from dinner, as soon as you sat down in my office for coffee, you excused yourself to make a phone call to England."

Theo apparently did not hear the acerbic tone of the Director's voice. He nodded his head slowly and said, "Fax, not phone. I had to resend it. I remembered it hadn't gone through, and I had to have it at the British Museum when they opened."

"I hear Reiko is being questioned by the police," I interjected. If anyone knew more, it would be these two.

"Yes, Berenice, I'm afraid she is. She's now being interrogated," Luykes said. "She was working late and I saw her up here in the lounge. I asked her to make the coffee."

*Chapter*
# 6

~~~

## Tuesday Afternoon

B ack in the workroom Jen had roused Zoe and Heather out of their concerns for an upcoming TV rerun with an invitation to lunch, and asked if I wanted to join. "Anything to get off-campus," I replied, and added, "I mean, thanks. I'd love to." If I could bear to eat after my abominable morning. "I'll find something to talk to Z and H about."

"You'd better. Why do you think I invited you?" Jen winked as we charged up the corridor.

She drove the ten minutes over to West 10th, the closest shopping street with no campus quirks. We settled for good cheap Chinese, and my appetite was restored. Asian food was next to chocolate in my major food groups. Chocolate. Of course. After deciding on the house special soup I got up to dash across the street to the gourmet chocolate shop. No need to stumble through artificial conversation with my young workmates if I could say it with chocolate.

I almost ended up hurling myself into the traffic because inside our restaurant, at a small table by the door, sat Max Turpin, reading. My eyes had been riveted by a gleaming plate of mixed mushrooms, greens and . . . chopsticks lifting morsels into an unmistakable mouth. With my head turned sideways, my feet tobogganed straight out the door onto the road. I found myself between parked cars, catching my breath, and awkwardly dodged to the opposite sidewalk. In the chocolate shop, I bought five dark truffles instead of four. The last one in a separate bag. Crossing back at the traffic lights I had the time to shake off my jitters, and ambled through the restaurant door to deposit the small white bag.

"It's probably been one of those days for you, too," I said to the curator, and headed back towards my chair. Was it the reply or the three sets of greedy eyes from my own table that made me blush?

"What an unexpected pleasure!" Max beamed. "You're a silver lining in a charcoal cloud. Thank you."

With a nod and a smile I went to my waiting wonton. When I didn't gossip, Heather couldn't hold back. "Can you tell us about the cops all over your lab? I hear they want to talk to you and Reiko about your chemical cupboard."

"Where'd you hear that from?" I hid my mouth behind the soupspoon.

"Coffee room," Zoe said, fiddling with her fluorescent green moon and stars earrings. "Has Conservation done something wrong? I mean, like, not deliberately."

The whole coffee room must be buzzing with rumours, insinuations. I said, "I don't know what someone new like me could tell them."

"They already interviewed you," stated Heather. A museum might have territorial departments, locked doors and displays, but none of that guaranteed privacy at MOA.

Jen intervened by turning the topic back to the one really on their minds. "Max. Has he said anything?"

"Yeah, he sure liked that chocolate," Heather grinned.

"Look, he's getting up," said Zoe.

"Now you can invite him over," said Heather.

"He's finished."

"So what? Invite him over!"

"These wontons are good." I replied. "I'm ravenous."

"Well, it's one o'clock. What time do we have to be back, Jen?"

"Gutsy," said Jen to me. "Max adores chocolate. He says it's an aphrodisiac."

<hr />

In the MOA parking lot I was finally able to get Jen on her own as the Collections Assistants raced towards the building.

"They're eager to get to work," I commented.

"They're eager to get to a mirror first. Good you didn't say anything more to Z and H about the chemical cupboard. They'd love a scandal."

"There's absolutely nothing wrong in Conservation."

With no more than thirty seconds before we reached the door, I said, "Jen, tell me about MOA's poison arrows."

"You tell me about Cupid's arrows—you and Max, eh? What's up?" Jen stopped, blocking my way.

In the remaining time this was not important. "For God's sakes. Nothing!"

"You didn't bring that truffle for nothing."

"Information." I hoped this sounded plausible. "I wanted to ask him what he has against Reiko's research. Now what about the arrows?"

"Curare? Ask Reiko. Max? Ask Reiko too." I kept my mouth shut about Reiko already telling me a few details about her and Max, and grabbed the door so Jen couldn't open it. She was right on the scent. There was a lot I didn't know about Max, and my curiosity must be evident. Was I actually, as Jen proposed, flirting? I repeated, "The poison arrows."

"The big bad arrows? You owe me another truffle. Dark chocolate with brandy, please."

"Done," I grinned. "Why were the arrows beside the Classics artifacts Foley was working on?"

"Like I said, they were on the table because I had nowhere else to put them while we made the final loan corrections. End of story. Then Theo spread out the Classics pieces so Foley would have more room."

Theo? This was not the end of the story.

---

All afternoon I bent over the ceramic sherds one by one, gently levering off micro-fragments of dried skin and clotted blood. Whole geometric and figurative designs surfaced on the earthenware, slightly darkened. My mind focused on Reiko. She did her conservation work in the interests of the collections, the public trust, rather than backing personal staff ambition. Reiko's refusal to compromise if she thought the collections would suffer must have made her more than a few enemies in the years she had been here. Would her enemies consider her intern their foe too?

I looked up to rest my eyes on a distant focus, and caught the policeman at my table flexing his arm muscles. In his twenties, I couldn't fault him for finding Heather and Zoe more interesting than me and my old bits of pottery.

"This must be very boring," I said to make conversation.

"It's my job, Ma'am."

Police actually still said ma'am?

"Can I ask you a question, or aren't you supposed to talk?"

"Sure, go ahead."

"In your experience . . ." I began, then changed it and said, "From what you know . . ." and added, " . . . or have heard or read . . . do the perpetrators of crimes usually use poison these days?"

"Some. Mostly women."

This was not what I wanted to hear.

"Okay, here's a scenario," I said. "Person A asks Person B to prepare some food, say. Would B be likely to put poison in it if she figured A knew she'd made it?"

"What if A's dead? Who's the intended victim? You'd also have to establish who else knew. Even if A's not the real victim, maybe he's dead because B poisons everyone associated."

"What else would you investigate?" I silently apologized for pegging this young man as a dumb cop.

"Lots. What kind of poison, where'd it come from . . ."

"Let's say Person B was known to have poison in her house. Maybe to kill rats. Would she go ahead and kill someone if people knew she kept poison? Her house would be the first place to look."

"Motive," he answered. "What was her relationship with the victim? Was it accidental or deliberate poisoning? Means, motive, and opportunity."

He was right. Anyone who knew about the pesticide residue research could find the means in the museum, but who really had it in for Foley? Aboriginal people who felt their family had been cheated? These days they could easily go to the media and expose him, or organize boycotts so no one would sell him anything. Deduction Number One: the person would have had to be in the museum last night. Brilliant, Cates.

But maybe Foley's death was an accident. Maybe Reiko had inadvertently gotten some of the arsenic on her clothing when she was testing the samples for the report. When she made the coffee she might have wiped her hands on her lab coat and some arsenic fell into a cup, and Foley's death was all a horrible misadventure. Like the figures in the wrong columns in the files I gave Constable Frick. Reiko was so careful, though; the research was valueless without precision. She would never have spilled the quantity of arsenic needed to poison anyone in one go. Well, how much would that be . . . what did I really know about arsenic? Nothing. But I knew about tea and coffee. I headed upstairs for afternoon break.

⁕❦⁕

The voice was loud. Not as in yelling, but as in operatic, filling the whole upper lobby by the reception desk, its carpeted floor becoming a stage. The extras on the sidelines were being played by museum visitors stashing their knapsacks in lockers, coming out of the washrooms, and kids fingering the tourist brochures. All were attentive, barely moving, careful not to steal the scene from the baritone at centre stage. I recognized the other characters around whom this scene revolved: Sergeant Daley; Lorna, the Northwest Coast curator; and Mama, the guard. The casting director of this opera had done well. The man with the deep rich voice was towering over the sergeant. Lorna, ramrod-straight as she came up behind the baritone in her Thunderbird-crested vest, looked the heroine. Mama wouldn't need to sing a word; with her folded arms and immutable face she barely needed a uniform to signal her role. I slid over to join the audience, or maybe it was the chorus.

"I dashed in to pick up an umbrella I left last night," the tall man said. Modern opera, then: not quite the drama of Wagner. "I have no time right now, Sergeant."

"Just a few questions, sir."

"What's all this about?" The baritone swivelled to Lorna, but before she could open her mouth Sergeant Daley pointed to the open classroom door.

"In here. Please." Daley did have a strong voice when he wanted.

"Is this an order?" The baritone was angry now.

"Not yet."

"I've absolutely got to go." Polite but livid. He gave Lorna a peck on the cheek. Mama stepped forward as if to escort him out. She had placed herself in the path of the sergeant. Another incident at MOA. How much did I actually want to know about this place I work in, the word "museum" I now spelled as M for Murder, U for Unsolved, S for Secrets, E for Enemies. And then a second U and M for Ugly Mess.

"One very quick question, sir," Daley persevered. "You're on a MOA exhibits committee. Do you agree with your heritage being in museums?"

The man wheeled around. "Salish culture is not in museums!" The volume of his voice reverberated through the lobby. "Our culture is not for sale."

This anger wasn't about Foley's murder, but about other things in museums' closets. I straightened up to clue in.

The sergeant adopted a mystified face. "Surely, sir, there are artifacts in . . ."

"Artifacts? That's a museum word. We don't have artifacts."

"Objects, then. Cultural property."

"My culture is not your kind of property, to be bought and sold. My culture belongs to me, my family, my community, my ancestors. And the generations to come. Sure, my family has a mask in the city museum. But my grandson won't learn his culture there. I'm head of Lorna's advisory committee because museums have a purpose, if they listen. If they don't, I don't care what happens to them. They can vanish from the face of the earth and maybe should." He smiled. "As long as we get our stuff back first. But remember one thing: my grandson will learn his culture from the Longhouse, not the museum."

There was silence. Several bystanders looked poised to applaud.

"Are you acquainted with Cuyler Foley?"

"Hah. How do you think our mask got in the city museum thirty years ago?"

"There are a few questions . . ."

"Here's my card. Call my cell. Give Cuyler my regards." The tall man turned on his heels and strode out.

Sergeant Daley gave him a good twenty-pace lead, pulled out his cellphone, and started punching in the numbers.

———————— ⚬☙☙☙⚬ ————————

The staff lounge was crowded and I didn't want to make nice. I snuck my steaming tea past the visitors in the lobby and sat outside on a shady bench banked by cedars. Anyone on staff could have taken the arsenic out of the cabinet in Conservation, wanting Foley dead. Or Luykes or Theo dead. That person knew where the arsenic was kept—well, the whole museum knew about the ongoing pesticide residue research—and could have put it in the coffee. Or the cream.

Or the sugar. But Sally Luykes and Theo were the only two officially with Foley last night.

When I started out in Conservation, if anyone had asked me to, I would have kissed a museum floor every day for finding myself halfway through my life in a new line of work I loved and was useful. I blushed with the memory of crowing to my Toronto friends when I landed this internship, "A conservator preserves a country's heritage. Collections give us what's real about the past. They're authentic. Witnesses that remain long after we're gone." That memorable evening when I was leaving Toronto for Vancouver, we'd toasted, "To a life of preserving good things."

My view of museum work and that toast rang hollow now. I should just finish the job, forget Cuyler Foley, forget cleaning flesh and blood, and forget that other queasiness in my stomach when my mind asked what was going on in this museum. Just move on, Cates. But it didn't work that way. How could someone implicated in a murder scene, however wrongly, simply go on with her normal work? I emptied my remaining tea on the ground, sat like a forgotten antiquity for a good five minutes, then trudged inside.

At my worktable I began to think through the mess. Either I should leave MOA right now while I could extricate myself before things got worse, or I should figure out the facts. Put the pieces together like any conservator restoring a broken artifact. Leaning over a pad of paper, I pencilled notes the policeman might think were conservation treatment summaries. "Motive," I scrawled, and "Opportunity". Then, "Means" and here I filled in "poison". Listing "Theo Younge, Sally Luykes, Reiko Smithson" under "Opportunity," I wrote under "Motive," "unscrupulous art dealer?"

That was all I had, and immediately began rewriting it because the list should have started with "Victim." We all knew the answer, but I had to ask myself if Cuyler Foley was the intended victim.

Someone planning to kill Luykes rather than Foley could have slipped a little arsenic into her office coffee tray's sugar bowl. A white powder goes into a white powder. But who would want to go so far as to kill the Director? Well, metaphorically, everyone talks about getting back at their boss at one time or another, but really. Here? In a non-profit museum? Murder Dr. Sally Luykes, whose major fault as far as I could see was that she was simply head and shoulders above the rest of us? Did she even take sugar?

More questions sprang up. Under "Opportunity" I added, "confirm nobody else in museum". Under "Means" I put in the details: 1. arsenic, 2. curare, and then remembered the Roman cloak pin that had lain hidden in Foley's pocket.

Another kind of brain light went on. I had spent the last how long in this once-coveted internship in a state of nauseous questioning. Was it because, in the careful process of a conservation treatment, sitting over broken sherds, swabbing and lifting, lifting and swabbing, there had been far too much time to ponder and obsess? The full inner life. But I knew I couldn't stop myself. And didn't want to, either. My brain was set on sorting this museum out. Saving Reiko's skin and my own. I had acknowledged long ago that my mind liked putting sherds together.

"Jen," I called down the length of the workroom. I had to discover who else knew about the curare on the arrows. And ask her why Reiko disliked Foley. Or was a better description "hate"—enough to want to kill him?

"Not here," came carolling back from the far end.

That was close. Why give clues to anyone that I was sniffing around, since the death had too many unknowns.

And so far all clues pointed to a deliberate act. Murder. By a perpetrator who had been in the museum that night.

———————— ❦ ————————

By 5 o'clock I had managed to lose myself in cleaning most of the red figureware and the amphora. The delicate designs of men and horses were beautifully evident once more. Apart from the big scratch I'd done well, but I hadn't yet started on the third drinking cup or on the bronzes. Work stopped, though, when the constable stationed at my worktable got a message on his walkie-talkie that I was wanted at the front desk, and he escorted me upstairs.

There was a man waiting for me. Daniel! Today he was all in black, linen jacket worn like a cloak over his shoulders, black pants and fitted long-sleeved jersey, and one vivid cobalt blue fringe of a summerweight muffler hanging down his chest. "*Que t'es beau,*" I murmured under my breath. "You are so handsome."

Daniel and I often spoke French together. I'm a Poirier way back on my mother's side, and I still remember solemnly repeating French phrases to my grandmother when I was small. I had always explored the francophone part of my background, and it had led me to study French at a university in Quebec and eventually tutor French when I settled in Toronto after my marriage. As Daniel's mother tongue was French, he relaxed into it. Many residents of Vancouver are bilingual, but one language is usually Mandarin or Cantonese or Hindi, and it was a pleasure for both of us to live a little bit *en français* here.

Daniel had come to meet me for our beach walk and dinner. I couldn't believe, even given the emotion of the day, that I had forgotten about it. The memory of the whole weekend came surging up, Daniel outside my door late Friday, flushed, jabbering about his new promotion. All I heard was "return to Québec" and "very soon." When my unwilling mind asked him to repeat this great news, he humbly emphasized that the job as lead investigative reporter for a new show was in Quebec City and not Radio-Canada's mothership in Montréal, but it was truly "*une belle job*." I was overwhelmed, sandbagged by a heavy, familiar despair. He was walking out the door. So our hot date on Saturday night had not exactly been a big success.

This had been our first real date, too, to my way of thinking. Way in advance Daniel had asked me out, and even on Friday when he'd told me he was leaving, he said he was glad this new assignment didn't start until after Saturday, that we'd still be able to go out together. He had said early he was taking me to a club but that I didn't need to dress up. So of course I'd spent considerable time as I drove back and forth to work in the preceding weeks stopping in consignment stores, comparing what I saw with my own old outfits, which ones I had shoes for, which looked too dowdy, which too "mutton dressed up as lamb". I almost went into some real stores but, after two years of being a student, I succumbed to my better, cheaper judgement. In the end, I chose an old fave but still unseen in Vancouver: a slimming black velvet A-line skirt with an unusual hem that gave life to the whole ensemble, and a flashy brown and black almost off-the-shoulder top that changed colour as it moved. I spent hours on my hair and nails. That sure was wasted time.

Daniel took me to a comedy club. It was a pub-and-theatre. For amateurs. I might as well have been wearing sweat pants and running shoes. Eventually, though, I got into the comedians' jokes; some were so funny the audience gave standing ovations after the act. Once I found myself nearly burping up my beer when one woman, doing both voices, was describing going back to school after her kids had grown up. She portrayed being in the professor's office with a "C" on her essay on early childhood education. The prof was saying, "if you'd read the text more closely . . ." The woman howled, "But you're a baby! You're just a baby! And I'm a Mom!" The prof then stood up, emphasizing his full height, and answered, "I graduated over five years ago." The comedienne replied to this, acting with her whole body, "Your point? YOUR POINT?"

It had me laughing, and when I turned to see if a man like Daniel had enjoyed it as much, he was gone. Washroom, another beer, I didn't know. I turned back to the stage, but when he still wasn't there after the next ten-minute shtick had finished, my own beer began to sour in my belly. It wasn't going to be a big bill he was sticking me with, but what had I done now? I had taken the club venue in stride, I'd thought, obviously surprised but joking about ordering a velvety liqueur to match my skirt. The two of us had had fun talking right up until the acts came on.

I started to get up to move around, stretch out my annoyance. A good time to go to the washroom. I heard the master of ceremonies announce, "And now *notre comédien favori,* Daniel Tremblay!" I foundered in a wave of applause and sunk back onto the metal chair.

"*Allô, allô!*" Daniel, lit up onstage, grinned and waved at the audience from an oversized red-and-black plaid lumber jacket, a string of small deer antlers dangling from his left hand. *Le beau* Daniel who usually dressed with flair in the most tasteful, intriguing clothes. His alter ego had certainly got his part right.

"*Allô, allô!*" yelled the audience back.

"*Comment ça va?*"

"*Oui! Bien! Allô! Allô!*" shouted his audience, who may or may not have understood what he said. But they knew him. Daniel was a regular here, then.

"Let me tell you about my time up north," said Daniel, and a peal of laughter and more applause erupted. It sounded like this was the way he always opened his act.

"Let me tell you about my time up north," he began again. "There's this new service up north, you know. It's a 1-800 number and you gotta be an adult to use it, eh." Daniel was exaggerating his francophone voice, but was speaking with a Native accent as well. I squirmed. He thought this was funny? Who was this guy, this neighbour I had been fantasizing about? Inviting me, proud of working for a museum whose motto was "Partnerships with Peoples," to a performance where he made fun of Quebeckers and First Nations? People could turn out to be so different from what you thought.

"So last weekend I dialled up this 1-800- . . ." He did a stage whisper for the last part of the number. "You see me after the show for the rest. I gotta see ID, make sure you got enough age on you." He paused to scrutinize a particularly beautiful young blonde at a front table. Laughter.

"This is the deal," he continued. It came out, "Dis ees le dil." Let me leave now before this stereotyping gets any worse.

"It's like phone sex," he went on in his stupid voice. "Only better. It's phone hunt!" I looked for an exit.

"Dial-a-Mammal!" Daniel shouted it out and rattled the antlers. He pulled an animal horn from under his plaid jacket, wrapped its braided cord around his arm and blew a long moose call. I'd had enough of this pseudo-woodsy Canadiana from my "*beau* Daniel." But there were too many people between me and the exit to leave unnoticed, and I wasn't trying to be nasty to him. Daniel's surprise for this date had appalled me, if I was honest with myself, but I didn't think of myself as mean. It took all my willpower to remain mature and seated.

"Line cut out. Up north you gotta punch in the full number each time, eh. Takes a long, long time and if you make a mistake, you can end up calling your auntie instead." There was some laughter. Not much, I silently applauded, but I peeked around and the audience was rapt, waiting.

"Hey, hi, this is Jim. Is this 1-800 . . ." and he whispered the rest. He was now speaking into the horn as if it was a phone.

"Jim. This is Auntie Mabel. What on earth you whispering for? Why you calling me this time of night?"

"Ooops. Sorry, Auntie, I was just trying to order some pizza, eh. Bye now. Bye, Auntie." He hung up by dangling the horn on his sleeve.

"Boy, that was close. Try again. For a real good hunt, call 1-800- . . ." Daniel made the sound of beeps as he slowly pressed each digit into the phone.

"Hey, hi, this is Jim. Is this 1-800 . . . whisper whisper whisper?"

For the response he put on a sultry voice. "Well, hi Jim. What would you like today?"

"I'd like to get a big one."

Eewww. And the fool audience was laughing.

"Big Jim, is that what they call you? Tell me what you like, Big Jim."

"I like caribou."

"Mmmm. I like caribou too."

"You know," Daniel addressed the audience, "the best thing about this hunt phone line is you get a real mammal on the other end." Delighted shouts and a few whistles.

"And you're sitting inside, eh? You're not out freezing your butt in some snowbank. It's all cosy, you're even getting hot, man. Real hot. It's like the caribou is right in your hands. And they deliver. I mean, they really deliver."

(Sultry) "I could have a hundred pounds of caribou at your door tonight, Big Jim."

(Jim) "Ohboy. Ohboyohboyohman." (Begins breathing audibly. Caresses the horn.) "So how much? Maybe I want two hundred pounds."

(Sultry) "It's only $1.79 a pound, Big Jim."

(Jim suddenly looks at audience.) "Boy is this tempting. But then she wants cash, eh." I was laughing now. Daniel was right on target. He talked into the "phone," "Naw. You got pizza? Yeah, double pepperoni, make it all-dressed."

"That'll be $44.95, Jim. Delivery extra."

Daniel let the horn and antlers drop on their strings, and put his hands on his hips. "Boy, you all know that's a good deal for up north. Let me know if you want the number."

He bowed and exited to a loud ovation. I clapped too.

<hr/>

When Daniel finally made it back to his seat beside me, bits of make-up and sweat still on his face, clapped on the back by the crowd as he passed through, he couldn't stop grinning.

"You really got me laughing," I had to admit. And I leaned across and kissed him. He cupped my head and kept my lips to his.

We sat in silence after that, looking at each other. I didn't know what to say, and maybe he didn't know either, although I was hoping he would lead off. Finally he said, under cover of his stage accent, "So you liked it, eh?"

"You were very funny, although in all honesty I was a bit worried at first." I could see by his look that this wasn't the best time for honesty, but I was in too far not to finish. "I didn't know if you were making fun of aboriginal people, with your accent."

"What about Québécois?" he returned.

"Them too," I said. "But you're Québécois, so you can make jokes and get away with it. I think an insider can make jokes I couldn't, even with my mixed background."

"How do you know I don't have some mixed background, too?"

"I thought the Tremblays were all '*pure laine*,'" I said, using the Québécois expression "pure wool", the equivalent of "came over on the Mayflower." And generations never marrying those who didn't, or in this case, weren't Catholic like themselves.

"Sure, *pure laine*," replied Daniel. "But even wool has to be spun. And you spin with different strands." I looked at his dark hair and blue eyes and remembered the poster at the museum, of the Salish weaver working on her traditional loom and her child with the red plastic truck. Nothing was simple, even this Saturday date. Just yesterday, Friday, I was floored when I'd heard he was leaving; two hours ago I was disappointed in him, dressed to the nines as I was, heading into a scruffy club; little more than a half hour ago I was writhing in my seat hearing him begin his monologue and glad it was all going to end soon. Now I'd kissed him and depression was sinking back in because he was leaving.

"A penny for your thoughts," said Daniel.

"Let's go," I said, and took his hand.

As we exited I saw Theo, of all people, at a table at the back with a young blonde woman, one of the students in the museum classes.

# Chapter
## 7

## Tuesday Continues At
## The Museum

I pulled Daniel into a dark corner of the club where I could get a better look at Theo and his date.

"They were here last week too," said Daniel as he followed my gaze.

My jaw dropped. Here, in this corny place, a MOA Classics professor? Or was this some crazy doppelganger with his beer and a blonde? But bald and wearing a shabby tweed vest? The young woman tossed her hair, and her face was spotlit for an instant in a shaft of light.

"Ah," I said, shoulders dropping an inch with my sigh. No funny business here. I'd met the young woman at the museum's student get-together. Theo was having a night out with his daughter. But why at an amateur comedy club? Likely I didn't want to know the response. It had taken me long enough to answer that question for Daniel and myself. I waved but they were engrossed in their conversation.

Back at our building Daniel kissed me warmly, but in the French fashion, on both cheeks. Maybe he was just being the gallant. Then he said, "Good-night," and headed up the stairs to his apartment. I stood frozen at my open door. Half-way up he saw I was still there and said, "*Merci, ma belle*. A very fun evening. I am going to miss you and this house very much." And that was that for the big Saturday night date.

---

Here it was Tuesday, a lifetime away for Cuyler Foley and a changed time for the rest of us. And for my image of MOA, no quiet dusty temple to the past as museums have been labelled. The past here held secrets vile enough for murder. No wonder Daniel and the end of the week hadn't entered my thoughts all day. Friday Daniel would be flying out on his new assignment. Even his cat would fly out; Daniel's aunt was in Quebec and said she'd be glad to keep Faux Paws anytime.

Seeing Daniel at the museum, I smiled in spite of myself. The beach walk and *haute cuisine* at the French restaurant was to be our last outing. Tomorrow was his going-away party at work. Thursday his new boss was passing through Vancouver. Friday he was gone. And I had forgotten!

"*Bonjour la restauratrice!*" Daniel exclaimed, and gave me a light kiss on each cheek. Then his smile faded and his face screwed up. His hands gripped my arms.

"What's wrong? What's the matter?" he said in rapid French. "You look awful. Why the police?" he said at a higher pitch, as he fully comprehended my escort.

"I'm fine," I replied in French, and then my knees sprawled. "Coffee," I said, comprehensible in many languages. I put my arm around Daniel's shoulder and half-supported myself into the lounge. We sat down in one corner, he tactfully got all the necessities together, and I began to break down. Not in a major way—my generation learned, like my mother's and hers before her, to soldier on—but I pulled out a tissue for my nose and an inconspicuous eye dab. Daniel sat down beside me and held my hand. I could barely hear myself speak as after-images flashed into my head while I described arriving to a death scene and all day cleaning human flesh, blood, and vomit from broken sherds.

Gradually my voice regained its normal pitch. Even so, inside I was a mess. Acid sloshed up and around in my gut. My heart had begun to race, as if only this action would keep the disparate parts of my body from trying to flee an embedded sadness, disgust, and anger. It didn't help that Daniel's professional journalist's interest started to get the better of him. His eyes glinted with curiosity when he heard about Foley's death; he interjected questions, and his hand unconsciously went to his pocket for a notebook.

I made a decision and interrupted Daniel before I could change my mind.

"Look," I said in English, "I don't think I can go for dinner."

"What?" Daniel repeated it as if I'd insulted him.

"I can't go. I won't be good company, and really, I can't leave. I have to finish cleaning the objects. They need them, for evidence," I said, even though it was a lie, "and I'm supposed to have them done." This I was sure of.

"But this is impossible. I have not another time." Daniel's expressive voice was almost whining, and it gave me a small measure of satisfaction. He was the one who had chosen to leave.

"What about Thursday evening, after you finish with your boss?" I said.

"It is impossible now."

"Give me a call anyway."

"No, it is not working this way anymore. Why do you have to stay *au musée?* You're not well. Finish tomorrow. I will take you home."

"I can't, Daniel," I replied, not knowing whether I was speaking against or with my better judgment, only that I was too vulnerable right now to make any good decisions around this man who was leaving my life. "I have to finish here. Especially if it's a murder investigation."

"You don't want to have dinner with me." Daniel was not stupid.

"I do, I do, but not right now. I'm too upset. I can't eat. And I have to finish my work. Anyway, you've decided to leave town, and this death has nothing to do with you."

"That is a lousy insinuendo," Daniel broke in coldly, and I smiled in spite of myself at his new word. "You can make your work," he said, dropping to the direct translation of the French verb *"faire"*. "But when I do the same for mine, something is bad."

Before I could muster a reply, Daniel continued, "This afternoon was a phone call. Big scandal breaking in Québec. Now I leave tomorrow morning, eight in the morning. If you decide to go home, call my cell." He stood and walked out the door.

Able to rationalize almost anything, I was already saying, "He's leaving Vancouver anyway, I really am not hungry and I don't feel like talking." I was going to pay no attention whatsoever to my stomach, my breathing, my heart. Instead, I indulged in memories of my Quebec student days and tutoring French in Ontario. Daniel's English was fairly good, completely comprehensible, but definitely not perfect. I used to tell my language students, "Don't be stopped by your mistakes. Sure they're humiliating, but look at them as your original contribution to the spoken word." For all of us who attempted a second language, or at least for whoever heard us, words like "insinuendo" were delicious. Daniel's mistake had brought back the memory of the time I was studying French at Laval and was explaining to the elderly aunt of a Quebec City friend that my father's people had come from the Isle of Man, famous for the cats there being tail-less. I mispronounced the word "*queue*" for tail, and it sounded like "*cul*" for "ass". "*Oui, Mme Simard, c'est vrai*—It's true, Mme Simard, cats without assholes." This was not nearly as embarrassing, though, as when my francophone friend came to Toronto and went into a hair-cutting establishment and asked for a "shampoo and a blow job, please". Both of us now could laugh at these unplanned "insinuendos". It was, I kept telling myself, asking too much of yourself to be perfect. If only I could do as I said.

I was just escaping into reminiscence. But my stomach had settled down. I was not submerged by feelings of abandonment, reactions if not over-reactions I appreciated only too well were linked to my pre-50 existence. Formerly known as life. I was feeling calm. Maybe I just wasn't feeling yet. Or maybe it was because a decision had been made. Daniel was . . . had . . . left, period.

I glimpsed museum staff walking past the coffee room with their coats on, heading home. Already? I'd better get on with it since I'd been so clear with Daniel. Without knowing he was leaving tomorrow, dammit. What would "Ms.-I'm-in-control-of-my-life" have done if I'd known first? Well, I wasn't going to be humiliated. I wouldn't call him. Buoyed up by my narrative, I relished being alone downstairs to pursue my work, with only a bored policeman who didn't know what my work was except not running off with any pottery sherds. I knew that my job tonight included more cleaning at least, and figuring out Reiko.

While I was preparing the files for Constable Frick, a frightening series of notations had jumped out at me. Like the mercuric chloride readings in the arsenic column. It wasn't just that Reiko had been working unusually late, and working on arsenic research on the precise evening when a man had suffered an attack in an adjacent room as poison worked through his body. Part of the research notes Reiko wrote that evening were confusing, and there was some routine information that looked just plain wrong. Why would the readings be higher on the inside of the lab coat and gloves tested at the end of the day than on the outside? This mistake was incomprehensible. Had Reiko been poisoned as well? Was that why she was sick?

The police constable came into the coffee room.

"I'm outta here," he announced. "You're on your own."

"They aren't replacing you?" I could hardly mask the pleasure in my voice.

"Cutbacks. Lemme remind you that the stuff downstairs is all numbered. I'll be counting each piece tomorrow morning."

"Have fun." Maybe he would think I meant now, after work.

I jumped up. I'd won the lottery. Budget cutbacks had for once worked to my advantage.

---

It was almost 7:30 before I looked up from the cleaning. I may have overdone my "good intern" work ethic; my eyes were popping. "Another visit to the optometrist," I groused.

Keeping up with eye aging was prohibitively expensive. Think again about leaving this job. "Need a hearing aid too." I'd missed Sally Luykes coming into the workroom earlier. What else am I not aware of? Slowly reaching for my tools, I wiped each one and placed them in order for tomorrow.

The door opened, and in walked Reiko. When she gave me a wink and a short thumbs-up she didn't look sick or as if she had spent God knows how long being questioned and still had two RCMP constables walking beside her. I adjusted my glasses.

"Reiko!" I walked quickly alongside the tables to greet her. She gave me a strong hug, and it took Constable Frick tapping both of us on the shoulder to get us to separate, gently reminding us that this was not "ahem" a normal situation. Even though Reiko wasn't under arrest, she was nevertheless here to show the police where everything occurred, to give evidence, and all of this was being recorded.

"I don't care," I whispered to Reiko, "I've got to talk to you."

Up close I could see Reiko did look tired. Under her eyes were dark stains and her jaw muscles showed through pale skin.

Turning to Constable Frick, Reiko said, "I need to talk to Berry before I lose my voice with this stupid cold. I need to make sure everything's okay in my absence."

"Go ahead then, but out loud, in my presence," was the reply, and Frick moved between us. I involuntarily looked down to see where the puck would drop.

"What can I do for you?" I said to Reiko. I thought this was a good first question, nothing to arouse suspicion.

With Frick's young keen ears so close, I couldn't ask the real questions. About the pesticide residue notations and poison arrow research project, her thoughts on Foley's death, and who in this museum might have wanted to do what to whom, why, and what about the insinuations involving her and Conservation. Instead, we went over a few details of ongoing artifact treatments, meetings, where she kept a house key hidden and medication I might have to get for her. "Can I keep in touch? Email or phone?" I expressed worry about her health, and eventually did slip in that I noticed the mercury readings had been put in the arsenic column last night.

"Oh, I'll make a note." Reiko dismissed my concern. I wasn't put off; it was understandable her mind was elsewhere. I'd broach the question another time.

"I saw everything, you know." Her voice broke. "I couldn't reach him in time. I was in Conservation and heard this awful crash. I could see Foley through the door. He was half on the table, vomiting, trying to push himself up, grabbing at anything for purchase. Then he collapsed. Smashing whatever was left. He twisted. I was almost there." She pulled a shredded tissue out of her pocket. "Foley was, like, reaching out to me with one of the bronzes in his hand, and the next instant blood was pouring out of his mouth. He grabbed his throat. He started convulsing with this terrified look." I hugged Reiko tightly and this time Constable Frick stood and waited. "I was too late," Reiko whispered. "He fell. I rolled him over so his blood and vomit wouldn't block his throat, but I don't think he was even breathing."

For a few minutes I whispered, "It's okay, it's okay, it's going to be okay" over and over, and at one point I put into the singsong, "did you make coffee, coffee for Luykes, coffee for Luykes?"

"I'm glad he's dead," came her vehement spit of words, jumping me back. "What a bastard. Cheater. He exploited everyone." Reiko straightened her back and brushed her straggling hair from her face. "I finished up the evening's work after Emergency came. I could easily have screwed up the wrong columns for the readings."

Scrutinizing my face, Reiko said, "Look, I'm in the middle of research, working late for a non-profit museum that can't pay overtime, with about an hour more before I can go home, and the Director asks me to wash cups, kiss ass. No, as I told the police last night and today, I refused to make the coffee when Sally asked."

# *Chapter*
# 8

## Tuesday Evening

Constable Frick had already begun to take Reiko's arm and move her towards her research table. "I'm sorry, Berenice," she said, "but I'll have to ask you to leave. Please don't stay in the next room either." I hurriedly gathered up my jacket and bags and tried to catch Reiko's eyes. I don't know if she looked at me or not.

Security would have a record of who had been in the museum last night. I took the stairs to head straight to the guards' station. If Reiko hadn't made the coffee, who had?

Operatic theatre, though, was unaccountably still in progress at the top of the stairs: Act V, or an encore at this late hour. This was the evening the museum stayed open late, and a crowd stood in the margins ogling the unusual scene. The stairs up from the basement workrooms emerge into the part of the lobby where I'd witnessed the baritone's matinee performance. The baritone wasn't there now but the theatrics continued. Centre stage was still anchored by Sergeant Daley. He stood where he had earlier, but gripping his hands behind his back as he conversed with one of his constables. I recognized a new actor, his tall skinny frame slouched outside the classroom that had been taken over by the police. The thin man was contemplating the clock on the wall, then Daley's back, the clock, the Sergeant. The end of the normal workday had not stopped the police interviews. This time Sergeant Daley saw me, broke his conversation, and hauled me on stage.

"Ms. Cates, glad you're still here." I had to advance to hear him better. "Don't bother with the whole run of those arsenic figures."

"Arsenic figures?" I searched my menopausal memory for my conversation with Daley.

"You were preparing a report for us on the amount of arsenic your lab purchased and the amount used up in your research. Forget the figures before, say, six months ago."

"Because?"

He shook his head. "Reiko's concern, not yours."

The lean figure said. "With respect, Sergeant, I want those figures."

Sergeant Daley flushed. He took a deep breath before he shifted to face Ed, the Exhibits Designer. Nonchalantly Ed continued, "I took some of your arsenic, Berry." Daley grabbed his elbow to turn him around towards the interview room.

"What's going on?" The Director's voice cut through the ambient noise. I looked over, and Sally Luykes, here late too, was escorting an older man out of her office.

"We're just heading into the classroom to sort out some information, Dr. Luykes," replied Daley.

"Is everything all right?" she persisted.

"Fine," said Daley. "I'll fill you in shortly."

Sally Luykes appeared satisfied, but the silver-haired man with her was eyeing Ed and me, not the sergeant.

He looked like an old-fashioned gentleman, quality hat in hand, dapper dark coat. "Does anyone here need a lawyer?" he asked in a toney English accent.

"We're fine," said Daley.

"If you don't mind, sir, I'd like to hear directly from the two people with you," replied the man with practiced authority.

Ed shrugged. I shook my head, hoping to God I didn't need a lawyer.

"If you'll excuse us then," said Daley, and pushed Ed and me as civilly as possible into the classroom and shut the door.

"Sorry, Berry." Ed slumped into the nearest chair. "I took some arsenic from your lab, but Reiko knows all about it. The figures'll back me up, too."

"Ed, my God, what on earth for?"

"A cat."

"You poisoned a cat?"

"Hell no. I preserved it."

"You stole arsenic?"

"You can't buy it any more. Berry, cool it. I spent half my career in the natural history museum. Arsenic has been used in taxidermy for a hundred years."

"You taxidermied a cat?"

"My neighbour's."

I collapsed in my chair.

"Look, Harry was dying and alone, and his beloved pet ate antifreeze."

"From your car, was it? Decent of you to rescue the body. Who got to keep the arsenic-ed cat?"

"Well, it was buried with him."

"Goodie. Let's exhume the bodies to see how much arsenic was used up. Did he pat the cat?"

"Please . . . ladies, gentlemen," interjected the Sergeant.

"It's not the kind of conservation you know anything about, is it Berry? Natural history specimens. You take the innards out through the anus." Ed watched my face.

"I have my own history with cat's assholes," I said. "And the two-legged kind." Rather than stick my tongue out at him, I made it say, "That's all?" to the Sergeant, and stomped out of the room.

———— ⁓⊙⊙⁓ ————

"Hi," I began to the young guard at the Security desk. I didn't recognize him and I didn't know if he recognized me. I made a mental note that since I seemed to be sliding in deeper here rather than leaving MOA, I'd make more of an effort to learn names and faces. Luykes I had heard of even before I came to Vancouver, but I knew many of the others as "the receptionist", "the guard," and "the cleaner". "How are you?" I asked with a brilliant over-compensatory smile. I was verging on either the politically correct or the condescending, and I said simply, "I hope you weren't on shift last night."

"No," he replied, "It was Mama."

"Just my luck," I thought. "How the hell am I going to get someone like that to say anything?" Maybe it was my luck, though, because at least Mama was on duty again tonight. The museum was open until nine, and Mama was somewhere patrolling the floor. I left to find her.

I walked down the main gallery's carpeted ramp past Northwest Coast feast dishes and painted chests made of huge planks bent to form boxes. The ramp ended at the Great Hall with its imposing totem poles. Through the huge window wall of the Great Hall vestiges of the colours of the day illuminated treetops and the ocean beyond. In the evening light I could see that the "Musqueam Museum School", a program for Grade 4s from everywhere in the city, was finishing its celebratory final session. The parents had formed a wide circle filling the hall to see what their kids had done. The Museum of Anthropology and the University of British Columbia stand on the traditional territory of the Musqueam, a Salish nation. At the top of the ramp MOA's first displays showcase Musqueam past and present with the community's own words describing their society and sovereignty. I stopped as a Musqueam elder gave a closing prayer for the museum school.

As she prayed in Hən̓q̓əmin̓əm̓, I meditated on the totem poles. Everyone thinks of totem poles when they think of British Columbia, but the Musqueam Salish did not carve big poles like the nations further to the north. I had seen, in my walks through the museum, many Salish works of cultural significance, smaller and more inconspicuous than a tall pole but just as powerful. The idea visitors have that "BC's Indians carve totem poles" is true and at the same time not true. Contradictions like this made me think how many black and white, confident assertions of my youth turned later into grey "yes, but"s and "on the other hand"s. Two sides to every question. Cuyler Foley was both a respected colleague, according to Theo, and an unscrupulous art dealer, according to others. Is Reiko not who I think she is?

One huge clue had gripped me as I was hurriedly stripping my lab coat off with Frick's orders to leave the room. Where was Reiko's own lab coat? The one that must have been covered with Foley's bloodstains. Did the police take it in their investigation? Or had she hidden it because it was evidence of something else? Either way looked bad.

Mama was sitting on a stool in front of the few remaining open sections of Visible Storage, near my favourite object, an Inuit stone sculpture of a music group, a literal rock band complete with all the wires to the amp rendered in sinew. It made me smile every time I saw it. Mama looked like she couldn't care less.

"Hello," I said, "Remember me? Maybe from Sunday? I'm the new intern in Conservation."

Mama regarded me, perhaps rather quizzically like everyone else, since grey hair is not the hallmark of a new intern.

"I need help," I said. Weren't museum guards supposed to give help?

Mama continued to look me full in the face and say nothing.

"Something has come up and I need to know who was in the museum last night." Was this too direct? Maybe she would ask me what had come up.

She didn't. I tried again.

"My name is Berenice, Berenice Cates. I work with Reiko Smithson." I folded my hands behind my back. "You probably know she's in custody right now, well, actually she's downstairs right now, but I mean she's with the police, she's being questioned by the police." Mama might have looked mildly interested in this information but didn't say so. After a pause, I levelled with her. "It looks like poisoned coffee might've killed the man who died here. Reiko says she never made the coffee. I'm wondering if you could tell me who else was in the museum last night?"

"Looks like you got a big job ahead of you."

Mama spoke! I could have hugged her.

A long silence ensued. I didn't know what else to say but I had to say something. "I just want the assurance there was someone else in the museum, other than Reiko and the man who died. And Sally Luykes and Theo he was with. And Security of course. I came to Vancouver to work with Reiko, and I need to know . . . she's not necessarily guilty."

Mama appeared to be considering this but continued her silence.

"Shit *de merde*," I swore under my breath.

I noticed a twitch at the corner of Mama's mouth.

"I never heard that one before." Her twitch almost became a smile.

"I said it to my grandma once and had no dessert for a week."

"How old?" said Mama.

"I was six."

"You're from the big city," observed Mama, "In my house that would have been a month."

I laughed. Mama grinned, but it didn't last long. Now I knew why. Her mouth closed down over a scattering of brown and crooked teeth. I said, "I didn't get into much trouble as a kid. Wish I could say the same for my life as an adult."

"Different kind of trouble now, eh?"

"Wish it wasn't."

"Sometimes it's good to stir things up." Mama looked at me carefully. "Is that why you're here?"

"Here to see you?" I stalled. Mama gave an almost imperceptible nod.

As new staff in an intern position, I had tried to adopt as smiling a persona as my personality could muster. As a woman more than halfway through her life, I'd rather have used a little more lip. Would Mama open up better to a person who was assertive and in your face, or orderly and nice? I said, "I'm too new to stir up things with any wisdom. I just want to know that the people I work with aren't murderers."

"Sounds like someone here is." Mama was not going to let me get away with politely evasive conversation.

I nodded, wanting to ask her what she thought, but I was afraid she would just clam up. I forced myself to chit-chat and hoped it would lead to more conversation. "I don't know what to think; I've heard the guy who died was an expert who came here a lot to work with Theo Younge, and I've heard he was a really unscrupulous dealer." Mama said nothing.

"Art dealer," I clarified. "I guess I just want to know, first, that it wasn't Reiko."

"What if it was Reiko?"

I froze. "If it was Reiko, that would change everything for me here."

"Well, there were a lot of people in the museum last night," Mama offered.

"Aren't we closed Monday evenings?"

"Sure, the galleries are, but there was a night class up in the seminar room, a bunch of graduate students in the Archaeology lab, and then the staff working late, like Ed all the time on that exhibit's supposed to open in two weeks. There's always someone working late. Except Max Turpin. Signs out five sharp most nights in tight white shorts, claims he's playing tennis." Mama almost grinned again. "But everyone was out of the museum by the time the ambulance came, except Reiko downstairs and Theo of course. Even that advisory committee of Lorna's had finished up."

The First Nations Advisory Committee. The baritone was on Lorna's committee, the head of it, he'd said this afternoon. A committee now in trouble. Their meeting meant that there were six or eight aboriginal people in the museum on a night when a dealer in Native art as well as Classical artifacts had been killed. How long does it take poison to act? From what I had heard of Foley's business methods, if someone had met him last night in the hall or the washroom there could easily have been a *crime de passion*—but there are a lot better weapons than arsenic for spur-of-the-moment efficiency. For whoever did it, last night did seem to present an ideal situation to pin the crime on a number of someone elses, in case one or two proved able to easily clear themselves. My "Opportunity" list had just stretched like a wet wool weaving.

I thanked Mama for the information and walked slowly back towards the guards' station, bone tired. Tomorrow would be bad, the pressure on to finish the treatments on the Classical antiquities, and then having to catch up with my normal jobs. Before this horrid cleaning I was about to work on the "Beads and Seeds" exhibit pieces. The objects needing restoration were in the Conservation lab. All my supplies were there too: Japanese tissue paper, fillers, pigments, matting agents, and the special adhesives and threads. What workspace would I be given now? Would I even be let into the lab to pick up the supplies, or was I going to have to make a list and give it to a policeman for retrieval? A cop would find a name like "B-72" on a bag of hard resin pellets, a bottle of the resin diluted with acetone to use as an adhesive, and a jar made up with xylene for coatings. Reiko and I labelled our materials for ourselves, not for the untrained non-conservator. My future held more frustration with the police.

Energy level sputtering even more, I signed out, asked the guard to watch the rear parking lot on his monitors, went downstairs, out the back door, and drove home. I'd call a few friends back in Toronto to soothe my spirits. That idea ended when I remembered that with the time difference it would be midnight in Ontario. As I neared home, not trying to do anything but stretch out or sleep seemed an excellent alternative.

Or something like home. The few belongings I'd brought and the few gleaned from garage sales barely covered the empty space in the small, east end, ground floor apartment colleagues told me I'd been lucky to find. And I had felt lucky when I signed the lease on this imperfect Vancouver apartment because I'd won the perfect internship. Tomorrow I'd better do my damnedest to get that back on track.

I couldn't hear any noise from Daniel upstairs, and this left me both grateful and disappointed. Calling Reiko about her lab coat was impossible if the police were still with her, and I was too exhausted to strategize. I put on a CD and relaxed into the gentle Bach sonatas for cello and piano.

Many old houses in Vancouver that have been turned into apartments have one furnace in the basement with big wide-open heating ducts between the floors. If I had wanted Daniel to know I was home, this music was a perfectly effective yet subtle way to go about it. I was too tired, though, even to muse about whether my conscious or unconscious mind had put on the sonatas. Instead of eating dinner, I poured myself a small rich sherry and fell asleep on the couch.

# Chapter
# 9

### Wednesday Begins

I woke up at 2:30 A.M. to go to the bathroom, nocturnal excursions being another after-fifty side-effect. It took me a while to get back to sleep, to push the day's events far enough away. When the alarm went off at 6:30 I had at last been soundly dreaming.

I stumbled through the routine decisions. Whatever I wore would be covered by a lab coat, so that wasn't a problem. A loose skirt would keep any tightness away from my stomach, flamingly annoyed at having had sherry for dinner. Can a person "haggard around" in the morning? I desperately needed caffeine, so I poured out some cold cereal first to calm body parts that would otherwise get offended. All this took time, and then driving through Vancouver morning traffic added a guaranteed irritant. I arrived at MOA at 8:45, ready to snarl at whichever policeman would escort my morning's work. There were, though, no police there. I was told I would have to wait until 9 for their arrival. I had a quarter hour for the worn, blessed coffee lounge, in which to intake more caffeine and, paradoxically, calm myself down.

Instead, I went for a walk outside even though a student mentioned some hot tea already brewed in the lounge.

Despite the June mist, the stroll allowed me to feel good about being at this museum, as well as giving my rational self the high moral ground for being so wise and healthy. And I did feel better. The Museum of Anthropology is on a cliff surrounded by scenic paths and woods and spectacular views of the sea and mountains, and close by is a meditative Japanese Zen garden. The mist covered the sea view, so I walked over to the garden, but it was still too early for the gate to be open. By the time I wandered the flower-bordered paths back to the museum a light rain had begun to fall. The tall coniferous trees along the road looked soft and magnificent. I was ready to begin work.

First, though, I poked into the Design area and told Ed that no one from Conservation could be at the 11 o'clock meeting. "Can humidity controls for the display cases for 'Beads and Seeds' be left until next week?" Then I tied up another parcel of conservation business. I'd hardly seen Oscar since Sunday, the young public programs assistant known in-house for his old-fashioned moustache and to the larger world for the spelling on his press releases. I assured him I'd take Reiko's place at the public "Care and Identification Clinic" next week if Reiko couldn't make it. There were other people in the photocopy room where I'd found Oscar, so we didn't discuss Cuyler Foley although it must have been on his mind as much as it was on mine. At 9:30 I collected my RCMP escort, and inveigled my way to the computer in the Conservation lab for ten minutes. I downloaded my emails to clear my mailbox, knowing what a time trap they could be if I so much as opened one, and remembered to post a message saying it might take me a few days to reply. I did the same for Reiko's account, happy we had needed to share passwords during the pesticide research set-up.

The phone rang. Forget it. I'm in the groove. I yanked my lab coat on, pumping myself up with extra self-congratulation for having accomplished so much already today. It was not that three months in Vancouver, "British California," had converted me into a serious self-help advocate reciting affirmations each morning. It was just that the spattered bronzes in front of me were a tangible reminder of the difficult day ahead. I wanted to take every opportunity to tell myself that the glass was also half-full. Calmly exercising my fingers, I waited for the policeman to finish a call on his walkie-talkie.

The cop stared at me. I checked my blouse buttons.

"That was the sergeant," he said. "He tried to phone. He needs you upstairs. Now." He hurried me out.

<hr />

The door to the classroom was closed but Sergeant Daley opened it seconds after the policeman knocked. I was led to a chair at the head of tables rearranged to form a large circle. Daley sat down beside me. Seven pairs of silent eyes witnessed each move. There was one smile—Lorna. I recognized two other people, Uta Vickers whom I'd met on Sunday when she wanted to borrow the weaving, and yesterday's "baritone".

Daley started. "Let me introduce Berenice Cates. She can answer your questions about pesticide research." Turning to me, he said, "Ms. Cates, this is Lorna's Exhibits Advisory Committee. We were discussing the tragedy that occurred here. I told them we were looking into various possibilities in Mr. Foley's death, but there is nothing conclusive yet.

Poisoning was part of the discussion. The question of why arsenic might be on Native heritage items came up."

This was not going to be a warm, fuzzy conversation. Daley paused, giving time for any immediate intervention, and then asked the committee to introduce themselves. I was not good with names, so I grabbed a pad of paper, found a clean sheet, and charted the table. "Please call me Berry," I said when it came around to me. Daley said, "First question?" and lost no time in lifting back his pad, tearing my paper off, and stuffing the others with his notes in his file.

"Thank you for speaking with us, Berry," began the baritone, whose name I now knew was Basil David. "It's been a bit of a shock to all of us to hear that arsenic was routinely used in this museum on objects from our cultures." His voice was magnificent even in the small room. "Could you please tell the committee when and why something as lethal as arsenic was used?"

His question ended and pairs of silent eyes turned towards me. What could I say? When I hesitated, Basil David's question was reiterated in plain words by a woman who had been introduced as Vera Brownlee. "Why have you poisoned our ancestors?"

I turned to Daley and smiled sweetly. "Since I've just come in, would you mind giving me a recap of your conversation about the arsenic?"

I jotted notes as Daley briefed me, and admired how he continually rechecked his understanding of the discussion with the people at the table. Then Basil David took the floor. He gave a speech about the importance to his people of what was in the museum. He made sure I understood. In my mind I replaced "baritone" with "orator". He was a traditional speaker. Now it was my turn, and I was not.

"Thank you for inviting me," I began. "Thank you for your explanations," I said to Basil David and then nodded, looking at the whole group the way I'd seen Daley acknowledge everyone. "Let me clear up one misunderstanding. Arsenic was hardly used at all in this museum to prevent insect infestation, but it doesn't mean that it wasn't used by collectors or dealers. We don't know which pieces it might have been used on. This is why we're so concerned about finding out what pesticide residues remain." I paused. "History collections, art museums, all kinds of heritage items were treated. Not just your heritage. I realize this is cold comfort." I stopped.

Vera Brownlee spoke up again, "You took our old masks, our sacred items, to put in museums to preserve them. Now you're saying that you couldn't preserve them unless you poisoned them."

"It was unfortunately common practice. Against insects."

"We don't use arsenic. We store our regalia in cedar boxes."

There was a long pause. I must have looked like a deer in headlights.

Uta Vickers said, "Museums say they're the professionals. They know how to look after heritage. As if we don't. It seems our choice in museums is to have the objects eaten away, or poisoned."

"Not exactly *our* choice," said a man on my right.

I looked towards the end of the room, appealing to Lorna. She met my eyes, then gazed calmly at the others around the table. She was right. Why should she intervene? It was my move; I had chosen the profession of conservator.

"Conservation's first mistake was to not keep you in the loop, explain the whole pesticide residue research project.

To you and the other aboriginal advisors the museum works with. I can't think of much more to say right now, except I'll get the information together. Let's meet again." Short and sweet. Soon I'd try sound bites.

Basil David rose. "Thank you, Berry." His eyes met mine. "Sergeant Daley told us you've only been here three months. The arsenic use on our regalia happened long before your time. For something you had no responsibility for, I like your answer. You didn't excuse the past, defend the museum; you proposed for the future. I look forward to our next meeting." The committee members lightly applauded. Grinning with relief that we'd found common ground, I pushed myself up to go while others stood to stretch and get a coffee from the side table.

Vera Brownlee came over and shook my hand. "Thanks for listening. It's sometimes pretty rare in big museums."

"It's me who thanks you for listening," I said, squeezing her hand too hard.

The man who had commented about choice joined us. "Hey Vera, that's what museums think they're all about—rare." His handshake was firm.

I turned towards the door, and Uta Vickers stepped right in front of me.

"Are my auntie's blankets poisoned?" she demanded.

"No," I said. "Everything recent has no chemicals on it." This I knew, that the contemporary weavings would have none of the older arsenic, mercury, or lead residues. But were mothballs ever used, for instance? I had more research to do, and amended my pronouncement with, "I'll double-check and give you a call."

Vickers said, "I'd like that. My daughter's sick again. I was wondering if it was from holding her at the funeral."

Someone at the funeral easily could have had a cold, but Vickers knew this as well as I did. Her concern lay elsewhere, and it was a good one.

"Does anybody," I said, "use household stuff like mothballs to help keep regalia?"

"Sure."

"Do you have a few minutes? If you want, I can tell you about the chemicals in mothballs, and how we protect wool without using them now." We sat in a corner, me explaining the differences between mothballs and moth crystals, naphthalene and paradichlorobenzene, and their ratings as potential carcinogens. Sure these chemicals evaporated, but into someone's surroundings.

Vickers thanked me with a "I hope you'll come tell everyone this. The museum should let the community know." But she was smiling. I wobbled out of the room. This internship was a rock climb in resolving the museum hard stuff. Which would be more difficult to scale—museum and aboriginal concerns, or murderous office politics?

---

Downstairs I found a short message from Reiko. "I'm fine, but don't call me," she said, and then riffed, "Officer Bluecoat is here again". She continued with, "When this baby . . . leaves me," and added in a hurry, "hope all's well," before hanging up. I pushed a swell of anxiety from my mind, and turned to focus on work.

The bronze statue in front of me was a grizzled old Pan, with his goat feet and pipes and salacious grin, still able to dance and play with gusto, except he was almost broken at one ankle so he danced parallel to the tabletop and his panpipes were bent in half. Part of his face had caved in from a type of corrosion called bronze disease. But for something so ancient, the Pan had been in marvellous condition when Theo first purchased it. It had also never been overcleaned; in fact, much of the surface still showed the corrosion and embedded dirt from its previous archaeological environment.

I love the colours of corrosion, especially the sea greens and azure blues. This bronze had formed a beautiful patina of age. Some areas were smooth, and others showed raised patches of mottled green encasing sandy-coloured dirt. But today the surface colours held no beauty. The dirt was blotched with reddish-brown dried blood, and even the adjacent green metal seemed stained. The worst were the areas of dirt-roughened corrosion; minute scrapings of flesh had hardened around the small sharp edges. Under the microscope, I could see that a particularly bad area of Pan's torso held what might have been skin from a finger. Foley had had a death-grip on the statue.

I could sense someone at my side, and rapidly brushed my free hand against my cheek. It was Oscar, though, leaning over to see what I was so interested in. I pushed the microscope away. He didn't need to remember Foley like this.

"Did the statue have a bent leg before?"

I shook my head and changed the subject. "Need something for the Artifact I.D. Clinic for the public?"

"Can I see through the microscope, too?"

What excuse could I give so he didn't see enlarged bits of flesh? "I've finished. I'm about to start some cleaning tests. What's up?"

"Ugh," he winced. "The cleaning. I just wanted to ask if . . . and I thought, you don't have an axe to grind about Foley . . . if you think he was as bad as they're saying?"

"Well, I've heard one nasty story. What've you heard?"

"Not much. But I'd noticed before, in public programs Foley's done for us, like when Theo organized the Archaeology in Greece series, that everybody kind of avoided Foley. You'd be in the coffee room and Theo would come in with him and people would look away. Like they were hoping he wouldn't sit down at their table."

I didn't say anything. Oscar ran his fingers over his moustache.

"Oscar," I changed the subject, "there's an older gentleman I saw with Dr. Luykes the other day. Do you know him?"

"Oh yes, the lawyer, you mean? Saul Samuels. He's a big MOA supporter. I hope I look that good when I'm old."

"I thought you might have noticed him." I didn't say, "Because with that big moustache of yours, I think you hanker after the era of well-dressed gentlemen." Old-fashioned propriety confirmed in my mind that Oscar was better off without the magnified details of death I was getting acquainted with.

"I've got to get back to work," I said. He knew I hadn't answered his question. We stared at each other. All I could think of to say was, "Are you growing it out to be a handlebar?"

Oscar's eyes sparkled. "Do you like it?"

"Sure."

He sighed. "Do you think it's okay to say this, I mean just to somebody on staff, or is it too crude—'I'd rather be anachronistic, than be history like Foley?'"

"I like the colours of corrosion on antiquities," I tried, "but I don't want to be corroded like them. Your line was better, but I don't think it fits you." At MOA we all liked history for our own reasons, and I enjoyed Oscar's old-fashioned tastes.

---

I started the tests for cleaning the statue. A poultice tech-
nique lifted a bloodstained area with partial success. For a
thin bit of dried flesh, I had to soften it first with a drop
of hot water before I could get it to lift off. Microscopic as
it was, there was a vile stench. Good thing Oscar had left.
I soldiered on; I had chosen the most damaged of the two
bronzes to begin with, so as not to be left with the worst
problems as the day and my well-being wore down.

The repair to the statue would happen later, but I began
its full condition report as the test patches were drying. The
police had taken numerous photos of all the objects and
Constable Frick had suggested I would be able to get copies
for my reports. This came with the unspoken rider, "if I co-
operated". An oblique hint, an implication, an "insinuendo"
in fact. I laughed out loud, and just shook my head at the
confused look of the cop at my table.

I examined every angle of the bronze, measuring each
damaged area and noting the extent of the corrosion. Normally I dislike this ultra-picky job, but today I was almost
enthusiastic about these tiny details. That was all I wanted
right now, a demanding task to keep my mind occupied. I
was recording the corrosion in the broken left ankle area
when something was distinctly wrong.

Glaringly wrong. At least to a conservator.

This kind of detail might hold no interest whatsoever to
the vast majority of the population, but I could barely catch
my breath, and bent down so the constable across the table
wouldn't see my expression. His eyes were again on automatic, flitting between the tabletop, the doors, and Heather
and Zoe organizing files at the far end of the Workroom. My
right hand reached out to bring the high-powered microscope into position. I upped the magnification and started,
objectively, scientifically, to scan the entire area of the break.

There was absolutely no trace of a layer that should have been there. Copper alloys form a liver-red layer of cuprite before the familiar green crust starts. Always, if the corrosion happened naturally over time, as it did in archaeological situations. You didn't usually see the red because it got overlaid by other corrosion, but it became visible when a break, like this one in the ankle, revealed a cross-section of the layers. No red layer, no natural process. This new acquisition I was holding was a fake. A fraud. A forgery.

Many museums had fakes, whether they knew it or not. Inexpensive replicas, and take-offs like the Haida bear in velvety plush that Foley had bought for his grandson, were sold in museum giftshops around the world. I'd also seen serious exhibits about historic reproductions and interpretations. But forgeries were intended to deceive. MOA's bronze was bought recently at a high price. Theo must have been duped. Did Foley know? Was this a motive for murdering him?

I got up and found the other lenses for the microscope to view the bronze under still higher magnification. I peered through the black tubes at small multi-coloured hills and valleys, boulders and crystals, until my eyes hurt. There was no trace of a red layer of cuprite. Also, the corrosion seemed to be fairly even—I hardly had to adjust the microscope at all to keep everything in focus when the depth of field changed.

I needed to talk to the police. I wanted to tell Reiko. This was key information. I wasn't going to tell my RCMP escort, though; he had a lot on his mind with Zoe and Heather. I'd find Constable Frick. First, however, I wanted to find Theo. If anyone deserved to know, it was him. What if he looked like he knew already? I would run very fast in the other direction.

Would letting Theo know get me and Conservation into deeper trouble? I had been determined to restore

Conservation's good name by proving Reiko had nothing to do with Foley's death, and by being the perfect intern, helpful and above suspicion. In this attempt I had damaged ancient pottery, found wrong entries about pesticides, and discovered a fake in the museum, a forgery revealed solely on conservation evidence. If Reiko was disliked before, and threats had been made to close our department, and if someone was trying to shift the blame for Foley's death onto Conservation, what would they do now?

I had to concentrate on the forgery. As I turned around to head to Theo's office, Max Turpin entered the far end of the room and waved at me. I grinned, mainly at the sudden disappointment on both Zoe and Heather's faces as he walked right past them.

"Ber-nice!" he greeted me "How goes?"

"All right," I said.

"Just all right? What's up? What's happenin'?"

"Tired," I replied. The stress of the fake was probably showing on my face, but this was Theo's territory, not another curator's.

"Well, sorry I can't help, but I came down to invite you out for lunch. You've got to be under a lot of pressure, too. Least I can do is provide comic relief. Free today?"

"I'm not sure," I stuttered. I had planned to spend my lunch hour at the library looking up arsenic. "I don't really need comic relief. I had some on the weekend." I stopped. This was not where I wanted to go.

It seemed like Max intuitively understood. He held up his hands in a "go no further" gesture. "Just lunch." How could I say no to a workday lunch when having time to indulge my curiosity about Max Turpin was what I'd been relishing?

On my first day of work barely three months ago, I had seen a man swing into the coffee room to gasps of "Your

beard! It's gone!" and, "Your hair! It's black!" from every female latte lover in the place. I had taken an immediate dislike
to this ego's star-itude, and simultaneously developed an appreciation for it. The middle-aged man had gone into a camp
vamp down the aisle between the two rows of lunch tables,
and then, to cheers of "You look ten years younger!" "No,
twenty!" circled and took a deep bow, without a word, at the
exit door. He was only stopped by Reiko calling out, "Max!
Wait a sec! I want to introduce you to our newest intern for
the year, Berenice Cates. Berry, this is Dr. Max Turpin. His
specialty is Native art based in tradition, but that aesthetically
isn't traditional." I must have looked confused because Reiko
added, "You know, contemporary, like works in plexiglas.
Have I got that right, Max?" Turpin nodded and I was hon-
oured that he actually took off his sunglasses at this point. He
gave me a bit of the once over but also quite a genuine smile.
I smiled back at the trim handsome body. He was a looker in
his red T-shirt and well-tailored grey jacket. We shook hands.

He said, "Pardon me for being so direct, but aren't you a
little old for an intern?" He smoothed over his curiosity by
adding, "You should be on regular staff instead."

I replied, "I'll try shaving. Maybe I'll look younger too."
I was way too new to have the guts to add, "And I'll dye my
hair. That always helps."

---

"Lunch? Sure!" I said. "I have some things to do first,
though, so I may not be free till . . . 12:30?"

"Okay by me," said Max. "Meet you in the lobby." I had
just hooked my second date in Vancouver where the man
had asked me out in advance. What a big menopausal deal.
I wondered what he wanted this time.

# Chapter

# 10

∽◯∽

## I tell Theo

How long would it take to get confirmation I was right about the missing red corrosion layer? The Canadian Conservation Institute in Ottawa would know the science. But given the three-hour time difference between BC and Ontario, staggered schedules and demanding workloads, I wasn't surprised to reach only the voice mail. With no excuses any longer to put off my impending mission here, I went in search of Theo: an intern letting the senior curator know there was a large problem with one of his artifacts.

Theo's daughter Elena, blonde hair and a remarkable resemblance to Marilyn Monroe, was coming out of his office as I approached.

"Hi, Ms. Cates," she said. "Can I talk to you? Here," and she waved me from the public area in through the adjacent MOA library door.

"How's Reiko Smithson?" Elena whispered inside the small library, its shelves smelling like vinegar from the deteriorating old paper.

"I think she's okay," I whispered back. "It's nice of you to ask."

"Go ahead and talk, ladies, no bribes required," the young librarian belted out. "You're the only ones here, and do I look like I wear my hair in a bun?" He ran a hand over his shaved head. "Thanks, Pete," I said, but we kept our voices low.

"Reiko spoke in our class last term," Elena said. "She's cool. She hardly knew me but let me come and talk to her outside of class."

"Are you going for a career in conservation?"

"No, well, I was having trouble with the museum course. I'm in Theatre actually, not Museum Studies, but I took the course to get to know my dad better, understand where he's coming from. I'm Theo Younge's daughter, did you know?"

I nodded. We had been introduced at the student get-together, but why would she remember me? "Theatre" made me want to ask, "Are you going into comedy?"

But Elena continued. "Reiko brought up some really interesting stuff in class, like about a painting that had two signatures. I want to maybe take the intro conservation course from her next year. Or from you, if you're teaching," she added politely.

"Reiko is the main instructor," I said. "I'm slated to guest lecture. If I speak to Reiko, I'll tell her you were asking."

Pete began shelving books, creating some background noise, but he was moving closer to us as he worked.

"Please say hi," said Elena. "She was so supportive to me."

"Unfortunately," I said, "I can't really contact her right now. It's hard."

"You're telling me," said Elena. "Mom and Dad separated when I was five, and Mom and I moved to Santa Fe. It's like I had to come here to UBC or else I wouldn't have known Dad at all."

"It's rough," I paused. "Separation can be very rough." My conscious mind thought this one statement, spoken aloud, wouldn't matter, but I was left almost gasping by a tide of memory. After my husband had walked out I'd spent three days on the kitchen floor with my hand in the liquor cupboard. At some point I puked up the truth that the pain was getting worse, not obliterated. There was truly no point in spending the next thirty years in a funk. If anyone was going to make me laugh again, or buoy me up when I was sad, it was not going to be my parents (now deceased), nor my children (non-existent), nor my friends who had held me tight way beyond the call. It was going to have to be me.

I'd had the locks changed, and was delighted by a concert we hadn't been able to afford with two tickets. Norm left appeals on the voice mail about "acting our age". I heard "I need my computer and at least the spare bed", and refused to talk. To him. I found a therapist and stuck buddy-the-ex with the bill. To a career counsellor I said, "I need a radical lifectomy." She showed me books and web sites, and the museum visits started as I got more focused. Salsa dancing and swimming kept my bod loose. And when bleak November days set in and Christmas carols were already playing in the malls, I put on my turquoise-tinted goggles and swam in clear water, and organized Latin food at the salsa classes. I couldn't claim my heart kept pace with my organizational skills; it did the crawl and the backstroke most days, but it kept afloat, and finally one day it went swimming because it simply felt good.

I said, "But sometimes you can turn separation to your advantage. As you've done, Elena." I turned to leave but instead said, "Did Max Turpin speak to your class, too?"

"All the staff did."

"What was he like? Let's talk in the hall."

Pete saw our turned backs and yelled, "Before you go, Ms. Cates, the police were in here asking about you and Reiko."

"Asking you about us?" My mildly curious tone masked a large lump in my throat. I'd hardly used the MOA library, which for the most part collected books for curatorial research and the Museum Studies students. But Reiko had needed information for her research projects. "Elena, would you mind waiting for me outside?"

The door shut and Pete said, "Is Conservation being investigated about Foley's death?"

My head managed a firm, definitively negative shake. "But there are some ugly rumours." Pete would have heard the coffee room gossip too. "What did the police ask about?"

"They wanted to know if I'd helped research poison."

"Curare?" The knowledgeable insider.

"No, arsenic. They'd already found the reference search I'd printed out for Reiko's curare research."

"Arsenic? The pesticide residue project? What about mercuric chloride?" My effort to make this conversation sound matter-of-fact was brave, but going nowhere I wanted. "Had you done research for Reiko on arsenic?"

"Oh sure."

My stomach went into spasm.

"They asked about you too, and I told them you hadn't been in much. But if you need me for any research," the librarian said with pride, "if Reiko hasn't shared it all with you, just ask."

"Thanks, but not right now. No need for more gossip about Conservation," I said, and pushed the library door open, hoping he'd keep silent in the lounge, and hiding my own eagerness to lighten up the day with Elena's gossip about Max Turpin. And Elena was there waiting.

"Oh, Max Turpin was awesome," she said. "Really funny. I'd love to be on stage with him. He spoke about contemporary art and traditional art and copyright on images. But he's . . . kind of a sleazebag, you know what I mean?"

"Oh?" I prompted.

"Well, he came on to me at break. The class goes from two to five, and at coffee he comes over and says, 'Was my answer to your question sufficient?' I was flattered. I thought for once I'd asked an intelligent question in this museum class. Then he says in his loudest voice that we should all meet in the pub after class to continue the discussion. And we do. And he sits beside me. And when it dawns on him that I really am Theo's daughter, or maybe that I do love my Dad despite not being with him since I was five . . ." Elena ran her fingers through her hair. "Dr. Turpin gets up to go to the Men's, and when he comes back, he sits with someone else. Female of course. Mind you, most of them are in Museum Studies. And they all adore him. He sure likes to be in the limelight—but wow, was he funny. I was kind of upset when he ignored me, but not really. He's twice my age, and Dad had warned me about him anyway."

I'd been fairly warned about Max Turpin too now, by both Elena and Reiko, but after we said good-bye I scooted towards Theo's door, relishing the thought of lunch afterwards.

──────── ⚬⌣⚬ ────────

Theo was alone in his office, reading and making notes. His desk overflowed with printed pages, and his bookshelves were layered with volumes stacked spine out, spine up, spine down. One gilt-framed photo of Elena sat beside a collection of contemporary Greek ceramics and statues. I wondered if curators affected a "curatorial look" the way artists unconsciously or on the advice of their agents created an artsy identity. Theo greeted me warmly while leaving the impression that he was annoyed at being disturbed and this had better not take long.

"I have good news and I have bad news," I said, not having come up with a better plan of how to tell him his prized antiquity looked like a fake.

"Good news first," said Theo, playing along. He capped his fountain pen.

"I've finished everything but the bronzes, and the cleaning tests are going well."

"Good. I imagined that. You obviously came here to tell me the bad news."

"Well, yes, I did." I concentrated on his face. "There are problems with the corrosion on the Pan. I'd like you to have a look." So far I couldn't detect anything but curiosity.

"Of course. What problems?" Theo shuffled a few of the papers on his desk to one side, as if clearing room for what was coming.

"The corrosion. It doesn't seem natural."

Theo's hands stopped. He leaned towards me. His eyes weren't leaving my face.

"What are you saying?"

"I'm waiting for scientific confirmation about what I'm seeing," I answered, giving myself wiggle room, "but there seems to be a layer of corrosion missing. This never happens unless the object has been restored, or made recently." I was having a hard time saying "fake".

"Are you sure? Who's confirming this for you?"

He looked unsettled but his voice had a coldness in it, a tone more inquisitorial than upset. And shit *de merde,* what kind of a reply was this anyway? I'd just told him, well, insinuated, that one of his prize bronzes was most likely a forgery.

"Scientists in Ottawa. Maybe there are situations when this corrosion layer doesn't form." What would be his next move?

"So what you are saying," Theo stated, still leaning across the desk but gazing now at the skylight, "is that if your supposition is confirmed, the Pan may have been restored, or it may have been made recently. Not be what it is supposed to be."

I murmured yes. He was dragging out this discussion and I wanted some clear sign he either knew or didn't about faking.

Theo returned his gaze to the vicinity of my face. "Can you tell if it is restored?"

"In the area of the break, where I can see that the layer is missing, it's not restored. Or if it is, the object is restored to the point of deception. Theo, it looks as if the Pan has been faked."

There. I'd used the "F" word.

Theo sunk into his worn chair. His face became red, and redder. He was deeply disturbed, or was it embarrassment? If embarrassed, was it because he had been duped by a forgery or because I knew something he wanted kept secret?

"I need to see this," Theo said. He actually looked upset. Or he was a good actor. Why did I believe I'd be able to tell the truth from someone's face? When did I ever have that talent?

"But," his voice continued, "You have the police down there, don't you?" I nodded assent. "I don't want them to know about this. Not right away. I can't face it." He was back to looking at the ceiling. His voice strained. "I'll have to tell Sally. We spent twenty thousand dollars on a fake. I can't imagine how I'll tell her. Please," Theo said, anguished now, "I'll be down in a minute. Set it up so I just have to ask, you know, hi, how's it going, can I see what you're doing.

Show me the part where there's the missing area, but don't say anything. Is that all right?"

"Sure," I replied, "but I will, you know, have to tell the police what I've found as soon as I hear back from the scientists."

"Of course." Theo attempted a smile. "But I'd appreciate it if you could wait a little bit." He looked at his watch. "Ottawa's in an earlier time zone. They might not get back to you today. Can you wait until tomorrow?"

He must have read the scepticism on my face. "I just need some time to pull myself together," he murmured with a shy shrug. In a voice now barely audible, he said, "Please, would you mind leaving and closing the door?"

Theo looked and sounded crestfallen, but was this the whole story? He might have other reasons for wanting me out of his office. I rose, resolving to keep an eye on Theo Younge.

"I can probably wait," I said in the doorway. He did look exhausted, and somehow small behind his old oak desk. I put out an offer. "You mentioned Sally Luykes. I guess she should know right away, too, before the police. Will you tell her or shall I?"

He came alive at the suggestion. He'd tell Sally Luykes and then let me know it was okay to inform the police. This could buy him time until tomorrow.

He had his own reasons, but I would find them out.

Standing by Theo's open door, I knew the pathway to surviving the secrets of this museum would not be smooth. Discovering the truth about the Pan was urgent. At any time Reiko's and my fate might hang on the actions of curators or the Director. Had this also been true for Cuyler Foley?

I felt like an archaeologist on a site where I was trying to analyze the layers of soil covering a mummified corpse, and discovering that there was more dirt than I ever imagined.

Just doing my work meant I was digging in this dirt. Here I couldn't retreat from the inescapable discoveries each layer was revealing about a museum and its staff, about integrity, honesty, and death.

But a dig might as well go deep. I sat down again opposite a startled Theo. "There's one thing I'd like to ask. Were you ever the curator for Native material too?"

The Theo I had judged as exhausted lunged forward until there was only a foot of dead desk air between my words and his glare. "And why does this matter?"

I put on my sweet intern smile. "I upset you earlier in the coffee room and don't know why. When I mentioned that Classics and Aboriginal expertise together were unusual?"

"What've people said about me? Tell the truth, now. The Romans made sure their foes were cursed if they didn't kill them. I can make sure this is your last conservation posting."

My chair screeched back. All I had wanted to explore were background links between him and Foley.

"People've said nothing!" I opened my empty hands for emphasis. "Why?"

Theo looked like a petulant kid who thinks he's being lied to. "What's your ancestry? English?"

Now I really was confused. "Isle of Man and French-Canadian."

"Nyeh nyeh," Theo sang out in a ten-year-old's voice. "You're weird. You eat pea soup. Your cat's got no tail."

Words from the long-ago kid inside me spilled out. "I'm telling!"

Theo grabbed my arm. "Gonna tell mummy?" His smile broadened. Not into a smirk, no victory shout, now just a teacher who's made his point. "I was the child everyone made fun of. I hated it and still do. Childhood lives on in the adult, age taught me that truism."

"What are you talking about?" I understood, though, even if it had been almost half a century since I'd been caught using the phrase, "I'm telling".

"I liked school. Loved reading. But I was captured by Pallas Athena, Apollo, King Midas. Not Gitchi Manitou." Theo closed his eyes.

"I read those Greek and Roman stories too."

"But your Cree grandmother hadn't married the manager of the Hudson's Bay store. My father got a teaching certificate and spent the rest of his life in the city. I grew up near a library. I had an ancient world I could escape to. But it wasn't the world of my Kokum, and it killed her I wasn't interested in those traditions. Luckily there were other children who were. Me, I just didn't belong there."

"You'd become acculturated?"

"Don't you understand? Do you eat pea soup all the time? Dump the old stereotypes! As if to be a real Indian I have to like hunting and hate the written word." Theo grimaced. "I was never Indian enough for them. This is a global world. Why can't I enjoy Homer and be accepted?"

Theo caught his breath, rolled back his chair, and asked me to describe exactly what he should look for and what was missing when he came downstairs to see the Pan.

---

Max was waiting for me in the lobby.

"Good to go, are you? Wearing that lab coat to lunch?"

"Five secs!" I waved my fingers, turned on my heels, and disappeared. Damned if when I took the lab coat off the light didn't show a pilled skirt and a creased blouse. "So just sit in a dark corner, then. Nothing you can do about it, Berry. You wanted Max Turpin and you've got him."

# Chapter
# 11

∽∽∽

## The Wednesday Lunch

The cool mist felt good on my cheeks as Max and I walked through the Rose Garden to a campus restaurant. The air was spectacularly fresh after being inside the museum.

"What's so funny?" he asked. Max had been commenting on changes to the campus since he'd come to MOA, and I wasn't following very well the differences between the Asian Centre and the Liu Centre and Asian Studies.

"I was just reminded of your, well, outrageous brushing of my cheek when you and Luykes and the rest were in the workroom yesterday."

"Outrageous?" Max smiled. "What reminded you of that?"

"Oh, the air. It's fresh."

Max opened his mouth, then he got it and let out a hoot. "You really are something, Berenice. Who ever thought a conservator could be so witty."

"That's rather a backhanded compliment," I replied. "But then, I hear you play tennis." He laughed at my poor pun and I grinned back. We arrived at the campus' classy restaurant, and from the foyer with its log fire I could look down on the dining area and see its beautiful view over Howe Sound. Much of the mountains and sea, however, were obstructed by the long line-up in front of us. Max hadn't reserved.

"I never reserve," he said to my worry. "The bar's better anyway. There's still too much tweed per table in the main restaurant." With that, he marched into the bar area and claimed a prime location by placing his thirties-style fedora on one chair and his silvery grey raincoat on the other. Then he rejoined me in the line-up in front of the hostess. When we reached her and were told we would have to sit in the bar since we hadn't reserved and to seat ourselves, Max winked and made sure I had the seat with the better view.

The bar area was indeed comfortable, with its own gas fire aflame in a not too kitschy fireplace and a waitress Max was on flirting terms with. They joked about needing a fire even in June, and insinuations about "hot" circulated. He ordered fresh wild salmon with spring vegetables and white wine, and had somehow caught my student-remnant hesitation about spending a lot for lunch. Without making a deal of it, Max insisted that this was his treat; he'd invited me, after all. I didn't want to be beholden, though, and I didn't have much appetite after the morning. I ordered a spinach salad and tea. Max insisted I accept one small glass of wine. He was the perfect host: generous, offering intelligent conversation and amusing anecdotes. At some point Max had the waitress refill our wine glasses before I could say no. I found myself leaning back in my chair, undoubtedly creasing my blouse and pilled skirt further, enjoying the conversation. When he laughed at another of my bad jokes, I said, "You're very witty your own self", and added with a grin, "for a curator". The wine was obviously working, but the comment he had made about conservators' wit as we were walking over still waltzed around in the back of my mind.

"Can I ask you something personal?" I said, glass in hand.

Max smiled. "Try me."

"You're at a high point in your career. Do you every worry about aging? Losing your energy or even just losing your memory? Not being able to do your job as well as you do now?"

"I think of it every time I can't find my keys. Seriously, though, you probably have more difficulty with aging than I do." Max flinched. "I don't mean because you're a bit older," he blurted, "but because you're a woman. I mean," he reddened, "society's emphasis on beauty, child-bearing."

I wasn't going to ask him if he worried about losing his own good looks. For an instant, I pictured him as Mama had described him during our conversation in Visible Storage: in tight white tennis shorts.

"What about old fogey professors, ones that people can barely tolerate until they retire. How do you know when you've gone downhill?"

"Leukemia," Max said. He looked at his plate, and moved some food around. Was this an unspeakable joke? "Took my brother when I was twelve. The little kid I didn't want hanging around. At sixteen I lost my best friend to cancer. Writhing in pain. I didn't have the guts to visit him at the end." Max lifted his eyes and they pierced my face. "I've seen downhill early. I consider myself lucky. Louie and Freddy knew what downhill really means."

"You were so young. Don't blame . . ."

Max held up his hand. "I did not do everything I could have. Young people are capable." He winced. "Sorry, you

weren't expecting this when you asked about 'personal.'"
Max bent down to cut his food, then lifted a wet-green asparagus tip on his fork and rotated it in the light. He sighed. "We spend our lives trying to keep control, make our world a certain way. Sometimes we just can't. Aging is in that category."

I swung the conversation back to neutral university territory and asked about his teaching.

"Love it. The students keep me on my toes. Perceptive questions. Impertinent kids! They're really asking why I believe whatever I'm talking about is important. That kind of reflection should be forced on everyone."

"Mmmmm," I managed. I was finding the serious side of Max Turpin as attractive as his wit.

He continued, "At the museum, an exhibit takes years what with all the research, writing the grants, setting up loans, writing the text. It's a slog. With teaching, the 'why I do this' reward happens every Tuesday and Thursday."

"The university's lucky. So's MOA." I wasn't just brown-nosing.

"I enjoy being with the kids, too," he continued. "Excuse me, young adults. They're so alive, so certain they can make a difference. Like I said, young people are capable. And they're aesthetic. Look at the group over there," he gestured at another table. "They're all so beautiful, and it's ephemeral, God damn it. Young lovers, get out and enjoy it now!"

I flashed on my conversation in the library with Elena. Max's ratings took a plunge.

"I know what you're thinking from my last comment. Berenice, let me tell you straight out," Max looked me right in the eyes, "There's a side of me that people gossip about. They've made me into some kind of dirty old man because

I get a kick out of life. Very unprofessorial—to have a body and not just a head. To have passion like an artist as well as passion as an intellectual."

I nodded. What I wouldn't give to feel truly passionate and alive right now. Maybe I'd made the wrong choice, remaking my life by choosing a profession centred on minuscule procedures and finicky details. By having the perfect work placement mean a museum with its storage of creepy secrets. Ones I needed to ask about at this enjoyable lunch.

Max continued, "Sure, I enjoy being in the same room with those in their twenties, but I'm enjoying this lunch with you, too. Yes, they're aesthetic, but if you don't mind me saying it, you have extraordinary green-grey eyes. And I don't want you to think I'm coming on to you when I say that. I simply notice colour, and beauty. Just so you know, I've never had an affair with a student, or a co-worker, and never will. I simply," he paused, "enjoy." Max shook his hands in a gesture of frustration. "I hope you can understand," he finished.

"It must be difficult." I squirmed, trying to sort out my feelings. "If a prof comes on to a student, there's a power relationship involved, and it's harassment or worse. If a prof isn't actually coming on to a student, but is seen enjoying being with them . . ."

"Exactly," said Max. "Suddenly every old guy's a predator. I'm a curator!"

"Well, it rhymes."

Max rolled his eyes. "Some days I wish I were a nerd. Please, God, make me a geek, a nerd, a nebbish, a schnook, a schlemiel, but not a schmuck. I've been learning Jewish expressions from my tennis partner. Anyway, why I am going on about all this now? Here, you must taste this delicious salmon," and he forked a moist slice onto the side of my plate. I transferred it immediately into my mouth. It was excellent.

"Ber-nice," he began.

"Berenice, actually," I corrected him, using the French pronunciation. I was going to get personal too. "But call me Berry."

"Berry," he said, "What a great name. Berenice is nice in French and sort of old-fashioned, but I guess I'm too much in the business of the contemporary. Mind you, I wish I'd been called Maximillian and shortened it to Max." He sat back, lifted his glass, and his eyes behind it sparkled like sun patterns on ocean.

"Berry, maybe I shouldn't even say this after what I've been talking about, but I'm enjoying this lunch. Getting to know you. You're fun. Thanks for coming to MOA. You're a breath of—dare I say?—fresh air. I hope you stay on after your internship. You'd be an asset here."

"Thank you," I said, wondering what he was getting to know about me in this conversation other than my French background. "Maybe there'll be new jobs because of the renovation."

"Well, you're here now for what, a year? Let me know if you need a recommendation from a senior curator. It will undoubtedly be a pleasure."

"Thank you," I grinned. "Much appreciated."

A reference from Dr. Max Turpin would open doors. But there was one question I couldn't let his conversation camouflage. My picky conservation brain had kept hold of the disparaging comment he had made earlier: "Whoever thought a conservator could be so witty?" I needed him to talk about what he really thought of Reiko. I couldn't figure out how to get him to do this.

My other urgent topic, the murder, was impossible to avoid.

Max opened it with, "Did the police interview you?" When I described the arsenic research, more questions followed. This guy could have been an investigative reporter, or maybe he was just nosy. Why did the police want to know this, know that? I was flattered that he was seeking my analysis, nodding, taking my thoughts seriously. Then I remembered Elena's experience in the pub. My inner tube deflated. Max saw my face and immediately asked if something was wrong. I thought, "*This man's observant, and he's really been listening—maybe he is like me, a detail person.*" I went on the offensive.

"Why do you want to know all these details about our records and our XRF measurements and our sample sizes? Why are you so interested in the arsenic project?"

"Well, curiosity, what can I say? I know a little bit about the Roman pin, the arrows, and the arsenic research, and one of them might be the cause of death, and you're the person to ask about the arsenic."

This was my opening. "Reiko's in charge of the research. You've had months to ask her. You don't seem to like her very much. How come?"

"Ah," said Max. "I can see why you were looking uncomfortable. Why do you say I don't like Reiko?"

Nothing goes past him. I didn't want to tell Max how I knew, from Reiko herself, and from insinuations I'd picked up on. I was brilliant. "You yourself made a scurrilous comment about conservators just when we were coming in the building. Don't think I'm going to forget."

Max laughed, one of those deep free belly laughs that makes heads turn. "Scurrilous comment, eh? Outrageous brushing of the cheek? The lady doth exaggerate, methinks."

"How come you don't like Reiko?" I smiled back.

"Like a terrier with a bone. All right, I'll tell you. Understand, I know she's your friend, boss, saviour, but this is my story." He ordered a fruit plate for dessert, expecting me to share.

"Sit back. This all began long long ago, when God was a girl and dogs slept outside." I don't have a belly laugh, but sometimes I'm overtaken by an uncontrollable smile. Max grinned back and continued. "We were all in it together, you know, all there at the beginning. You probably didn't know that our esteemed Director, Sally Luykes, was a grad student in linguistics in the early '70s up in Alert Bay, earnestly comparing verbs in Kwakwala with some other language, at the same time that our esteemed security guard, Mama, was being helped by a toney British lawyer there to get out of a fucked up—excuse my French—stage of her life in that very same village, at the same time . . ."

"Max," I interrupted, "I like your story, but I have to say this now. I do not excuse your French. That's a real slur. Either you say the word fuck or you don't."

He stared at me.

"You don't pretend to make it okay with the innuendo that it's another language, or, 'Oh, it's French, you know what they're like.'"

"You're right. I stand linguistically challenged and corrected." Max bowed his head and took a sip from his glass. He didn't worm around with excuses. It impressed me, coming from a man I had pegged as used to being admired.

"Isn't Turpin a French name?" I asked into the silence.

"Maybe. My ancestors were dissenting Englishmen."
He picked up the conversation. "As I was saying before I
erred"—erreurrred he corrected himself in Franglais with a
smile—"Sally, Mama, and I were all up in Alert Bay at the
same time in the 1970s. I bet you'd never guess that Sally and
Mama are friends from way back? Or that I know all kinds
of things about them from those drunken days, even about
the reticent Mama (giving it the French pronunciation), but
I'll be fired if I tell you that Sally and I once shared a bottle
of vodka, followed by brandy, followed by crème de menthe
to cleanse our breath." His face had a mischievous grin as he
concluded, "And that's all I remember of that evening."

"Was Reiko there, too?" I asked.

"No, she was still in her crib, picking out dirt from her
dolls with a pair of tweezers."

I gave him a glare and let him continue. "I'd just graduated, and I'd landed a job with an excellent private gallery
here in Vancouver. I was up in Alert Bay looking at art. Cuyler Foley was there too, asking about artifacts. I ended up
buying a painting called 'The Big Creation'. It was beautiful,
luminous, and it spoke to me because, well, this was a new
world for me, after university, although I did eventually go
back and get my doctorate. But then, it felt like I was on the
brink of 'Creation.'"

Given the stage, Max was not going to relinquish it.
"What a painting!" he continued. "The colours of dawn—
reds, blues, and purples lighting up the sky. A universal
statement—Anishinaabe creatures with all their innards
showing, Northwest Coast figures transforming into each
other, a Christian-like ark of every living thing as seen on its
inside and its out. Recklessly magnificent, I said about that
painting, and I still stand by it." I signalled for a fresh pot of
Earl Grey.

"I suppose it was a conflict of interest, buying for my-self when I should have been buying for the gallery, but I loved this painting. Later, when I joined the museum after the Ph.D and some rather plum curatorial stints in Los An-geles and London," Max glanced at my reaction, "I decided I'd make good my little conflict of interest dilemma and be-gin my career here at MOA by making a fresh start. I'd . . ." and he almost doubled over before he repeated, "fresh start, well yes, I guess I've done that, as you so kindly pointed out as we were coming here." Max enjoyed my amused expres-sion as he finished with, "I'd give the painting to MOA."

"Now, let me backtrack for a minute. 'The Big Creation' was by Norval Morrisseau, you know him I'm sure." Max didn't stop to find out. "The Anishinaabe artist who had this magnificent, sinuous skeletal style of painting creatures. Traditional yet modern. It was perfect to start myself off with as MOA's Curator of Contemporary Art. Terrific ques-tions, you know; how to put contemporary art in an anthro-pology museum: is it art first or Native first? What do the artists say? Does the contemporary art we collect here have to look at least somewhat traditionally Native to be recog-nized by our visitors as something we should have at MOA? But anthropology is supposed to embrace all cultures, so why aren't we collecting, I don't know, Vancouver's hot-test young artists, aboriginal or not?" Max was gesticulating and his wine spilled over onto the table. He checked to see it hadn't hit me, and continued while he and the waitress mopped up. "So Morrisseau's painting . . ."

I broke in. "Why was an Eastern Woodlands painting in Alert Bay, BC? Morrisseau's Anishinaabe from Ontario, I thought."

"Don't know exactly, he's not someone I've really delved into or written about, but Morrisseau spent a long time on the West Coast. Died here, in fact. More than a few young aboriginal artists imitated his style. Max continued with a grim face, "I paid a fair price for 'The Big Creation', but I guess in the end the middleman always makes the most profit." Max halted his narrative: we were getting dangerously close to talking about an art dealer. About a Cuyler Foley.

"Anyway", he continued, "the painting went on the 'Consideration for Acquisition' table at MOA, and I guess one evening Mama saw it on one of her security rounds, with all the paperwork beside it saying 'Morrisseau'. And she went to her old friend Sally Luykes who was Associate Director by now, and said, 'That painting's not by Morrisseau. It's by Graham Bells in Alert Bay. I was given one just like it. I know it's by Graham—whom we all knew when we were up there, poor guy died the next year in a fishboat accident—because he uses a particular blue.'" Well, Mama didn't exactly say it like that; she probably said, 'He uses that funny blue' or 'He uses that traditional blue,' but it's true—my painting had a bright blue—don't know if it was the laundry blueing artists used to use—and I noticed, after I heard this piece of news, that a lot of Graham's work I saw had bright blue, too."

Max had the courtesy, after lecturing me on art and anthropology in museums, not to begin lecturing me on laundry blueing, but to ask first if I'd heard of it. And I had, as a conservation student in my Materials and Techniques course. So I showed off. "Sure," I said. "In the nineteenth century a lot of aboriginal artists used commercial products, and one of the most spectacular blues came from the blueing sold to make laundry look whiter. On the Northwest Coast, it was first imported from England." In my three months here I'd already seen it on hundred-year-old masks and imitated on new art.

Max grinned and nodded. He held up an approving finger to signal he had more to add. I poured the last of my tea. The waitress had come over, and Max said, "Just the bill, please. No, wait, I'll have a quick coffee too." I politely accepted her offer of more hot water for the teapot, even though I should have ordered a fresh bag. Earl Grey is my favourite restaurant tea, the pungent bergamot flavour hiding the worst abuses of commercial establishments: water not brought to the boil, bag not in the cup before adding water, and equipment used for both coffee and tea. Sure enough, by ordering a fill-up of water I was soon sipping a weak liquid tasting like the coffee thermos it was kept in for table service.

I caught myself making a face. "It's hard to be a tea drinker in a coffee-coated world," I explained. Max looked at me quizzically. "Tea not up to ANSI standards, then, madam?"

I almost spit my mouthful in his face trying not to laugh. Max had just quoted the technical agency that sets standards for such products as archival-quality paper. Conservators are always referencing these exacting standards, but I didn't know a curator would appreciate their importance. He understood our field well enough to banter about it. Yet he had harsh words for Reiko and Conservation when the poison arrows had came up.

"Touché," I said.

"Where were we? Yes. Sally Luykes called in your friend Reiko to see if she could do a quick technical analysis on my 'Big Creation' painting: was it a Bells or a Morrisseau? Reiko's not a fine arts specialist, as you well know, so she suggested someone else in private practice. At the time this would have cost more than the painting was worth, Morrisseau or not. So MOA refused my painting, and I took it back." Max sighed. "But it was kind of tainted for me now, so a few years later I put it up for auction. I did tell them about the blue being used by Graham Bells, and as I said, I haven't looked into Morrisseau's palette in any detail. I was going by style and signature. Plus, I have no control if a company prints 'Morrisseau' in its auction catalogue, but Reiko must have thought I did. Before a month was out, your friend Reiko," Max jabbed a finger at me, "went to the auction house and said, 'From the point of view of a professional conservator, this is probably not a Morrisseau. Buyer beware.' It ruined the sale."

I didn't know what to say. I didn't have to. Max continued, his fist opening and closing. "But that's not the worst of it," he said. "It ruined my biggest opportunity. A few years ago the job of Director here came up. Sally and I were the two internal candidates. She had an edge as Associate Director; I had an edge in publications, research, the things that count at a university and that Sally hadn't had time to keep up with because of her administrative duties. Someone asked me in the interview, 'Didn't you once try to sell a painting by saying it was done by a better-known artist than in fact it had been?' That question, that phrasing, lost me the job." Max ground the words out.

"So you were damned before you'd even had a chance to explain?"

Max nodded but his fist hadn't relaxed. "Sally's been a terrific Director. She's a very good administrator; frankly, she's better than me at it. I begrudge her nothing. But Reiko, she's gotten under my skin. Here, let's stop this now. The conversation is probably making you uncomfortable." Max took any awkwardness out of my having to respond by gulping his coffee and rising to go. I looked at my watch; it was after two.

"Don't worry," said Max, "the lunch was on me, so it was on curatorial time, too." An ego who could make fun of himself—this prof got full marks.

"I was hoping I'd have time to go to the library," I said. "What was I thinking?"

"Go!" said Max. "You work in a university museum. Going to the library comes with the job description. If I were director, anyway. Go!"

"Thanks," I smiled, and couldn't think of how to say what I really wanted, so resorted to the well-worn formula, "Thanks for lunch. I really enjoyed talking with you." I charged off, going over in my mind how enjoyable it had been to chat comfortably with a senior male academic— dare I presume to call him colleague?—who spoke so openly, so honestly, and with at least a bachelor's degree in self-knowledge.

It didn't take me long to look up arsenic. The medical library was too far away, but from what I found in the undergrad stacks, it appeared that arsenic poisoning, as the amount of arsenic increased, could cause extreme discomfort before it caused death. I had no idea what medical state Foley's heart or blood pressure had been in, but it was credible he had felt something enough to panic him and precipitate a heart attack, if not more.

# Chapter
# 12

## Wednesday Afternoon

I walked back to the museum thinking about arsenic, about the lunch, and helplessly, about Daniel. Would I ever see him again? Catching myself, I focused on the tall straight fir trees instead. "Instead?" whispered a Freud-like voice with Daniel's intonation. I looked ahead at the distant view. It finally hit me that the morning mist had burned off. I'd been seeing mountains even in the restaurant. It was sunny now, gorgeous and not too warm. The kind of weather we'd had when Daniel first took me to Lighthouse Park on the North Shore. A picnic, the two of us nestled out of the wind on warm water-smoothed rocks, the freedom of the ocean in front and a forest older than the province marking the trail we'd hiked through.

I went down the steps from the campus terraces and flagpole to walk back through UBC's formal rose garden before crossing the road to the museum, and was rewarded with another unbelievable view of range upon range of mountains cascading into the distance beyond the water. When I'd told people I was coming here, some of them had referred to Vancouver as "nice but dumb" and I'd been offended. Now I understood. As a city, Vancouver was new, with most of its growth occurring in the last forty years. I had yet to meet anyone under sixty who had been born here. There appeared to be no unifying urban identity, no soul that was Vancouver. But the setting! The mountains, the beaches, the overwhelming greenery and flowers all year round stood in for a soul. City planners apparently knew this, and even the downtown was bordered by long seawalls for leisurely strolling.

Vancouver was a city to grow old in. Except I didn't have a job . . . yet. I had decided already that one goal in my professional life would be respect from Max Turpin. And the way I felt? Grow old in Vancouver when Daniel had left, damn him? If Daniel could do this to me in three months—and even after lunching with my would-be collegial crush—what a hold he had on me. I had better shore up my heart. The wall life's disappointments had already built should have by now been strong enough on its own, but evidently it was not. I saw the museum entrance and made myself laugh to break the depression rolling in like a breaker; next time I wouldn't coddle his damn cat either. It didn't work. A good actor might be able to pretend, but I wasn't even a good liar, especially to myself. I remembered what I'd been thinking, that Vancouver was a city to grow old in. Unless you were murdered. That worked. I concentrated on strategy.

Theo had appeared upset, but not nearly surprised enough when I told him the bronze was a fake. So he knew. He used delaying tactics. What was Theo up to, what was he doing right now, what was he covering up? I decided to walk through the museum galleries, which meant I looked like I could be working, monitoring the humidity levels for preservation standards or something, while keeping a lookout for Theo without raising suspicions.

The museum wasn't all that large and there wasn't much thinking space. I bypassed the Great Hall to make a circuit, such as was possible, through Visible Storage and Gallery Ten that fronted on the same corridor, both still roped off. Wires hanging from the ceiling tangled into unnameable equipment, as if a team of workers who thought they knew what they were doing had all given up. If this chaos was what laying high-speed Internet cables looked like, what would prolonged renovations do to a visitor's sense of this world-renowned museum? A moot point if stories about Foley's death at MOA made the news.

Was that an artifact case open? The workers in this gallery usually had one of the Collections people with them to make sure nothing was harmed by the construction. A few of the heaviest artifacts remained roped off in their cases here like trees at a construction site surrounded by fluorescent plastic fencing, until a mechanical lift could be brought. The staffperson must have left in a hurry. Nobody was here now, and it looked from where I stood as if the case with the log drums was half open. Carefully I picked my way over to investigate. The consummate intern.

A noise like ripping canvas made me look up. A crack was snaking along the ceiling beside one of the light fixtures. I grabbed the worker's safety ladder beside me just in time to hide under it. Stupid. An earthquake would topple it easily. But the ladder stayed steady. No earth tremors. Useless protection anyway. I sprang away just as a light fixture came crashing down, bouncing off the ladder, debris missing my spot by inches. My scream penetrated the clouds of dust.

A panicked voice yelled, "I'm coming!"

I stayed rooted, heart pounding, my one rational thought commanding me not to move if the wires were live. A thin figure broke through the dust. Ed, the Designer, leapt right over the fixture and wires, enfolding me, words stammering out. Was I all right? He started patting down my shoulders and arms before I could stop his mobile hands, and even felt my nose as if I were a cat. It made me laugh, and the look of relief on his face was so tender.

"Oh my God, oh shit," Ed kept repeating, and between the apologies that tumbled out I understood that this was his ladder, he'd been installing new bulbs and noticed the fixture was coming loose. "I went back to the fuse box to double check the circuit was shut down. But for changing lights I wait anyway till everyone's on break and the area's roped off. So there shouldn't be anyone here. It sure hadn't looked loose enough to fall."

"It's not your fault, Ed. I'm okay, just a bit shaken. I was looking for Theo." I told the straight truth because savvy, worried Ed would have asked, since it wasn't visible, if the light fixture had destroyed my humidity monitoring equipment.

"Theo came by awhile back to let the workers know he'd probably be Acting Director while Luykes is off lecturing, wanting to see if everything's on track for the next few days. He likes to plan and avoid problems."

Me too. I told Ed I needed to go to the Ladies and clean up. Stopping as soon as I was out of sight, I caught my breath and leaned against the quiet wall behind Visible Storage. I had almost just been killed. It looked like an accident. How convenient. Reiko was silenced, effectively in the custody of the police. Me, the one other member of the Conservation department, had been enticed to verify a display case that happened to place my body directly under a loose ceiling fixture. The display case with the heavy drums—yes, the consummate intern had better go tell Collections: their turn now to check it.

I couldn't move, though. This was fear, not a hot flash flooding me. Was someone actually trying to get rid of me? Because I might be in cahoots with Reiko? Because of the fake Pan? Because they thought I knew something about Foley's murder? What information was I supposed to have?

I'll discover it. You want to wreck my ship, I'll weather the storm. I haven't come this far to be put off course. Sunk with all hands and cargo? But I had to admit Ed's story hung together. Was the whole incident nothing more than a complete accident? Or did some sociopathic pirate have it in for me?

———— ༀ☙ ————

I couldn't come up with a plan that gave me a logical excuse to monitor Theo. Damn this fuzzy brain. It's just shock, I told myself. To hell with it. I headed back through the galleries towards Theo's office. I would just keep popping in on him all afternoon—nothing he could do. Ask him questions about the last bronze, tell him it was for the condition report.

Theo wasn't in his office. Or the other offices I passed by, and the coffee and photocopy rooms. Security should have a record of Theo signing in or out.

Beside the desk, turning in his visitor's pass, stood the fancy older gentleman I had first seen with Luykes, a good friend of the museum according to Oscar and the man who had asked Ed and I if we needed a lawyer when Sergeant Daley wanted to question us.

"May I ask again," he said as he eyed my dishevelled appearance, "if you would like to talk to a lawyer?"

His voice was soft with concern, but he had one of those classy British accents that sounds arrogant to North American ears. I shook my head.

"Is that a yes or a no? My name is Saul Samuels and I've done work for this museum and members of its staff. If it is an issue of money, we can make arrangements. My priority is to assist if there is trouble."

The way his long coat draped and his bespoke hat showed no wear, I was not going to talk financial arrangements. Free advice, though, was welcome after my recent brush with disaster and paranoia. Lowering my head as if wanting to talk to him confidentially, I moved further away from the Security guard.

"A conservation analysis—I'm Berry Cates, an intern here under Reiko Smithson—has made me think one artifact is not as ancient as we supposed. I'm new here. Do you have any advice if further work shows there's been a breach of museum ethics like a forgery? Has there been one in this museum before?"

"There was a questionable painting many years ago, but if you work for Reiko, you probably know about it."

"A dispute with Max Turpin?"

"Disclosure is up to the complainants and the incident is long over."

"Would you say this museum is ethical?"

"Sally Luykes would want to know if there was any deceit going on. Is there?"

"Is there at other museums?" I could be as evasive as him.

Saul Samuels pulled out a handkerchief and delicately wiped a drop of spittle that had formed in one corner of his mouth. "Museums with their valuable collections present enormous temptation," he said, carefully refolding the white linen. "Museum procedures and records are one effective guard against fraud. But there are many kinds of deceit: financial fraud, looting sites and selling the antiquities, and for instance forgeries or otherwise making up an artifact or its context and stating that the piece is something other than what it is. Some of these represent crimes, some may be only misinformation. You can be sure that whatever the case, the perpetrator will justify his or her actions."

"How can you tell if it's criminal then?"

"Ms. Cates, that's why you have the police. And lawyers. May I suggest that you talk to one of us?"

"If and when I know enough, I will."

"Of course. Evidence is the key." He extended a thin hand to shake mine. "If you need to get in touch with me, just ask Sally."

At lunch Max had told me a toney British lawyer had been in Alert Bay when he, Sally, and Mama were there. Saul Samuels must be the man, and in Sally's inner circle, to talk like this. The old gentleman would certainly know more about the museum's hidden history, but to get definite details out of him I would have to have a reason, and money to pay, or a lawyer's knowledge of how to question.

⋅⊙⊚⊙⋅

Theo had signed in but not out with the guards, although that could have been deliberate, to be passed off as a slip. No one would call a senior curator to task. At least I had a plan for contacting Reiko and a growing list of all I wanted to talk about. I'd phone at midnight. The call might catch her asleep but there was less chance of having a police guard there. I went back downstairs.

Under the unwatchful eye of my cop escort I worked on cleaning the last bronze. Conservation was problem-solving through paying attention to details. Yesterday Sergeant Daley had struck me as the type who could be a good conservator. Maybe I would succeed at detection.

I took advantage of a coffee break at 3:30. Many others had done the same, though none of them was Theo. My green mug wasn't in sight so I grabbed a cup and a tea bag from the generic box and waited by the kettle. Any tea would do right now.

Seats at the biggest table were all taken and there were only two free chairs left in the lounge: one at a table beside a curator and some archaeologists I didn't know well, where I fitted in with the age group but not the status, and one at a big table with an overflow of young museum assistants and students. Not planning to tell anyone about my near escape from the falling light, I sat down with these other recent grads, hoping they would gossip about the murder and not cool music, models or, well, a long list was already reeling off in my mind of their generation's leisure topics I had heard discussed, about which I knew nothing, couldn't join in, and couldn't care less. Sometimes I wished I'd had kids and could enjoy this stuff. Did Max ever see this side of them?

Luykes did. I stared at the big table, at the seated figure who had her back to me as she talked to Theo's daughter. It was the Director, in concentrated conversation with Elena, advising on course options for next year. Two others at the table had already taken the program and had firm opinions. Luykes listened and inquired. Everyone was very circumspect about the profs. Then Zoe asked the unspoken big question, "Have the police found anything out?"

Luykes turned to Oscar. "Have Public Relations had any media inquiries?"

Oscar shook his head, fiddling with his moustache. Either the news wasn't out yet, or the museum was only an incidental backdrop. No one asked the table of curators if they'd had any calls to outline their praises for an obit.

"Have the police found anything out yet?" Zoe pumped.

All at once no one was speaking. It was as if a blanket of snow had fallen in the room, quieting the universe, freezing people to their spots, and making everyone's ears red.

"Well, there is one bit of news," said Luykes, looking now around the room. Several chairs scraped. "Our conservator, Reiko, has been asked not to come to work. I've given her leave with pay. We're to have no contact with her until the police are through their interviews. There'll be an all-staff email about this shortly."

Then Luykes looked directly at me. "Berenice, if any questions come up in Conservation, do come and see me, or the Acting Director while I'm away." I nodded, searching her body language for any clues as to whether she really expected problems, and searching my mind as to whether I'd obey her command to have no contact with Reiko.

There were plenty of questions that had already come up in Conservation that I needed answered. Did the police actually suspect Reiko of murder, or only of having ties to information they needed? Maybe Reiko was an incommunicado suspect because she hadn't divulged a motive yet. Because she had none, not being a murderer. Or perhaps her missing lab coat showed evidence of something else.

Luykes stood up as if she was about to announce something. An almost imperceptible shiver shook her body and face, and for a second her head bent down. One hand went out to grasp the table. Then she looked up and surveyed the room. My eyes followed her gaze. Theo was standing in the open doorway.

"We are in the midst of a very difficult and tragic situation," she said. "Some of you may have heard about a Roman pin that was in Mr. Foley's breast pocket when he died, with the theory that this may have caused his death when he collapsed. The police have discounted this theory; the angle and the bluntness of the pin could not have caused . . . anything lethal. But I do not yet know what the coroner's report will say. So for now, there is one thing I want all of you to keep in mind. Our sympathies are with Cuyler's family. Whatever you may have thought of him, whatever you think happened to him—and I know there's been gossip in this very room about poisons—at this point the police have not revised their statement that the cause of death was a massive heart attack. There has been a tragedy at MOA. A terrible loss for all who knew him." Luykes glanced around like a teacher at her class, and exited the lounge, Theo one step behind her.

Conversations bounced around the room as staff washed their cups, break time over. My tea was gone and I needed to finish my work even if gumshoe Berry Cates' first choice would have been waiting with an eye on Luykes' office door for Theo. At the far table one of the archaeologists rose to go and the empty corner revealed my green mug shoved to one side. I leapt for my love object. The check-shirted man apologized for not knowing it was mine. The mug had been on the table when they arrived, full of hot tea, waiting for its owner, and eventually they had put the mug aside when no one claimed it. I nodded and took a sip anyway of the cool but well-steeped liquid. It tasted funny.

"This is very sweet."

The archaeologist handed me a small canister of stevia, explaining that the natural sugar substitute had been on the table along with my mug when they'd come in. I would have thought nothing of his statement except that, in a version of a story becoming increasingly plausible, someone had just attempted to kill me with a falling light fixture. Now the mug I regularly use had been waiting for me, filled with my favourite beverage, but heavily sweetened. Why? To mask a white powder going into a white powder? I stuck the stevia into my lab coat pocket, asked if anyone had seen who had made the tea—which they hadn't—and took my mug to find the police to analyze the tea and the canister's contents.

∘◦⟨⊙⟩◦∘

Close to 4:30 I phoned Theo's office, focused and calm. What had he been up to immediately before and after I'd seen him following Luykes out of the lounge? His phone went to voice mail. I checked around the offices and walked the main corridors of the galleries and still couldn't see him. Several meetings were going on behind closed doors, though, and I went back downstairs to proof the last bit of the last bronze's condition report. The police would now be taking all the artifacts away unless they were stored in MOA's high-security lock-up. Either way, it would be good to pack them up properly so the handling and transportation wouldn't damage them further. I proposed this to the police escort, who phoned Constable Frick, who phoned back with a yes. Meanwhile I had found several sturdy boxes—not made from acidic cardboard either—tissue paper and bubblewrap. I glanced at my messages and knew the Canadian Conservation Institute in Ottawa had called back, but it was again too late to phone them. I might as well go and photocopy my documentation next, since the police would likely take this too.

Where on earth was the report I had done on the faked bronze? Maybe I was more upset than I admitted, my brain behaving a little like Gallery Ten with all its loose wires. By now my search through the pile of documentation was the opposite of methodical. Putting the files aside I went to gather the artifacts, figuring that the whereabouts of the report on the bronze would appear in my frazzled brain sometime around 2 A.M. I started to pack up the pottery, and glimpsed a few staff putting on jackets and coats. All the meetings were over. In fact the day was over; it was way past five. I had been doing a poor job of following Theo this afternoon, although there were good reasons for it. But I had to find him.

Going through the galleries to Theo's office would be the quickest way to lose my escort and avoid curious staff. I phoned up to Security. "Are the alarms on yet in Visible Storage?"

"You've got another hour. Need more?"

"Can I? I thought the alarms were automatic."

"Usually yeah, but Theo is working in Visible Storage so they're on temporary override."

Excellent! I banged through the lab door that led directly into Visible Storage and made my way towards the "Mediterranean Collections" area.

Theo wasn't there. I scurried and ducked, leaping around wires, pegboard, studs, trim and plasterboard. I scrambled in and out of the remaining bays that make up the large Native American and Canadian areas, and then through the rest of Visible Storage that encompass world collections. No Theo. MOA may not be a huge museum, but it has its quiet corners; these had become a labyrinth. My mind plotted a message I could leave on Daniel's phone later. I would tell him of my global search through North

America, Europe, Asia, and Africa. Exiting Visible Storage into Gallery Ten, I debated telling him about the crashing light fixture.

The darkness was sudden, and for an instant I was reliving the earlier horror. But now there were no lights at all. Maybe Theo had finished and the guards were closing the museum and about to set the evening alarms? I glimpsed the skylight-lit main corridor, and moved towards it. A pile of twisted wires caught my foot, and, trapped, tumbling, the broken coils enveloped me.

Then silence. No slap of running steps, no help. I knew I had to move—if the alarms were on at least that would set off the motion detectors—but it hurt to lift myself off the floor. My head rolled around on dizzying waves. They've got me now. I'm losing it. A condition report. Now consciousness.

Deliberately I took several deep breaths. I wasn't going under. The fall had only pushed a panic button in me, ramped up by the events of the day. MOA has 24-hour security. There had to be someone at the guards' station, and surely I could crawl my way up there if nothing else. I wouldn't be locked in, unlike the countless faces in the dark cases surrounding me, human, bird, animal and supernatural, and all the clothes, fans, shoes, and toys now separated from their past lives.

"I need out!" My voice echoed through the darkness. With the silence broken again, some other part of my brain kicked in, or at least my body. A flash of heat, a quick surge of pain, and then these dulled. More scared than badly hurt, I figured, but in the gloom there was no trace of movement, no rescue. Nobody had heard me. Light poured down from the distant skylight. It wasn't much past six on a long June evening, and the sun was out. "I am not scared," I told myself. "This is ridiculous!" Half crawling and half slithering, I freed myself from the wires and stood, shakily, but more or less upright, then shuffled towards the corridor light.

Under the skylight, I inspected my wounds. There were cuts and some bleeding but nothing more than a bad-looking scrape, although a smart Berry would go for a tetanus shot. By the time I got to the guards' station, my joints were moving in a semblance of my old self, and I was able to pass off the young guard's concern with a breezy "Oh, nothing but a flesh wound," and glanced at the roster showing who was still in the building. Theo was. I scented blood, even if it was my own, and headed for his office.

"Of course he isn't here," I said to myself outside his closed door, pounding red knuckles on the wood. My fear voice rose. "Maybe he did it. He's trying to frighten me off. Go back to the guards and find out why the lights shut off, why the barriers to Gallery Ten were down. It was deliberate." My face collapsed as my eyes flooded. I want chocolate. I want Chinese food. I want Daniel to be at home.

———— ⚬⚬⚬ ————

Wiping the wetness off my face with my lab coat sleeve, I turned and went back downstairs, relieved that I would be alone at this hour. The calm routine of packing the artifacts, making them secure, would reorder my life. Seeing the objects in their boxes I would know that this disgusting, disquieting cleaning job was over. I organized the remaining packing materials and wrapped the pieces one by one. When I got to the bronzes, the Pan wasn't there.

I stared at the spot on the "completed" table where I had moved the bronze earlier, looking up and down the whole table and nearby surfaces. No Pan. I did it again, not trusting myself. No Pan. The adjacent artifacts appeared to have been moved so there wasn't a visible missing area on the tabletop. *"This is too much. Maybe I've mislaid the condition report, but now I can't find the bronze itself. I'm phoning Constable Frick."*

I managed to get right through to her. Something in my voice must have sounded urgent. Frick didn't interrupt as I told her about the missing piece. Not just one of the artifacts, but the one that might be fake. I had decided to tell her. Theo had had enough time. Part way through my description Frick started to reassure me. She'd heard the note of high energy frazz in my voice and I think she believed that more than my words. But I didn't humiliate myself by telling her my fears, that someone was out to get me. Incidents like tripping over wires were decidedly puny compared to most she must deal with.

"Probably the Collections people just put the bronze away while you were concentrating on the last cleaning," said Frick. "Don't worry, Berenice, I'll look into it first thing tomorrow morning."

"If the fake's gone, it proves something's up."

"Don't worry, it'll be investigated."

"It's very serious, don't you think?" If the forgery had anything to do with my "accidents", at least police would be investigating. "Can you let Sergeant Daley know?"

"Of course. We'll look into this fake business. It would be very important."

Stuff her anodyne assurances. Or was I over-reacting and maybe Frick did have the right take on it? But after having a light fixture practically kill me and the weird sweet tea, as well as the wires? I'd been tangled up in Gallery Ten for a fair bit of time. The coffee lounge would pull my brain together.

I hobbled first into the main office to pick up Conservation's old waiting mail so I had something from normal work life to read over coffee. "Coffee" in the generic sense; I was contemplating gunpowder tea, delicious round green balls of whole tea leaves, rolled, that must have resembled old ammunition. Or because they packed the wallop of caffeine I was desperate for right now. But there was no need for gunpowder. The empty room reverberated with another explosion. A loud "Damn you!" rang out from Luykes' adjacent office. The next instant the Director's door flew open and a livid Theo stalked into the main office where I stood.

Stomping towards the exit he almost missed me, and I wished he had. But he registered my presence, whirled around and yelled, "You! You're the cause of all this. Go in there and tell her your science."

When I didn't move, he took my arm and swept me into Luykes' office, plunking me down into the still-warm visitor's chair opposite the Director, the dark polished seat lower than hers, with the solid cherrywood desk in between. Theo loomed behind me, one hand on the chair back. He probably would have preferred pressing into my shoulder, keeping me securely in place. With a voice like paint stripper he questioned me on each segment of my suspicions about the Pan. "Have the scientists confirmed the corrosion layers? No? When did you graduate?"

"You're absolutely sure you haven't made a mistake?" Luykes' voice had that raw cracking that stress brings. I shook my head, saying that a chemist specializing in heritage metals had called back but I was in the galleries.

"Would Cuyler have known?" Luykes eyed Theo.

"I think his notes will show he had just started the bronze."

"Let's hope this wasn't what gave him the heart attack. Realizing that the bronze was new. Thinking that you, that the museum had just spent twenty thousand dollars on a piece that wasn't authentic." I could hear Theo's shallow breathing behind me.

"As I said, I have to inform the police." Luykes' voice rose. "This unfortunately makes you a suspect in Cuyler's death, Theo. Gives you a motive for murder. Embarrassment at your professional blunder, figuring Cuyler knew. He'd discreetly spread it around, too. Berry, you are not to repeat any of this."

Theo gripped the back of my chair, his heavy body rocking. Then Luykes said, "I'm sorry Theo, that was uncalled for. Nothing is proven. I apologize for this outburst. I'm shocked at myself these past two days. This situation has hit me harder than I'd like to admit." She looked straight past me and up at Theo. "But I will rescind your being Acting Director while I'm gone. I'll have to ask Max, and of course he'll love that."

She turned her eyes on me. "Berry," Luykes said, "are you deliberately looking for trouble with your conservation know-how, examining the antiquities to the nth degree? We don't need another conservator like that. Not trusting the curators. Raising suspicions at MOA when we have a far worse tragedy to clear up." She brushed an invisible strand of loose hair off her forehead. "A conservator's job here is to treat the artifacts so they're preserved. Any problems, you bring them directly to me." Her eyes glued on mine, making sure I was attentive, she said, "This has been a private conversation. Especially the confidence intended for Theo. Let me emphasize that repeating any of it could be cause for dismissal. Now please, leave. Both of you, just get out."

As we headed for the door Theo turned towards Luykes, almost spitting out his words. "Let me make this perfectly clear again. I did not kill him. He was a brilliant colleague. Better than some. Just because you never liked him."

I bolted across the hallway into the lounge, my heart flipping as if I'd touched a live wire. I didn't need any jolt of gunpowder tea. Theo scowled past and slammed his office door. He emerged, seconds later, coat in hand, but stopped short as Sally Luykes left her own office and headed towards the guards and the washroom beyond. Theo made a show of looking under his coat arm as if he'd forgotten something, and hurried back into his lair. I scuttled down to Security and signed off to exit through the back door. Rushing to my car, I swung out of the back parking lot since Theo's car wasn't there and headed towards the front. It worked. There were only four cars in the small front faculty-staff parking, and Theo's was one. Thank God the front lobby renovations hadn't started and MOA staff didn't have to go over to the parkade where Theo's car would be one of a thousand. Here I could see the faculty-staff cars easily from the public area, and there were enough night students parked where I was waiting, a camouflage.

To hell with Luykes' warnings. Being suspicious was better than being a suspect. Luykes was supposed to be going away to lecture. What would she know of my movements? I couldn't go and talk to Theo after the conversation we'd just had with Luykes, but I wanted to figure out what he was going to do next. See his face as he came out of the museum, when he thought he was alone.

And I did, but it wasn't his face that caught my attention. He was stressed all right, with his lips drawn tight, the muscles in his jaw working, and his shoulders hunched. He was distraught, maybe angry. What more? I hardly knew him. My time was better spent concentrating on the box he now carried under his arm, cardboard, recycled, and almost exactly the right size for a bronze of Pan.

# Chapter
# 13

## Wednesday Evening

Stoked by seeing the box he held, I instantly decided to follow his car. This was going to be good. I felt cocky. Could a woman really use that expression? What the hell, I felt great. My ribs and legs were painful, my muscles were aching, my brain was regressing, but hey, kid, this was where it was at. God, that must be an expression from thirty or forty years ago. All right, I had attitude. 'Tude. That at least was somewhat more recent because I'd heard it when I was studying. Maybe I would catch up with reality one day, and the truth about a fake and a murder.

Theo's sedan headed towards the exit. My rust-bucket, at least in West Coast terms, swayed out to follow. I'd only ever followed cars when somebody had offered to guide me on a new route, and I'd hated it. The person went through a red light, and what were you supposed to do? And this was when they knew you were following them. Tonight's traffic was sparse. My problem was now how to keep the sedan in view and not be noticed. But this was Theo, preoccupied and professorial; his mind did not include tailgating. There weren't too many directions to go in Vancouver anyway. I gunned the engine. I would never have the makings of a real detective, but right now I had the adrenalin, and was going to get some answers.

The sun was setting as we proceeded down along the water, past the modern mansions hidden behind their professional plantings and their private sea views of English Bay. Then came the three and four storey apartments, older and spacious but with no balconies, some of them co-ops, relics of Canada's "Just Society" decades. Theo signalled his lane change for the Burrard St. Bridge, and as we crossed False Creek towards downtown the view of the city was glorious, a shimmering Oz in gold and silver reflections. The avant-garde angles of tall new condo towers scaled down to stately townhouses, gardens, and public art. We skirted the water, bypassing the direct route to downtown, and then turned straight down Homer St. heading towards Gastown, an area developed for tourists and nightlife. Would there be any parking there this time of night? No worry, we didn't stop. Theo turned on the borderland between the reconditioned Gastown visitor section, all old brick, reproduction Victorian lamps and black iron, and the area of boarded-up storefronts and single occupancy rooms called the Downtown Eastside, the DTES. The shabby "hotels" and rooming houses were home to laid-off old loggers and those down on their luck, while the alleys sheltered down-and-out drug addicts and the otherwise homeless. As I parked outside a dark building a quarter block from Theo, I forgot our tour of Vancouver. I couldn't care less about its attractions, because I was a few blocks too far away. I had heard on newscasts about where I now was. Not only is the DTES the poorest postal code in Canada, it has open drug dealing at noon, and the police are swamped. It looked like everything I had heard. I was in an addicted, poverty-ridden, garbage-strewn ghetto, and I stuck out like a ripe peach tree.

I scooted with as much dignity as possible down to the doorway Theo had gone through. It looked like any of the other doorways on the block, paint peeling, old blackened doorknob, bricks on either side worn and disintegrating. A buzzer, but no name under it. I wasn't going to ring—to say, what? Standing in the doorway, in the shadowed street I wasn't feeling so cocky.

As usual these past few days my brain was sauntering a few steps behind the main event. I turned my back to the door and half slouched. Just hanging out. I could leave and look up the address tomorrow in the Criss-Cross city directory at the library. That sounded good. I could bring my car down closer and wait, do a real stake-out. With no bathroom? No food or drink? And all I'd probably see was Theo exiting with a box and heading home? Cop-out excuses, Cates. But a well-enough dressed woman sitting in a car for any period of time down here would probably be monitored by the police for drug involvement. I'd end up spending the night at the station, explaining away. That was reasonable. I'd better go home, a conclusion that made me happy until my body jerked to attention.

Wasn't that Mama, the museum guard? A short squat figure had crossed the road and was slowly walking up the side street. What on earth was she doing here? I didn't want to know. It was her. I was drawn out of my doorway, staring at her back, not wanting her to be here. My belly cramped. I didn't want her to be here for crack or smack or anything to do with the stolen goods that supported them. I didn't want her to be here for any reason I could think of. I didn't want her to live here, I didn't want her friends to be here. I couldn't help myself from following her.

Mama turned onto the main street and into a brightly lit storefront. I crept up to the windows. Not a bar, not a club. Huge bags of aluminium cans on one side, plastic bottles on the other way back into the far reaches of a warehouse. A recycling depot? Go down at night to the DTES looking for a recycling depot? Boxes of beer and wine bottles were there too. These you could get money for at the provincial liquor outlets. I couldn't begin to guess what was going on here, but there must have been close to ten people inside. Mama was talking to a bearded man and then suddenly she was out the door and facing me.

"Berenice," she said, "I saw you outside the foundry and now you're here. You okay?"

"Sure," I said, stalling while my brain tried to process something. "Listen, please call me Berry."

"Sure. . . Berry." Mama waited. She didn't budge. We stared at each other like kids trying to see who would blink first.

Foundry? Theo had gone into a foundry. Now that was interesting. How else do you make a bronze statue but in a foundry? Thank you, Mama. And thank you for being here—a familiar face was exactly what I had needed.

"Am I glad to see you, Mama. I was feeling apprehensive about waiting outside that door. It was locked and nobody was answering. I was wondering if I could use the bathroom wherever you were going." A half-lie would do.

"I'm surprised the door isn't open," she said. "It usually is when everybody's there. Bell doesn't work. I'll walk you down. They can't have a worse bathroom than us."

Mama marched me down the street and towards the foundry's door. There was nothing I could do. My brain whirred as I tried to think what to say when we got there. There? Why not right now? I slowed to keep pace with Mama's wheezier steps.

"Mama, can I ask you about a blue painting?"

"Nope." She chortled. "All questions go through my lawyer." We both laughed at the old standard. But there was a finality to her "nope," and I didn't press further. The next minute she said, "Go on ahead. Try the door. It should be open."

I walked on, tried the door, and it was open. What could I do? I waved at Mama with a silly grin and went in. Very quietly, and slowly, I poked myself into the building.

I was in an entranceway to a big warehouse. The entry space where I stood was bordered by raw studs and sacks of supplies, while a good thirty feet beyond was a much larger open area. There were no interior walls, just piled bags and bins. Smaller bags had been dragged into a semi-circle around the central concrete floor. Two dozen people sat there under a few bare bulbs rigged high up towards the ceiling. More people stood leaning against some far studs. No one even turned to look at who was coming through the door. Their attention was riveted by a burning cauldron being lifted from a furnace.

Slowly a block and tackle moved the cauldron forward.

"C'mon, guys, it's cookin'," said the man at the far end holding the long chain. The ceiling must have been twenty feet high; the machinery creaked, and the cauldron tipped a little as the chain slowly pulled the apparatus along the ceiling rail.

"One sec," came from the background. Now that was a voice I'd heard before. I crouched down near the door, behind a partition formed from a few sacks piled on rusty barrels. Looking at the cauldron was like looking at the sun.

The people had become black silhouettes its light was so intense.

Red hot, white hot. The cauldron was all the colours of flame and metal, mixed to become liquid fire. Black scraggy masses floated on the top. It was a volcano and lava, an intensity of primitive alchemy.

Two figures emerged from the dark background, wearing what looked like white spacesuits, complete with helmets and gloves. "Okay. Let's swing it," said the familiar voice, now muffled. One spacesuit grabbed a large pair of tongs and the other took the chain from the man who had been pulling it. Both then moved in towards the cauldron. I could feel heat even back behind my pile of sacks. Some of the people who sat closer were fanning themselves. The spacesuits must be asbestos-like protective clothing. The figures moved as if doing modern dance, beautiful and unpredictable, touching the cauldron with the tongs, pulling it up and down on the chain, tipping it until the incandescent syrup poured out.

On the concrete floor were perhaps twenty little mountains of sandy rough clay, every one with metal tubes sticking out at odd angles and a funnel at the top. The heavy cauldron was manoeuvred over each mountain and its fiery liquid contents flowed into the funnel, darkening as the temperature dropped even through that short distance. No one spoke. The two figures worked quickly. They had poured perhaps three-quarters when one of the funnels tipped. Sparks of metallic heat flew up a clear twenty feet to the warehouse ceiling. People screamed and dove behind their seats. Even the asbestos-covered figures couldn't help lifting their arms to shield themselves. It was finished in an instant, like a spectacular fireworks gone awry. "Wow" and "Oh boy" and "I'm okay" chatter started as people emerged and retook their seats, testing them first for hot spots and pointing out areas where the sacks had been burned. The spacemen were already back at work, probably sweating, I thought, dancing now in tight synchronized concentration, moving even more quickly to finish before the cauldron lost its heat.

Then it was over. There was a cheer from the sidelines. The cauldron was tugged back towards the furnace. The room lights seemed brighter now that the molten metal was gone. People started to rise, and I backed even closer to the door. The first spaceman removed his helmet, grinning and shaking his head. Not Theo. The second spaceman had taken his helmet off and his gloves, and begun gesticulating to the onlookers. It was Ed, the museum's Designer.

I stopped, transfixed. What was Ed doing here? For that matter, what was everyone doing here? My eyes roved over the crowd. Nobody was coming towards my door—they were milling about on all sides of the little sand mountains, talking and exclaiming in small groups. Somebody began passing beer around. Ooooh! I couldn't do anything except watch and thirst. A long time passed. My watch was unreadable in my dark corner, but it was over three beers for some, and since nobody made a move to leave, I didn't either. And I hadn't seen Theo.

Then someone yelled, "Okay?" Conversation stopped.

"Okay," replied Ed, and reached for his gloves. People crowded in closer to him, blocking my view. I could barely see Ed, now on his knees, something in his hand, leaning over one of the little mountains. His fingers picked away somewhere near the floor, by the clinking and clattering. A few minutes later came a cheer. People stepped aside as Ed rose, brushing off something he held up in his right hand. A statue. A bronze statue.

From where I peeked out the thing looked funny, rough and a bad colour, and there were bits sticking out at all angles where the tubes and funnel had been. It could have been a Pan—it was the right size and more or less the right shape. I knew from conservation school that a casting, even after the mould has been removed, still needed a lot of finishing work to make it look like what we thought of as a statue. It didn't matter about identifying it here. I would talk to Ed tomorrow. Why were two dozen people watching a Museum of Anthropology staff member manufacture fakes? Besides, as a door opened in an adjacent room, its light illuminated Theo walking towards Ed.

I shivered despite the lingering heat and craned my neck to see better. The corner of my eye caught motion—some heads turning, a wave of hands. Good-byes floated across. A couple were now walking hand-in-hand towards the exit to the street, the door behind me. Some people were collecting empties, others putting on their coats. I had to leave before Ed or Theo saw me.

The air outside smelled strong and clean. It had rained. The street was empty, but noise rolled out from a bar somewhere. I snuck down to my car, incandescent after-images flashing in my head.

⁐⁐◦⊙◦⁐

It was a few minutes before I could drive. My earlier worry returned, of cynical police coming to ask what a woman was doing sitting in this part of the DTES at night, and I hit the accelerator. And then braked hard. More people were now outside the foundry, talking on the sidewalk. I pulled over into a dark spot on the opposite side and watched. Why not? Would Theo come out with Ed? Would he carry a box with him? Was anybody saying anything I might like to hear?

Snatches of night time conversation filtered through my open window, as if the last two hours hadn't existed for these people once the spectacle was over, the movie finished. Time to get back to real life in Vancouver. "My men's group's meeting next Tuesday . . ."; "That dog cost us nine hundred dollars and the vet still isn't sure . . ."; "Have you tried phoning Gourmet-Gourmand for fig mustard?"; "I know a great consignment store for kimonos." My ears perked up at the last one, but the answer was lost to me as a car passed. Then Ed came out with the other guy who had been in a spacesuit.

They were crowded with "Great work," and "Thanks for inviting me," and Ed's voice rang out, "Glad you could come. Not something you see everyday, is it? As I said in the invitation, the school end of the foundry is an edu. . ." Another car passed. ". . . bronze costs a lot for a young artist. We didn't pass the hat tonight, but if any of you are so moved, we give tax receipts. We do private commissions, too."

"Weddings, bar mitzvahs." His companion grinned.

A young arguing couple squeezed out the door, each with two cases of empties. The former spacesuit opened the trunk of a big old American car parked just in front of the foundry, and he and the man loaded the beer bottles in. The woman had stationed herself beside Ed, waiting with her load. I could hear, "So what percentage of copper were you using again? I mean, my instructor said. . ." and her empties were lifted from her arms, the trunk slammed, Ed pulled her into the back seat, and all four were off with a wave to the sidewalk. The stragglers began dispersing in groups to newer cars all parked within an easy sightline of the foundry's door, pulling out to head down the one-way street that led west.

Theo was almost the last to come out. With a woman turned towards him, talking, both carrying boxes.

As they passed under the first streetlight, I saw a flash of blond. Theo's daughter. I hadn't seen Elena inside, but then, I hadn't seen Theo either until right towards the end. Did she know about the Pan? The boxes were the right size. What choice did I have except to tail the car? If Elena kept her box, tomorrow I would talk to her, too.

---

I was really wrong this time. First, I think they wondered about my tail; hands adjusted their rearview mirror at one point. I had to go past them when they pulled onto a side-street in the old funky residential area of Kitsilano, and the whole neighbourhood heard my tires squeal as I doubled-back on the next street over. There they were. Lucky for me they'd taken the busier Fourth Avenue most of the way, but now there were no other moving cars and no parking. I had to double back again and pass them, and I almost hit Elena as she ran across the dark street. She had one of the boxes in her hand. Stopping in the middle of the road, I put on my flashers. I was just delivering a late pizza. I watched Elena tiptoe up some porch stairs. Then she left the box at the door. And ran back to her waiting car.

Big decision time. Their car was pulling away maybe four car lengths to my rear, heading in the opposite direction. But the box was on the porch. They turned a corner out of sight, and I floored reverse towards their now empty parking spot. I was facing the wrong way from all the other cars, and I'd never been good at parallel parking when the space is on the driver's side, but I got within a foot of the curb. Running for the box, I barely remembered to tiptoe up the steps.

The old two- and three-storey houses in Kitsilano were built for wet weather. The ones from the early 1900s had cedar-wood shingles to side them, but most were now covered with coats of paint or stucco. All were similar: wide wooden front porches, broad steps, and pillars at the porch corners supporting thick roofs. "Basement" meant ground level; the main floor was raised six or eight feet up and that kept it dry. Each house had a front lawn or garden and with the wet weather, the shrubs were now trees and the trees the size of apartment buildings. I was shielded by bushes, but when I hit the porch, I was in the full glare of its light.

It is illegal to open someone else's mail. It is suspect to be on a stranger's porch in the dark of night. With a sealed box, trying to make no noise. The box wasn't very heavy, though, not nearly heavy enough for anything bronze. I'd better take this cold pizza away, and I slunk back down the stairs, trying to look natural.

In my car I needed to put the light on to see anything. But I couldn't, not in front of the house; what if my sidewalk scurrying had woken somebody up? What if the householder was expecting this box and came down to find nothing on the porch? Tough luck. I turned on the engine, and then had a truly lucid moment. Checking and rechecking the house number, I noted that the porch had a pottery planter. In a parking spot three blocks away I turned on the car light and wrote down the house number from memory. Not only would I be able to check out who lived in the house when I went to the library, but I would even be able return the box to the correct address.

The box was sealed with packing tape. If I wanted to see the contents, there was no choice but to take the box home.

I had already overstepped the limits by absconding with the box, so what difference would opening it make? Sherry in one hand, kitchen knife in the other, I made a neat slit up the tape. Inside was some bunched-up newspaper and a DVD in an envelope with a handwritten title, "The Story of Summer and Winter". An enclosed note read, "Dear Principal Thomas. We hope you like this. It shows an example of what we do. Please call me, Theodore Younge, at the museum and leave a message if you are interested." The note was signed "Sincerely, Theodore Younge and Elena Younge." So of course I had to watch. Luckily, my move from Toronto had included a small ancient TV and my laptop for DVDs. I couldn't move to a strange city and not be able to flake out in front of the tube. I poured myself another sherry.

The DVD wasn't like anything even remotely in my mind. I had pegged Theo as a fuddy-duddy professor and his daughter for a sincere young student. What I saw were two pros, real pros, theatre pros giving a riveting performance of an ancient Greek myth to a group of grade school students. Not a fake in sight. Nothing illicit in this picture.

Elena appeared first, in front of the kids sitting on the floor. They couldn't have been more than in Grade 3.

"When I was little," she began, "my Dad used to tell me stories. He didn't read to me from books, he just told me these awesome stories. Then when I was five I moved away with my mother, far away to Santa Fe in the United States where it's hardly green at all, it's desert, just the opposite of here. I didn't really see my Dad till I came back to school to study at UBC. I'm too old now to have bedtime stories. Am I too old to have bedtime stories?"

The kids yelled back, "Yeess! Nooo!"

"Well, this is my way of getting to hear those stories again from my Dad, and it's even better because this way I get to share them with you."

The camera swung to Theo who had been sitting in a chair to one side. He rose and strode regally out in front of the kids. He wasn't dressed in a costume, but he had a sceptre in one hand and a crown on his head.

"I am Zeus. You may also call me Jupiter the Great. I am the king of the gods of Mount Olympus, and I welcome you all to the ancient world," he intoned. Theo then began to tell the story of Persephone and how she came to spend six months each year in the Underworld as punishment for eating six pomegranate seeds. Elena had meanwhile moved to one side and wrapped herself in a shiny cloth for a flowing robe, and put a silk circlet of flowers and leaves on her head. I squinted my eyes and entered the world of ancient figures on red and black ceramics.

Theo and Elena played off each other beautifully, moving in and out of the "stage", using small props to show a change in characters. Theo couldn't keep the pleasure off his face as he watched Elena. At one point, Theo recited in Greek. If the kids couldn't understand, they didn't show it; the camera panned across rapt faces.

At the end Theo gave his sceptre to Elena, and as she exited to the side he put his crown on the floor in front of the kids and said, "Now our story is over. It is an ancient story. Imagine, it's older than the city of Vancouver, some say older than the pyramids of Egypt. It is a story about how the earth came to have both winter and summer. I hope you have enjoyed the Grecian world of long ago. My daughter Elena is named after Queen Helen of ancient Troy, and my name, Theodore, also comes from the Greek. The story you've seen is very, very old, but it is still alive, and as each one of you tells it to your family or friends, you'll continue to make it live." Theo began to smile as he looked around the room, and I could swear, each student smiled back. "I work in a museum and my job is to collect ancient pottery, perfume bottles, bronze statues, and much more that show the history and beauty of Greece and Rome. If you come to my museum, you'll see things just as old as this story." I smiled as the camera panned across delighted young faces. Here was Theo ensuring a good future for the museum.

I put the DVD back in its envelope. Elena would make a name for herself in theatre. Theo had come alive in front of those kids in a way I never would have guessed. It was way past my bedtime, the sherry had begun to take effect, but I knew I had to get the box back to its doorstep so Principal Thomas could see what a treat was in store for his students. Stuffing some bread into my mouth and carrying several slices out to the car, I hoped they would act as an alcohol absorbent. My stomach didn't like to drink alone anyway. During the drive I wondered again that Theo had the actor inside him, and the storyteller's instinctive sense of timing and music. Was it the kids that made him so exuberant? Was it being able to share his passion for ancient Greece with such an appreciative audience? Why had I missed the charm and uninhibited vitality in him? I dropped off the box and was skimming back down Thomas's porch steps when my feet stopped dead and I almost toppled. It wasn't that I had missed anything, it was just that I hadn't put two things together. Theo was a great actor because—what do actors do? They become other people. They enter fully into saying and doing things, and convince the audience that they are real. Actors are the consummate liars, the best fakers in the world.

# Chapter
# 14

## Wednesday Midnight, Thursday Morning

Pacing the floor, I waited for the right moment to call Reiko. Midnight was too dramatic, one o'clock too far away. At quarter after twelve the urgency of my news couldn't hold out any longer and I braced myself for an angry, sleepy voice. The Reiko that answered sounded wan and depressed. Was she still sick? I apologized for calling so late in the evening, making an immediate decision to go over to check on her.

"You can't. It's like house arrest. There's a car watching the house, or they take me to the station for interviews, or they show up here. For the umpteenth time, the same questions."

"Do they really suspect you?"

"Sure. Don't you?"

I caught my breath. The lab coat. "Should I?"

It wasn't the bitterness in her voice that caught me by surprise, but, when she said my name, the defeat. "Et tu, Berry?"

I yelled into the phone. "I just need to know some facts. And I need to tell you about a forgery and now it's missing and Theo and Ed are making fakes and I think someone's trying to kill me."

My news was greeted by a peal of laughter.

"Reiko! This is serious."

"Is this the scenario? Cuyler Foley looks like he was murdered, and he got what he deserved because he was sleazy. Now someone is trying to murder you because you're what, a menopausal conservation intern? Double standard for women again?"

Too outraged to laugh, I hissed, "Smithson, they make it seem accidental."

"They? Who? Berry, go to bed and sleep on it. Don't you think this's a bit over the top? You want facts? Here. It hurts me more than you can imagine that people think I've something to do with Foley's death. It's a complete trash on who I try to be. Principled, ethical Reiko Smithson—and the first person they suspect as a killer."

I was still furious with her and the outright dismissal of my news and worries, but I said, "It's the chemicals in our cupboard they suspect, not you."

"Who else is under house arrest?"

I tried to change the subject. When I raised my concerns again to get her take on the "accidents", she said, emphatically, "No."

"You won't even hear me out?" My voice had risen with that kind of ashamed anger you feel when a loved one dies and you're left feeling both bereft and pissed off the thoughtless person did this to you.

"I think they've tapped the phone." Reiko tried to laugh but it sounded more like a painful cough. "Seems you're already in trouble. It'll be worse if they catch you calling when nobody's supposed to make contact. Visiting's out for sure. 'Bye, bye, Berry,'" she sang.

"Wait. This is urgent. Where's the lab coat you were wearing Monday night?"

"I washed it."

"Reiko!" My voice squeaked. "Why?" I didn't know how to continue. What if her phone really was tapped? How could I ask if the cleaning had removed evidence that would have incriminated her in Foley's death?

"For God's sakes, there was blood and vomit all over everything. I couldn't stand it. After the medics left the police let me wash up. I put your lab coat on and threw mine and my dress in the washer while I pulled myself together. Yes, I used the museum's fancy equipment for personal use and not textile storage sheets or dust covers. Broke the big rules again. So I'm evil, the police figure that too."

I should have known better than to suspect her.

Reiko said, "You'll find the lab coat in the dryer. My dress I put on damp and went home."

In an attempt to skew the topic for any phone tappers, I said that when she was back at work we needed to talk about lab coat and glove readings in the pesticide residue research over the last few months.

"One more quick question," I added. "Has Theo ever been connected to fake . . ."

She didn't let me finish. "My only piece of advice, Berry, is do whatever you have to do quietly, and keep your eyes open."

The phone clattered down, and I was alone.

---

In my dream it was bells tolling, and the ominous ringing shook me awake. My bedside phone continued its noise. "Shit *de merde,*" I said out loud. "It's got to be four in the morning. Oh God, who's died." I croaked hello into the phone and waited.

"*Bonjour, ma belle. Ici Radio-Canada,*" announced a bright voice. "I have you wakened, *n'est-ce pas?*" There was a certain delight in this last statement.

I glanced at the clock. It was seven-thirty. I had slept through my alarm. "Oh, my God," I repeated.

"Yes?" said Daniel. "I am here, my child." Daniel had had a Catholic boyhood.

"It's so good to hear from you," I croaked again, and swigged water from my bedside glass.

"Drinking so early, my child? That is a sin, you know."

"Yes, *Mon Père,*" I said, even without a Catholic background. "*Père Radio-Canada*. But it's not a very bad sin. I can think of others I would prefer."

"So can I," said Daniel, and then laughed in what I swear was embarrassment.

"What are you laughing at?" I teased.

"Oh, nothing. I'm not laughing at you."

"I know. You always give that old excuse, you devil. You're laughing with me. So, what about me?"

"Well, I have this picture in my head of you in bed."

"Daniel, are you implying . . . is this an insinuendo?"

"Ah, *ma chère Berry,* I give you a big kiss in your bed from Québec."

I laughed too, with pleasure. "Now, this is getting to be a better in*sin*uendo." I heard Daniel erupt into more laughter. Upbringing from childhood showing itself in the adult, just as Theo had said. I threw caution to the wind. "I wish you were here, Daniel. I miss you. And Faux Paws, too," I lied, in case my id had made itself too clear.

"Ah, *ma belle,*" Daniel sighed. Like the displacement activities of a real cat, cleaning its fur when the bird was out of reach, Daniel continued by saying only that Faux Paws was doing fine, and chit-chatted about his new job. Wonderful as this was, had Daniel phoned just to say hello?

I interrupted, "It's great to hear from you, but I have to go to work. I'll call back later."

"I have one more insinuendo for you, very quick."

I'd guessed right. It would have been thrilling if Daniel had called just to hear my voice, but I was too eager to hear what he was going to say to be disappointed that he hadn't.

"I have looked up your Mr. Foley," he announced. "The files and databases we have for the news."

"And?" I said, forgetting "thank you."

"Six times he has sold internationally something of Canadian heritage." I could hear him pause and turn a page. "Six times a heritage agency has tried to stop him, but no Canadian buyer."

"Aboriginal objects?"

"*Pas beaucoup.* Some fine old furniture."

I sighed. "It's not illegal."

"Non, but listen. He has—had—an office in Vancouver and Montréal," and Daniel named two buildings I didn't know.

"So?"

"Very chic, both. He was doing well."

"I wish we had more to go on." The "we" was a slip I didn't notice till later as I was recapping, driving to work.

"We do," answered Daniel. "With the fine old furniture, the heirs to the estate accused Mr. Foley that he influenced their mother. They lost. The court said the evidence was not enough."

I hadn't ever told Daniel the Chief Joe story. Two incidents from across the country: enough evidence for me. Foley's reputation as unscrupulous was standing up. How did this tie into his death in the museum? If Theo was involved in fraud, was Foley, too?

⌘

I rushed through the good-byes, flew into the shower, dressed, bought some decaf coffee and a muffin en route, and hummed along with *Radio-Canada* whenever I could, all the way to work.

I arrived at MOA just before nine so I was fine, except for having had practically no sleep. It didn't matter, I was on a roll. I had work to do, people to talk to. I signed in and was told I could head downstairs.

"You're looking cheery this morning," said Jen. The Collections Manager often got in at eight and stayed until after six, citing a burdensome workload. Cheerfulness at work first thing in the morning was noteworthy.

"I've finished the cleaning," I explained. That was good enough.

I bypassed the murder scene area and Conservation too. "Good morning, Ed," I said to the lean figure bent over his drafting table.

"Morning. What's up?"

With deliberate unclarity I said, "I wanted to ask you about some technology."

"I noticed the humidity's bad in Visible Storage. I've already called Trouble Calls."

"No, not that technology, actually."

"The way you stomped right in here I figured you were angry I hadn't told you. But I didn't see you till now."

"Sorry," I replied. "I didn't mean to stomp." Nobody was used to an energetic fifty-three year old employee. "The coffee's gone right to my head and the muffin right to my foot."

Ed grinned. "So, what's up?"

"Ed, do you know much about casting? Metal casting, I mean, not fly fishing."

"Sure do, about both." Ed swivelled his thin body towards the wall and nodded up at the illustrated calendar that showed an enlarged delicate hairy bug. "Wait till November. I'm Mr. November. Well, my fly is." He turned towards me to wait for my reaction. Another damn insinuendo. I laughed, but only to keep him on my good side. Yuck.

"What can I do for you?" Ed was apparently satisfied.

"I'd like to take the museum class to a foundry." I was making this up as I went along. "After my guest lecture in January on metal conservation." That was far enough away that he wouldn't check up on it. "I figured as a Designer you probably have an art school background and might know an art foundry."

"Right, right, and right again," said Ed. "I could show casting to the class if you like. I instruct at a foundry."

"Really?" I said, with genuine interest in my voice.

"Sure. I was just doing some last night at a fundraiser." Ed was being very forthcoming. This wasn't going to be hard at all.

"Really?" I said again. "What were you casting?"

"Figures from the Classics collection," said Ed.

Oh goodie. I knew that. Did the two dozen funding targets know what they had seen?

"Really?" I enthused for the third time. "What for?" What would he say now?

"Repros," Ed said.

"Reproductions?" Where was a sound recorder?

"Sure," Ed said. "For the shop."

"The shop?"

"The MOA giftshop. Upstairs. We sell 'em." He looked like he was going to add, "dummy". "Haven't you seen 'em? We've been doing it for years. Makes us a lot of money."

"No, I guess I never looked beyond the Native art there."

"The repros are great, if I do say so myself. Look just like the real thing."

"Really?" I said, reduced again to my brilliant conversational gambit. Then I realized my chance.

"How can you tell them from the real thing?"

"They're all marked. We've got "MOA" and a date right in the mould, so it comes out on the bottom of each piece."

"Oh."

I took my leave of Ed, promising to talk to him again when I knew more about the January lecture. Amazing how it was going to get cancelled. School these days.

A policeman let me into the workroom. Then he left. The yellow tape was gone from the door to the Conservation lab. I ran to check the dryer and sure enough Reiko's lab coat was there.

My mind concentrated on the missing statue. The Pan bronze hadn't been marked "reproduction". I would have seen it, and noted it on the condition report. On the missing condition report. I leafed through the stack of "treatment" file folders for the fortieth time. I could check the bronze itself, if I could only find that too.

"Ms. Cates," said a quiet voice at my ear. I jumped, and files flew open.

"Oh, sorry, I'm really sorry," said one of the Collections Assistants, bending to gather the files up. As she leaned over, her too-short top pulled away from her tight pants, exposing a tattooed heart on unblemished skin.

"Don't worry, Heather," I said, guessing that it wasn't Zoe because she wore no large earrings. "I just didn't hear you coming." I bent down too. "I'll put the files together," I said a little too sternly, and with no mid-flesh showing.

Heather had the miserable look of a kid who could do no right. And she was drivelling more apologies. "No!" I wanted to say, "You aren't being bad. Get some backbone, girl!" Easy enough to pronounce judgments, Berry. You don't have attitude, you have platitude. What I wanted to say next was, "Who's abused your self-confidence?" but I didn't want to know. I've never been a mother, and rarely a confidante to a young person; I didn't have confidence in dealing well with this situation my own self.

Unfortunately, Heather was at my side because she did need a warm, competent mother-figure. Or at least Georgina, a graduate student upstairs, did. Heather had come to look for me, an older woman, because Georgina was "practically hysterical" in the coffee room.

"Where's Dr. Luykes?" I said, thinking of yesterday's comfortable scene around the coffee table.

"In Montreal," Heather replied, her voice thin. "She's giving a paper at a museum there."

Of course. I should have remembered.

"Nobody's upstairs, Ms. Cates. Could you please come?" I gentled down and dashed with her to the lounge.

---

Georgina was bent double on the reupholstered couch, sobbing into a wad of paper towels held by a young woman sitting beside her. Three others stood awkwardly in front, murmuring. I squeezed in on Georgina's right and put my arm around her, and held on tight. Georgina moved slightly towards me. As long seconds passed the sobs began to subside, and I asked quietly what had happened.

"It was the police," said one.

"They accused her," said someone else.

"No way," said the first. "They were interviewing her; then that policewoman came out with her into the lounge. She looked awful. Georgina I mean. The cop just said, 'Georgina's not feeling well. Can you stay with her?'"

"I got her a coffee," said one of the group. "But she wouldn't take it, she was just moaning and crying. I mean really crying."

"The cop said to come and get her if Georgina was having a bad time, but when I said, 'I'll get the policewoman', that's when Georgina started freaking out."

"Does anyone know what went on in the interview room?" I asked.

Several voices began to speak.

Elena was standing to one side, raking her hands back and forth through her blond hair. Even distressed, Theo's daughter looked like a movie star, and she seemed to carry it off without noticing. She said, "When Georgina started sobbing, she was saying something about coffee, and, like, 'I didn't do it,' so I checked to see if the coffee maker was working, but . . ."

"She was accused," maintained a strong voice. "That's what happened. The police think she murdered Foley."

"I didn't do it. I didn't do it!" A wet red young face looked up at me. "Honest."

"I believe you." I said. I gave her a squeeze. I smiled. I squeezed again. More tears. I waited.

"Tell me what happened," I encouraged Georgina. She looked down and shuffled the paper towels. I shunted a bundle of wet ones onto the floor.

Georgina slowly told her story, unravelling the details and her remaining composure as she talked. She had witnessed the Monday night scene between Reiko and Sally Luykes. Reiko had indeed refused to make the coffee. But her words had hit an office door already closed by Luykes, who had, apparently, just assumed Reiko would do her bidding. So Georgina, who had come up from the Archaeology lab where grad students had twenty-four-hour access to their research bays, went ahead and made the coffee. Why not, she said. Dr. Luykes was the Director of the museum, and she'd been great to Georgina. Not stuffy at all. The door was still closed, though, when Georgina had everything assembled. She left the tray outside Luykes' office.

My stomach gave an old familiar lurch. Someone at MOA was not only willing to let Reiko take the blame, but apparently, if need be, a well-meaning young grad student. If people thought Foley was bad, who was topping him, literally and figuratively, here at the museum?

"Don't worry," I said to Georgina as well as myself. "The police will know you've done nothing wrong. You had no possible motive." I figured that by now museum gossip, Heather and Zoe included, would have spread the rumour that Foley may not have died of a heart attack.

"But yesterday they took my stevia too. From the lounge."

"*Your* stevia?"

"I hate sugar. They must suspect me. Then they gave it back today saying there was nothing wrong, they'd been asked to check, but why would they have it?"

"I gave it to them, Georgina. Someone had put it in my mug of tea and I never take sweetener."

I expected the room to go silent, but nobody appeared concerned. There was a background of embarrassed giggles. One person said she was glad Georgina had gotten her stevia back.

"OhmyGod," Georgina said in one breath. "Yesterday somebody was, like, using the pot so I made tea in a big mug and was starting to pour it into our cups when Elena said it was your mug, but you like tea so we left it for you and I made new tea in a bowl. We all take it sweet. I left the stevia bottle so you wouldn't wonder why it tasted different. Stevia's awesome and it's no calories and natural. I never thought maybe you wouldn't take sugar."

Plausible, clear, and said with honest emotion, just like Ed's story about the light fixture. Was I paranoid thinking someone had been trying to injure me enough to get me off the scene? A threat with any weapon needs to be taken seriously until you know it can't fire.

I said, "Anyone could have come along and tampered with the stevia, or the stuff on the tray for Luykes. The police know that. They're just making sure. They seem pretty reasonable, the police on this case." What else could I say?

"Someone?" I looked around. "I think Georgina needs to go to Student Health. Let them know what she's going through. Any volunteers to go with her?" Heather offered immediately.

I retreated downstairs. I might have pulled Elena aside to talk about last night but she looked too distressed. Truth was, I was feeling fragile and worn down myself. The morning's energy had leaked away. Needing calm, I grabbed my jacket and went outside. Only after walking for ten minutes, looking at the sea and the trees, did I remember I hadn't even signed out.

My head wasn't clear and my energy was damped down in that emotionally tired way, but I did feel better. Slipping back inside, I deposited my jacket, found my big green mug, and headed for a cuppa. I wasn't getting much done today, work-wise, but I was certainly doing a lot, lounge-wise and just plain wise. Or wiser. Wisening up. Wizened old me.

———— ⟨∞⟩ ————

Walking into the coffee room, I saw Mama gesticulating to Lorna across the main table. My eyes settled hungrily on the beautiful black shirt with a red Northwest Coast hummingbird design Lorna had on today. Oscar was at the table too, wearing a MOA t-shirt with its latest Northwest Coast design. Another time the imagery might intrigue me but my mind was reeling. Mama rarely took coffee in the lounge and was never so animated. I walked over to the fridge where the milk was, a smile constructed on my face, listening to their laughter. Mama was saying, "We did one million dollars worth of business last year."

I cradled my full cup in two hands, balancing the weight smoothly just as if it were a precious sculpture. My mug was hot, but old habits died hard. The first rule of museum handling is to use both hands to pick up an object; my conservation training had seeped into even my unconscious body language. One day I would buy a carton of old pottery at a garage sale and deliberately smash it piece by piece against a big brick wall. That would be really living it up.

The outside of the cup was burning and I sat down at the table. Not beside Oscar, even if I usually took a seat with the newer staff rather than the experienced ones. Nor beside Lorna, a decade older than Oscar. I gingerly sat beside Mama, pushing my chair out at an angle so I could both watch her and the others.

"A million dollars!" Lorna was saying. "Tremendous!"

"A million dollars," Mama cackled.

"Is this the museum?" I broke in. All eyes looked at me. For a second my newness, my awkwardness about my place here reasserted itself. Maybe I hadn't understood and this was a private conversation. "Don't be stopped by your mistakes," I remembered telling my French language students, and gazed around as if calmly waiting for the answer to my question.

Mama's eyes crinkled and she almost smiled. I took a long sip from my cup.

Lorna said, "One million? MOA? I wish. We could invite every Native community in, then, to see their stuff." She shook her head. "No, not MOA. Mama was just talking about the recycling depot. She's on the Board. Did you know? The recycling depot downtown?"

Mama still had her bright eyes on me.

I tried to stifle a "shit *de merde*." I managed, "A million dollars from recycling? There are that many cans and bottles in Vancouver?"

"The Board met last night," said Mama, the corners of her mouth twitching, "and we are the most successful recycling outfit in the whole Lower Mainland."

"How do you do it?" I said. I hoped admiration showed in my voice, but it was probably continuing surprise, since I was still not really able to picture it, building up money like that on five and ten cent deposits.

"Everybody's from the DTES. That's the Downtown Eastside." Mama was enjoying herself, and I had to sit still. "The management, the binners who collect the cans. Just not the Board, or not all of them. A guy can double what welfare gives him and actually eat a decent meal."

"I should do an exhibit on the recycling's success," said Lorna. "It's the stereotype of urban First Nations turned on its head. And the stereotype of the DTES."

Oscar said, "Reality Museum." We all chuckled.

"Ever been to the DTES?" Lorna asked me. Mama sat back, close-mouthed but grinning now. She was really enjoying herself.

"Uuuh" I said, shrugging in a noncommittal way. I didn't want to explain what I was doing last night to anybody.

"You should go down," Lorna continued. "Go during the day. Don't be scared, and don't stare. Go to Oppenheimer Park. See the big totem pole there."

"Who carved the pole?" I said with relief. In my short time in Vancouver I had picked up a certain amount of what to say, the local lingo, and talking about totem poles fit that category.

"A community of eight carvers. It's a memorial pole. It was put up in 1998. Now that was a nice ceremony."

I noticed that Mama was no longer smiling. Her mouth had set in a hard line. Lorna saw me looking, and said, "One night Mama and I leave work here at the same time, say good-bye, and a half hour later we each show up for the totem pole committee downtown." Lorna grinned. "We've had a lot of good times there."

"Yeah," said Mama, "Arguing over whether the plaque should say 'to those' or 'for those'. Time of my life."

We laughed again. Lorna said, "The plaque turned out fine." She looked at me and then Oscar, and spoke slowly, "To our sisters and brothers who have died unnecessarily in the Downtown Eastside and to those who have survived."

Silence. Lorna might have been on the totem pole committee because, as a curator, she knew the artists, or because she was concerned with aboriginal issues. Mama was there for another reason, and I couldn't begin to guess it. I wanted to say something, anything to bring us back to our little table.

I said, "Did you know each other before MOA too?"

Lorna and Mama exchanged looks. I had crossed a line again. I was about to hazard something like "doesn't matter" when Lorna said, "I'm Kwakwa<u>ka</u>'wakw. I grew up in Alert Bay. Do you know it? Up the coast, on an island near the tip of Vancouver Island? I guess I really got to know Mama when I was about ten."

"Are you Kwakwa<u>ka</u>'wakw too?" I asked Mama.

She shook her head. "Married in," she said. "Married out."

"When I was little, ceremonial things that had been illegally seized were returned to us," said Lorna. "I was just a kid, but I think that's what made me go into museum work, seeing that." She looked directly at me. "You can't imagine what it was like for the Elders to see their old regalia come home. How important the repatriation was. We all cried." Lorna now turned her gaze to Mama, whose face was impassive. She had retreated into her accustomed mask.

Lorna continued, "In school, we kids would learn the traditional dances, and practice with all the repatriations on their stands looking at us. We had little masks and button blankets and we would be so proud."

She paused, holding Mama's eye. "Your ex caught us once sneaking back into school with one of our little blankets. He took his belt off and went after us, but when he hit, it was the trees or a wall. Still, he was a mean one. He had a bad time at the residential school, I heard." Mama gave an imperceptible nod.

"All the kids were afraid of him," Lorna finished.

I felt awkward again, afraid that these memories, brought to the surface by a question I'd asked, were too powerful, even for Mama, too close to the bone of survival, the plaque on the totem pole.

"When did you move to Vancouver?" I asked Mama, hoping I was on a better track.

"Long time ago."

"Yo, Mama," came a loud voice from the doorway. The red-haired guard whose name I could never remember was pointing at us. "You're fifteen minutes late. It's quarter after. And," he added in a mock whisper, "I gotta go to the bathroom."

"You men. Always thinkin' about yourselves and your . . ." Mama's voice dropped but Lorna had a big grin. Mama lapsed into a growl as she was getting up, "Go have your pee, and wash your hands, now."

<hr />

Back downstairs, my main job in the lab this morning, what little of it was left, would be to find the missing condition report and verify what I'd seen on the bottom of the statue. Even my Luddite soul was ready to make a pact with the devil if I could have looked up a copy on the computer, but we used only pencils and paper beside the artifacts. MOA's collections were incredibly varied, frustrating to describe on the kind of standardized formats developed for computer use. We'd keep on with the longhand at least until we could afford good software and a new laptop.

Contemplating upgrading the technology was a welcome diversion, but I was getting worried now. I had to talk to Constable Frick. She was supposed to be looking into the fake; she'd promised me. And I was bursting to hear if anything poison-like had been found in my mug of tea. Instead, Frick appeared to be constantly busy interviewing more people. Just keeping on with the regular investigation? I couldn't blame her; that was what was important, and that was what she was paid for. The tea in my mug must have come out clean; that's why Frick was in no hurry to see me. But the missing bronze and the missing report have got to be related.

I decided to find Jen first. Why embarrass myself in front of Frick if the Collections Manager had simply put the Pan away? Nobody from Collections was around, though, in the workroom, the offices, or the photocopy room and other common areas. I broke down and asked the receptionist.

"The Collections staff? Gone to the meeting with the bargaining unit. About those cuts to the benefits package. Hadn't you heard?"

It had gone completely out of my mind. I decided, before I forgot again, that I would phone the CCI scientists back. It wasn't even 3 P.M. in Ottawa, and it was worth a try.

A living person answered the phone; the voice mail loop must not be working, a small gift. He put me right through to the metals chemistry lab. And I got another real person. And she had the answer.

Citing some publications, the scientist agreed that cuprous oxide or cuprite, the missing red layer, almost always was formed as the first layer on bronze in archaeological circumstances. "No, not a hundred percent, but it would be unusual for it not to be there. And you're right, naturally formed corrosion's uneven. It bites in to different depths in most metals in a way fake corrosion doesn't duplicate. Can you take samples and put them under a scanning electron microscope? There's a powerful one at the university, isn't there, with that good operator who knows how to interpret historic pieces?"

The scientist made sure to remind me that not only would the SEM produce a picture of exactly how the corrosion had eaten into the metal, but it would give me data on the individual chemical components that made up this particular bronze alloy. She went into some detail about how the shape and make-up of the crystals of the metals that form bronze would be different in corrosion formed over time from corrosion in a fake. Why not sample at least a few of the areas? When I hesitated, she guessed at what might be bothering me, and reminded me that valid tests could be made from minuscule samples, so small they would be unnoticeable in a corroded antiquity. The tests would not cause damage. Well, I wanted to reply, fabulous information, and I would definitely pursue this sampling, except I can't find the whole damn statue, and that was noticeable. But I left my frustration unsaid and thanked her warmly. She promised to put a conference paper in the mail from one of the world's experts on artifact corrosion, and we hung up.

At least I had one answer, but I had to find Frick, and the bronze. And the missing report. I should download my emails, and Reiko's; the boxes must be bulging by now. I needed to look at my daily agenda, and listen to the lab's phone messages. God knows how much other regular work was crouched in the shadows. I needed to talk to Theo, too, see if he had the same story as Ed about last night. And I needed to eat.

I sat down at Reiko's desk, muttering "Where to begin, where to begin." I was paralyzed by the options. I did none of them, squirming my way out with the conclusion, "Work avoidance can be healthy, too." I put a clean sheet of paper in front of me, thinking "Frick is probably on lunch, Theo also. They're my priorities." I wrote down "#1" and "#2" and "Frick" and below that "Theo". Then, "and/or Elena". Across the top I scribbled "noon" and the hours of the afternoon. I would be organized, I was constructing a terrific plan; this was a managed situation. The lab already had perfectly good daytime schedules both on the computer and the desk agenda, and I was avoiding them. As well as being careful to look just at my paper and not at the blinking phone light to my right or the computer screen off to my left.

I was rationalizing my priorities by what I felt like doing, what was most interesting. Would I ever make a good employee? Or was this just being a typical employee? Tearing off the top of the page with my notes, I ripped it into bits over the recycling pail. If Berry Cates wasn't a good employee, why leave written evidence? And, why not keep snooping? Time to look for Frick and Theo and definitely for lunch.

The doors to both the interview room and Theo's office were closed. Elena wasn't in the lounge. I hurried outside and over to the cheap student cafeteria. A light rain was falling, the landscape now an intensity of greens and greys. The colours of UBC's abundant plantings ran up into the sky like a wet-on-wet watercolour. Amazing tones, amazing greys. I began to hum "Amazing Grace". Smart aleck. I opened the door to the stuffy cafeteria and got in line. This being the West Coast, the Chinese food special looked good, and I was gazing over a hundred heads to find a spot to sit when I heard, "Hey, Berenice Cates." Constable Frick was sitting off to one side, waving to me from her chow mein. She had one arm draped over a free chair.

We talked about the weather first, and this led to the air conditioning and humidification system in the museum that was continually malfunctioning and causing the temperature to go up and down unexpectedly. The coolness today was better than being too hot, Constable Frick said, admitting the uniform she was wearing wasn't comfortable in summer. I told her that at my age I was getting hot flashes and had to dress so I could quickly whip off outer layers.

"What do policewomen in uniform do when they reach menopause?" I asked.

"Oh, by then we've moved so far up the ranks, they give us an air-conditioned office. If not, we retire."

I laughed. She told me to drop "Constable" and call her Alice, and she called me Berry. We talked about the Chinese food (good for the price), about what I liked about Vancouver (I surprised her with all the places I'd been, but, then, I left out mentioning Daniel), and about why she decided to join the police.

"I was tired of being bullied," she said. "I grew up in a rough part of Saskatoon, always small for my age, a late bloomer. I got "hey, Frick off" one too many times. I was going to get strong, and have authority. And make the world a better place for little girls."

"Have you succeeded?" I asked.

"Somewhat. Better. At least I have to keep believing in that."

"Don't you sometimes see two sides to questions? I mean, the law says guilty or innocent, there's no middle ground. But you can understand why a starving person would steal a loaf of bread."

"I know. I used to think that kind of thing was just in Charles Dickens, but it's not. At least people don't get executed any more for stealing bread. There is a middle ground, though. Like, not all murder is first degree."

We had moved around to the topic we had both carefully avoided over what had become a pleasant lunch. "What's the difference between first and second degree murder?" I asked, to keep the topic on neutral ground. Just the facts, Ma'am.

"First degree is deliberate, planned. It's also for the killing of a police officer. Second degree is not premeditated. A more spontaneous crime. The sentences are quite different. Here you get twenty-five years with no parole for first degree. For second degree the sentence can be quite light by comparison, depending on the circumstances. And your lawyer."

"The lawyers make a difference?"

"You'd better believe it. We aren't in the Dickensian age of injustice, we're in the lawyer age of 'my client right or wrong.'"

"Isn't that their job? Their professional code of ethics—to give the client the best defence they can?"

"Sure. But it burns me to see a guy who you know has committed a very violent crime get off on a technicality"

"It's easy to lose the idealism you start off with, isn't it? The more you know, the more you see, and the more that has happened to you and yours. Maybe that's just aging?"

"Maybe. I can't wait to find out." Alice grinned. "But sometimes, I think, idealism about fighting crime just gets replaced by grim determination. You have to be satisfied you've done your best. Make sure justice works." I nodded, I hoped sagely.

"Speaking of making sure," I said, "Was anything unusual found in my mug of tea?"

"Unofficially, no. The written report'll take a few days."

Relief flooded me until I thought that a threat doesn't always have to be real to have an effect. As long as you perceive it as a threat, you react. Maybe what I need most is a good therapist out here. But was the rapid succession of incidents—the light fixture, the stevia, and the tangle of wires—simply products of an overstressed imagination fuelled by a real murder? I said, "What about the bronze? Have you found it?"

"I saw it in the cupboard, the one near the table you were working at."

It's not that I didn't trust Constable Alice Frick, with whom I'd been having a good down-to-earth conversation, but I felt a strong urge to run out the door. MOA has an extensive Classics collection. One bronze could look like another unless you were an expert. If it was the fake one, would Frick believe me? If it was real, I could swear there was a fake. Out of the frying Pan . . . smart aleck.

I excused myself and hurried out. Justice and injustice; at least Alice Frick had chosen a profession that dealt with it directly, not sneaking around like this conservator. Why was I so obsessed? Well, my mind, my physical body and my future might be in the balance. Wasn't that enough?

# Chapter
## 15

# Thursday Afternoon

S ure enough, the Pan was visible through the mesh that covered the workroom's cupboards. I fumbled the keys from the safe, scribbled my name in the sign-out log, and went for the bronze. I had to make myself slow down, be careful around the collections. Unrolling a pair of clean gloves over my hands, I found an empty trolley and some small pillows, and moved these to the cupboard, cradled the Pan out onto the cushioning, and paraded ourselves over to the microscope. Even without magnification, I glimpsed a red layer at the ankle.

The red copper oxide layer was there. No, it wasn't. Why couldn't I place the bronze properly under the microscope? I moved the cushions and upped the magnification. The red layer was showing, smooth. Why smooth? I refocused. Because it was paint.

Sometimes scientists get the results they seek because their assumptions are so strong. I was supposed to be looking at corrosion, so it looked like corrosion, until it glared back at twenty times its size: flow patterns indicative of dried paint. This deception was staring me in the face. In fact, as I stood up to breathe better, my eyes registered that something was wrong with the whole statue. Why it didn't sit on the cushioning like last time. The ankle was bent and almost broken off, but not quite the way it used to be. And someone had taken the condition report so I couldn't check. This flashed in my mind as glaringly as the paint. Why hadn't I thought of it earlier? Now I was seeing red, figuratively and literally. I was more than ready to confront Theo.

I had to follow procedure first, carefully putting the bronze back on its shelf, locking the cupboard, putting the key back in the safe, signing the key back in, and . . . damn! Going back through the whole business in reverse, my eyes fixed on the base of the statue. No indeed, there was no "MOA Reproduction" or date or any variant visible on the underside. This statue was a deliberate forgery. I might have no idea what was going on, but it was going on. Fishy stinko.

I did the security procedure once again and made a bee-line upstairs, knocking too loudly on Theo's door. A worried bald head peered out. The worry didn't go away as Theo said, "Berry, is it important? I've got someone in my office."

I could see who was in Theo's office. Not "someone". Ed. Good, these were exactly the guys I needed to talk to. I would catch them both.

Was I crazy? Now there were two of them. If they had made forgeries and perhaps committed murder, why not shut me up too? They weren't going to do it here, now, in the office. Not before tea, my dear. I would find Constable Frick right after this and tell all, get police protection. From what? Two sets of concerned eyes? Wondering why I'd knocked so loudly and was staring and not speaking?

My posture adjusted up to regal. Commanding. And svelte. When you stand tall, the body mass fat index drops to a better level. I took the edge out of my voice and put in firmness.

"Hello," I said. Now that was a good start, Berry. "Ed, glad you're here. I came to see Theo," I said, turning to look him directly in the eye, "but I've got a question for you," as I swivelled back to Ed.

"Shoot," said Ed.

"Come in." Theo looked around to offer me an uncluttered space. Ed motioned to the chair he'd been occupying. I shook my head. I wanted to stand over them rather than sit. I leaned back against a bookshelf. "I'm fine, Theo, don't worry, I've been sitting all morning." The men eased back into their places.

"Ed, those castings for the Shop you were telling me about." This was good. It didn't feed anything hidden to Theo. "How do you finish them?"

"I don't," he answered. "I never do. I mean, we do too many. I get enough finicky work in my regular job. Mr. November's a great detail man—you saw the calendar in my office—but not on two hundred bronzes a year. We send them to Quebec."

"Quebec?"

"There's a guy there who's real good. Makes things look like new or just like the old ones. He must have a great team working for him, all the stuff is always perfect."

"Ed," interrupted Theo. "I need to discuss some things with Conservation. Could we continue our conversation later? Over coffee?" Theo had a thin smile on his face as he turned to face me, "I trust this is all right with you?"

"Fine," I said, smiling back.

Ed's tall, wispy body glided out of the chair, and with a brief movement of his head he was gone. He swung the door closed as he left.

Theo said, "Sit!" Then amended, "Please. Please sit down." I moved into the empty chair, keeping my regal back.

"Why are you here?" said Theo.

"I need some answers," I said.

"To what?"

"I think you know what."

"What are you talking about?"

"You know exactly what I'm talking about."

"You'd better be a trifle more explicit than that, Ms. Cates." Formal now.

"I'd like you to tell me about the forged Pan."

"But you told me that it was a forgery."

We danced around like this for another minute or two and then I said, "Give me the condition report, Theo."

I was expecting another innocent "what condition report?" Instead, Theo hung his head. As he looked up, he composed his face into what seemed like a properly abashed countenance. Or maybe he really was embarrassed. He'd had a lot of embarrassment recently.

"I'm sorry," he said. "I picked it up and forgot."

"You were going through my files?" Let's see how well he could lie.

"I . . . the police came and questioned me about the current status of the antiquities. I told them everything was in your reports, and, well, I did in fact have one report with me. I'd gone back to the workroom for a second look at the bronze. You weren't there, so I took the report to make a copy for myself. I was only going to be five minutes, you know, and then . . ." He gave a sort of "you know what happens when you go upstairs" shrug, and smiled rather sweetly.

Not convincing, but plausible.

"I'm terribly sorry, what with one thing and another I completely forgot to put it back."

"Where is it?"

"Here. A copy anyway. I made it when the police wanted the original." Theo lumbered out of his chair and began to sift through the papers behind his desk. I contemplated my next move. I had to get to the red paint.

Theo turned to face me, eyes glinting as his arms moved forward, not holding the report. Instead, he levelled a gun. The one from Visible Storage. It was longer than a large duelling pistol and MOA had it because its stock was carved with Haida designs. Theo's finger was on the trigger.

"You're not handling it with blue gloves," I kidded as I rose from my chair.

"Don't you dare move, little Ms. Conservator," said Theo. "Sit!"

No way was I going to sit. Standing tall, I waited to see what Theo would really do.

"Sit," he commanded. As if he was talking to a dog. "Sit or I'll shoot."

"Theo," I said in a soft voice, "That gun won't work. It's an old flintlock. Besides, the law doesn't allow museums to keep guns in working order. For just this reason," I added.

Theo's face turned a dark red. "I've fixed it," he said, "I worked my way through university as a re-enactor at historic sites. I know all about flintlocks."

He probably did. I adopted his point of view.

"Don't shoot, Theo. Police're in the building, and it's your office. Your career'll end. For what?"

"One's career will end anyway if you keep up this forgery talk."

Forgeries weren't my idea of a good reason to murder people. But we'd had one corpse already in this museum—I wasn't going to take any chances. The gun looked clean and solid. I grabbed a large book off Theo's desk and hurled it while I ducked. The gun didn't go off, but I did score a direct hit. The flintlock clattered onto his desk then dropped to the floor. Who's he calling little Ms. Conservator now?

Theo bent to pick up the gun and had to scramble on the floor, searching. I dropped to hide on the opposite side of his big old oak desk, twisting my knees. All the pain of yesterday's fall came hurtling back, tenfold. I was on the floor, but the bookshelves were within reach. I began firing my only ammunition. One hand hurled book after book towards Theo.

Half the books hit the opposite wall, thudding open, pages bent. One slid across the desk top like a curling stone, striking his faience mug and sending it crashing to the floor. Muddy coffee spilled over open pages. I kept throwing, and the gun flailed this way and that as Theo tried to aim. I was sweating from pain. It crossed my mind that Theo hadn't pulled the trigger. Maybe I was right; the gun wasn't in working order. I threw with more vigour.

I was grabbing from the third shelf, on one throbbing knee, ducking my head between throws, and my aim was improving, except that the spines of the last two books had ripped off in my hands. Theo screamed. I could see two small eyes set in a dark red fleshy planet rising just over the opposite side of the desk, and I aimed straight. At the last minute a hand intercepted and the book went down. "Stop!" Theo yelled. "Stop! I surrender! Truce!"

I took the next book in my hand and my inner sheriff snarled, "Drop your gun." He put the flintlock down gently on the desk. Somehow we were moving back into museum space, and out of this insane childish scene, half cowboy half pillow fight. It had been real, though. I hurt too much.

"Don't move a muscle," I said, picking up the gun in both hands and placing it carefully on an empty shelf behind me. "Stay," I said. Doggy commands would do fine. He'd started it, anyway. This really was a kid's pillow fight. I was adult tired, though, and I wanted to be close to the door in case this white flag stuff was a ruse. Easing myself over to the chair Ed had occupied, I wheeled it a few feet back to be able to push the door open. "Okay," I said in the deepest voice I could muster, glad to have watched at least some junk TV, "You can come out now. Slowly."

From under the desk, Theo couldn't come out any other way. I heard his bulk heave this way and that and saw a hand piling books carefully off the floor. It took a long time for his head to surface again over the desktop. The sea lion emerged from his hole in the ice and whuffed into his chair.

Theo had an old leather book in his hands, one with its spine gone. He reached down and scrabbled around, emerging with the torn, gilded piece. "Chapman's translation of Homer's *Iliad*. A first edition. Very rare, you can imagine," he stuttered, anguished.

"My bones," I said. "Equally rare. Damaged."

"I do apologize." Theo hung his head. He was good at this.

He glanced up at me with that self-deprecating smile of his. Would I forgive him? His eyes caught the chaos of the room, and the smile faded. I looked around. The room was a mess, but then it had been a heap of papers and books before.

"It's not bad, Theo, it's just rearranged."

"Oh, shut up." He wasn't winning any points on the for-giveness scale. "I apologize", he said again. "If you hadn't gotten to my rare books, I might have had you." Once a cu-rator, always a curator.

---

Everything was the same as it had been ten minutes ago, yet everything was different. How could both happen at once? Another "yes, but" or "on the other hand" situation? Was this like Foley being a bad guy and a helpful expert? Like Theo being an amiable curator and a son of a bitch? One minute we were scrapping like dogs in a kennel, and now we sat across the desk from each other like two polite oppo-nents at a chess match. The chess match was okay, though; my queen had taken him.

"Are you hurt?" he inquired.

"Of course. But not as badly as your reputation is going to be if you don't start telling me what's going on."

Theo nodded. "Do you need a doctor?"

"No!" I shouted, meaning yes but not now. "Talk!" I hit the wall with my fist. A few books jiggled. I couldn't hit very hard any more, but Theo spilled.

"I don't want you to tell anybody. I will go to the po-lice myself and confess." I didn't budge. After a long silence, Theo continued. "I have made a couple of fakes. Not many. Had them made. The Pan was one. What a stupid mix-up. Imagine!" He slapped the desk. "I got the idea for the bronzes when Ed started doing them for the shop. I would take one or two and get the 'MOA' obliterated."

"Were you selling them?"

"Of course. I may work at a university, but I am em-ployed by a museum that is a non-profit organization."

"What did Foley have to do with it?"

"Nothing. Except that he found out early on there were reproductions being sold. Just once. You see," Theo grimaced, "someone brought one to him to evaluate, and he had done the same thing for us years ago on the original. He knew of course only one original exists. I told him the museum's ID marks must have been removed by an unscrupulous profiteer. I remember him just grinning."

"That was quite a risk you were running, forging unique pieces that could be identified."

"Oh, not really. They were sold in Greece and Italy, to tourists, not serious art buyers."

"Italy? How'd you get them there?"

"My dear," Theo sighed. "I have been going to Greece and Italy all my life. Naturally I know people there. I lead trips now for Continuing Studies; it gets me overseas once a year. I give one or two of the bronzes to a friend of mine in the bazaar, and a year later take the tourists to that shop. It helps his sales, I get a little something on the side, and if Betty or Bob chooses the piece, I can tell them it's very rare. I don't lie."

I swore to myself, *"Berenice Cates, never again believe you're the champion rationalizer,"* and said out loud, "So you were afraid Foley would tell Luykes?"

"Oh no," exclaimed Theo. "Sally knows I have a hand in the reproductions. She just doesn't know the whole of it. She lets me keep a few of the ones made for the Shop for teaching, as a study collection for students. And I do of course do that."

"But you killed Foley because he knew what you were up to."

Theo's eyes honed in on me. "I did not kill Cuyler. I repeat, I did not, would not, ever, kill him."

"You have a stellar motive, Theo." I couldn't help myself from grinning. I was, after all, talking to a Steller sea lion, the big ones in the North Pacific. Oh, bad pun, kid's humour, smart aleck. Maybe people age, but inside, they never feel like they do. I had been risking my life and job around this bronze of Pan; a statue of Peter Pan would have been more appropriate.

"What are you laughing at?" said Theo.

"Nothing."

"You're laughing at me. You don't believe me."

"No, I don't. But I'm not laughing at you." I added, "I'm laughing with you."

Theo looked confused. "I wasn't laughing."

"Never mind."

We sat in silence. I started another tack.

"You deliberately took the condition report," I said.

"Yes."

"You didn't want me to be able to recheck the details."

"Yes."

"You put the red paint on the bronze yourself."

"Yes."

"That was another one of your fakes."

"Yes. I had two replicas with the 'MOA' removed. This was one."

"How did you think you could ever get away with it? Do you think I don't know what I see? Do you know how closely an object is examined before a conservation treatment?"

"I should have known. You people spend days on those condition reports." This was a dig. Curators wanted us to work more quickly; all of us in Collections wanted to work accurately. I let the jibe pass.

"What was in the box you took out of the museum last night?"

Theo replied, "I saw you at the foundry, you bitch. Was that your car following us, too?"

Uh oh. Doggy talk again. So this dog has damn good eyes. Situation deteriorating.

I sat up very straight and repeated, "Theo, what was in the box last night when you left the museum?"

"None of your business."

I got up and unbalanced myself out the door. I was hardly through when Theo called me back. Easing back down into the chair, I waited.

Theo pushed himself up to hang over me. "Never repeat this."

"And if the police question me?"

"You refer them to me. Don't tell anyone. Is that a promise?"

"I'll do everything possible so I don't have to tell anyone." If I admired Reiko's honesty it had better be in practice as well as theory.

"Not good enough. Especially don't tell your boyfriend that reporter."

"What do you know about Daniel?"

"I saw you at the club, remember? When Elena was studying comedy for her theatre class. Your boyfriend was so Canadian. Then he shows up at Foley's lecture and it turns out in real life he's a reporter. Interviews us for French radio. If what I say is not kept private between you and me, I will make sure you never work again, in any museum. Understand?"

Luykes had threatened to fire me if I didn't behave. Now Theo was doing the same. No wonder honest Reiko was in trouble, divulging museum secrets and making curators toe the line. This museum was intent on keeping everything in storage.

I was too old to be intimidated this way. But not too old to be frightened of early death.

"How would you make sure I couldn't work anywhere?" My voice came out weak, like my bones felt.

"You won't know. Because you aren't going to tell."

Or I wouldn't be around to tell. I understood. An accident. A light fixture falling, a drink tasting odd, a heap of tangled wires in my path. He'd seen me with a reporter, and I was on the scent of a forged artifact in his collection. I had no real evidence whether my injuries were my clumsiness or his plotting, but my actions had threatened him enough to have faced a drawn pistol. If I placated him, I could find out why.

I said, "Daniel's not on the scene any longer." This was the geographic truth.

Theo sat, head bowed. "When I left the museum yesterday I had one of the reproductions of the Pan, the one you had done the report on." He raised his eyes to watch my reaction. "In the box. I went down to ask the foundry to cast it, gave them some excuse. Hard to find an object when it's covered by a mould."

"And you would leave me your second one, with the red paint added to look like the real thing," I reasoned out loud. "Where is the real one, Theo?"

"Being cast, too."

I looked up sharply. "What?"

"The Shop asked about reproductions. So last month I had my two Pans made, direct replicas without MOA on the bottom, ostensibly to show the Shop what the bronze would look like, and then to use them for teaching. The Shop liked them. I said I would have more made from the original, with their MOA mark on them."

"But how could you be casting the real Pan when Foley was supposed to be evaluating it?"

"That was my mistake. My stupid, stupid mistake. Imagine!" Theo slumped in his chair. "It was nothing. So much of nothing gone so wrong," he said. "Weeks ago I made all the arrangements with the foundry for the shop reproductions and with Cuyler for the evaluations the day after his lecture. The foundry had to cancel and reschedule that appointment so they didn't do the pour until last week, Friday, and were supposed to remove the casting marks Monday morning. In time for me to pick up the real one for Cuyler in the evening. But the bronze wasn't perfect enough for them, too many air bubbles. So Friday they'd encased it back in another mixture to form a better mould, ready for the next pour. How could they know my schedule or Cuyler's? I had to tell Cuyler that he wouldn't be able to evaluate the real Pan, but I did have a very good replica. I'd put it on the trolley Sunday so he could get an idea. Could the real one be evaluated a week or two later? But he was supposed to go off to Europe. He said that Monday night he'd evaluate all the other recent acquisitions so at least we could go ahead and get them properly recorded, and he'd look at the Pan reproduction and make a general statement that would be amended when he got back and could see the real thing. It all seemed so reasonable at the time."

"So," I countered, "how come you told Luykes you spent twenty thousand dollars on a fake?"

"What exactly do you think you know? You and that reporter, what've you been up to?"

"Nothing, and never mind," I said, and then, "you scumbag. You were going to sell the real one."

Theo glared at me.

"Since I discovered the one on the table was a fake, and you knew where the real one was, you could never bring it back to the museum."

"That's your theory. I was in fact afraid maybe I had bought a fake in the first place. Now that I knew, thanks to you, a telling metallurgical detail about what a fake looks like, I needed to check the one I'd bought when the foundry was done with it. And I had to explain something to Luykes in case you might be barging in there with the news. At least, I had to stave off Luykes until she went to Montreal. It would all be settled soon at the foundry anyway."

Theo continued his defence. "You see, initially there was some question about the provenance of the Pan, and I hadn't bothered investigating before we acquired it because the problem seemed legitimate. The market often is quite general. You know, 'Roman, second century' or whatever, but nothing more detailed. I was going to tell Sally when she got back from Montreal that I'd done research and it wasn't in fact a fake."

"Balls!" The older I got the less I believed what I heard, but what I did believe was with conviction.

"Your word against mine, Ms. Cates. Which do you think she'd accept?"

"And I wouldn't have had the report to back me up," I said slowly. "If you really were going to put the original back in the museum, you would just have made another switcheroo of the fake in the cupboard with it. If I'm to take your word," I was thinking aloud now, "how would you explain the good shape the original is in?"

"It wouldn't be in the cupboard. Not for a while. The Pan's gone, isn't it? Luykes will hear I sent it out after the castings were complete, for restoration at a specialist antiquities conservator I know. All on Greek and Roman's budget so no problem for Conservation. It will come back later."

"All that stuff's police evidence! You're going to say you sent evidence away without showing the police?"

"Don't be silly. The police don't want it. It's not evidence! Evidence of what? That Cuyler fell down? The police just want to make sure that right now everything associated with the case is kept. And Cuyler fell on the reproduction, don't forget. I can tell them why a replica was out for Cuyler." Theo shrugged.

I knew I had lost. He had an answer for everything. Except for the fact that he was dealing in fakes. It helped me understand Theo's relationship with Foley: both respected experts, both unscrupulous. How much had they helped one another, in either career? I'd tell Constable Frick everything I'd heard. And Luykes. But not Elena. That would be too awful. Because I would be finishing Theo's career. I wasn't looking forward to this, but once you knew something, you couldn't unknow it.

And I still had to prove Reiko didn't poison Foley.

Dial M for Museum.

*Chapter*
# 16

∽◦∾

## Thursday Evening

After my scuffle with Theo I hobbled into one of the little washrooms near his office. I took my time washing and straightening as best I could without a comb, make-up, or make-over. Limping over to the guards' station—here comes that woman again, even more cut up, what a job conservation must be—I signed out and dragged myself to UBC's health clinic. Nothing broken, the doctor said, but where did I get those bruises? I said I had gotten into a bit of a scrap, but it wasn't my husband or boyfriend, I had neither, and it was my own fault for thinking I could vault furniture. The doctor didn't press; she cleaned up the cuts and scrapes, gave me a tetanus shot and a prescription—starting now I could take the painkiller every four hours if it would help—and told me to go to bed when I got home. And no alcohol with the pills. She was persistent as well as thorough. She asked when I'd had my last check-up, whether I had any pains or distress, and when I answered honestly, commanded me to come back and soon, or else a gastro-intestinal specialist was in my future. For what it was worth, she also described a violent ischemic event when I asked if a heart attack or stroke could produce Foley's last moments. Yes, if the blood had come from injuries or had other external or internal causes.

Pain was my excuse to indulge myself. On the way home I picked up Asian take-out from a place right beside the pharmacy. Tan Tan noodles and a side of gai lan greens. My true Chinese food comfort dish was shrimp and lobster sauce, but unaccountably it did not exist in British Columbia. Until I'd journeyed the three thousand miles between Toronto and Vancouver I'd had no idea that the Great Divide of the North American continent meant shrimp and lobster sauce to the east, and we in the west unable to feed our habit. So I indulged in one half-sized sherry before dinner and savoured the food before me. Pain flared as I cleaned up afterwards. Pouring out three of the painkillers, I looked forward to twelve hours of sleep. It wasn't like I was downing a dozen, and dinner had been big. I would wake up refreshed, and then call Daniel and hope for sympathy.

I had just undressed and was extracting my nightgown's arm from inside out when the phone rang. Right now self-preservation meant ignoring any demands and responsibilities and just curling up in bed, but I had come to acknowledge that a ringing phone in my home-alone home was a power greater than myself. It mesmerized me, hypnotized any common sense out of me, and I was bound to pick it up.

The "Hello, is that Ms. Berenice Cates?" had a smooth British accent, perfect for selling or polling or otherwise scamming.

"Who are you calling at this time of night?" I barked.

There was a pause. "Excuse me. I have been asked to call Ms. Berenice Cates. Eight-thirty is usually an appropriate time to make inquiries. I apologize if I have disturbed someone else."

I stood still, naked there with my nightgown in my free hand. "Can you hang on?" I said to the man, "I'll get her."

I put the phone down and pulled the nightgown over my head, slid into my slippers, sat down on the bed, and giggled. "I hope I'll be able to get her but I think the pain killers may have gotten her first." An incoming tide of euphoria washed over me, whether from drink, drugs or the absence of pain, I didn't care.

"Hello, this is Berenice Cates," I said into the phone. I had meant to disguise my voice but realized, as soon as the words were out, that I'd forgotten.

There was a pause. The smooth voice said coldly, "Mama told me to call."

"Mama told me there'd be days da-da," I sang back.

"I beg your pardon."

"I beg yours, I'm sure."

There was another pause. "Ms. Cates." Even in those two words I knew that this was a voice used to being listened to, obeyed: the cold power of authority. The high tide wave drained away as quickly as it had come. I hugged my cotton nightie close.

"I apologize," I stammered. "I'm drugged. Do I know you?" There was something familiar about his voice but his name couldn't penetrate my fog.

"Can you understand what I'm saying?" came the even reply.

"Yes, yes, I mean I've had to take some pain killers and I'm not quite myself."

"It's a relief to know you're not like this all the time if you're a friend of Mrs. M's. Mama, at the museum."

"Mama? Is she okay? Why are you calling?" Then I lost it again. "I mean, you phone with 'Da boss sent me' and . . ." It was probably a good thing I didn't get to finish as the louder voice overrode mine.

"Ms. Cates, listen to me, please. I have gone out of my way to do Mrs. M's bidding. She asked me to call you and arrange to tell you some information. Do you want to meet?"

"No," I said. "Who are you?"

"You may remember we've met briefly before in the museum. Saul Samuels. I'm a legal consultant with the International Court. Perhaps I haven't explained myself sufficiently." Exasperation was seeping through the practiced voice. "I apologize."

I liked that.

"I have a message from Mama to deliver to you only, personally. I gather the message originated with your supervisor, Reiko Smithson. Mrs. M asked me to call."

I dove in. "Mama talked to Reiko? Can staff contact her now?"

"Mama wears a blue uniform, and is, as I'm sure you can appreciate, taciturn enough to convince the police she needed only to know if Reiko had made alternate arrangements for her dog. Since Reiko was often being taken to the station for interviews."

"I forgot Hound Dog! Mama's feeding Hound Dog? Aren't Reiko's siblings here?"

"This provided a way for the museum to check up on her, and let her know her lawyer was available. Now, I have been asked to tell you about a Graham Bells I was involved with."

"A what?"

"I was consulted about a painting by the artist Graham Bells. Tomorrow morning at eight I leave for the Hague. We can meet now, or at 5 A.M. I suggest, frankly, that it might work better for you at five."

Never in my life has anything worked better for me at 5 A.M., but I could see his point.

"Where?" I asked, gaining a little time.

"I can meet you at the airport, or I can ask my driver to wait for me at your place. I suggest the latter. What is your address?"

And I gave it to him.

"I'll be there at five. This won't take too long. I would appreciate coffee, black."

<hr />

What wouldn't take too long? For one perpetual minute I couldn't move from my bed: the phone by my side, arms hugging my nightie, my mind counting my stupidities. I'd invited this man my haze couldn't quite place over to my empty house in the pre-dawn. I had no phone number to call him back and say forget it. I didn't have Mama's home number either, to corroborate his story. Maybe Mama would be on the night shift at the museum. I called MOA security but of course she wasn't there, having worked the two previous "museum open hours" shifts, and no, I wasn't on the permanent staff phone list and they were sorry, they could not give out home phone numbers. What else could I do? Wobbling over to the table in the main room that served as my breakfast, supper, and desk surface, I produced three long sentences. The note went under the saltshaker for when they found my body; my tired, wired body, I realized, swaying towards the kitchen. I don't take many medications. Maybe the doctor I saw was an accomplice of this legal Hague man? In the kitchen I forgot what I was doing there.

"Berry, you need sleep," announced my one functioning brain cell. Hobbling back to the bedroom, I worked slowly through setting two alarms for four-thirty A.M. I got out a can of bear spray a Toronto friend had given me as a good-bye present for the wilds of BC's mountains. The bed shook with my shivering as I climbed under the duvet. Soon its warmth began to creep up, though, and I stretched out. The euphoria surged back. "Here comes the judge!" I chuckled, and then the alarm woke me.

Staggering out of bed, I just made it to the toilet to vomit. Every cell in my body was jangling. It was almost ten to five by the time I'd succeeded in my attempts to wipe up myself, my mouth, and the bathroom. Grabbing slacks, top, and an oversized jacket to hide the bear spray, I raced around opening the few doors in my apartment so it felt big with escape hatches. My sparse belongings did not include a coffee maker. Why I was actually worrying about this? I put the kettle on. The running water must have masked the sound of the doorbell. Down the hallway a dark head and hat appeared through the door window.

I stood stock-still and took three deep breaths. On the third I walked steadily to the door, putting on all lights within reach. My left hand held the bear spray under the jacket. I opened the door with my right. A thin man dressed in black slipped in. The nightmare was real. I screeched. He kicked the door closed. My fist shot out of my jacket but the bear spray was knocked expertly out of my hand.

An overriding male voice penetrated my shriek.

"Stop! Look at my hands. Nothing!"

I saw his open palms, and then light glinted off metal and I screamed again. It came out a near voiceless high mew.

"Please! Just tell me what won't frighten you." The man did a bow of servitude and removed his hat, revealing a bald head with a few wispy grey hairs, then a lined, pale face as he straightened. He was only my height without his hat, and at least eighty years old. I recognized the dapper gentleman I had seen coming out of Sally Luykes office, the one who had asked if Ed or I needed a lawyer, the one who later had lectured me on temptations and ethical practice in museums.

I could hear thick rapid panting and knew it was me. The man looked at my face, then thrust out a gentlemanly arm and took over, slowly moving my flushed, gasping self down the hallway. I folded into the one chair in the kitchen, keeping my eyes on his. He stood facing me, arms at his sides, palms outwards. My breath eased, and then the kettle's whistle jumped me out of my skin. Before I could rise he had turned it off and poured a little into the teapot by the stove. He was sideways to me now, concentrating at the counter, a black couture raincoat draping to tasselled loafers. If that metallic gleam was a knife, it was still hidden in the coat.

"Take your coat off," I squeaked.

He turned his legs to look at me, then allowed the expensive coat to slough to the floor. The man was gaunt even in his dark suit. He let the jacket drop to the floor too and began turning out his pants pockets, then patting down his Oxford shirt.

"I want to search your stuff," I said. "Don't you dare move," and before he questioned, I was scrambling on the floor at his clothes. His legs slowly twisted away from me, and I heard the routine noises of tea-making.

"I have no weapon, if that's what you're thinking."

"I saw metal. A knife."

"My ring?" He spread his palms again. "I do admit to some experience in hand-to-hand combat." His voice betrayed pride.

"I'm calling the police!" I began scuttling backwards, still on hands and knees, and at the safety of the door swung around towards the one sweet phone in the bedroom. If I live through this I'll get a cell. With a Bach ring tone.

"I will leave now, or, I can explain everything, give you the message from Mama, and then leave."

I stopped. Rear end in the air, crawling on hands and sore knees, I was about to phone the police about an eighty-year-old tea-maker whom I had invited into my home and who I wasn't even sure had intended to threaten me.

"What do you take in your tea?" came the calm British voice.

Face it, butt-in-the-air-Berry, he's got you. "Milk. Please." I rolled around to confront him, and he was holding out a steaming cup to me. His face betrayed nothing, not even a glimmer of amusement when my joints cracked loudly as I pulled myself up off the floor. I didn't take the cup. "You take that one," I said craftily. "I'll pour my own."

"Of course. Thank you," he said, and walked slowly towards the main room to sit at the table, using his foot to push his coat and jacket off to one side, smothering a half smile now.

"You attacked me," I accused.

"No. I do apologize, though. You were pulling a weapon on me."

"It wasn't a weapon. It was my defence."

"That is, I'm afraid, what they all say. What I saw was a metal canister, and I acted. It's an old wartime reflex. I apologize. They trigger . . . the memories are visceral. I can't seem to overcome them. Like Holocaust survivors still hoarding food. I'm eighty-two now, you know, and not as strong as I used to be. Not quite as confident I'll outwit the shadows. Nor as quick."

"You're not so slow. You got the bear spray."

"Is that what it was?" he smiled. "Splendid! I rather like being thought of as an old grizzly."

"You're much too thin."

"I am indeed sorry to disappoint you. Please sit down. I have to leave for the airport quite soon."

I saw my three-line note on the table as I took the chair opposite. I didn't want a war vet to see it, although it was crazy to hide this puny artifact attesting to my fear after everything else he'd seen. I started to laugh and couldn't stop. Staggering to my feet, I fetched a tea towel from the kitchen to wipe my eyes. I didn't care what this man was thinking now, I just couldn't get the image of myself out of my mind, on all fours on the floor, scared as a chipmunk, thinking my time had come when it was only my teatime.

The man waited without hurrying me. I asked my first incisive question. "Your name again is . . .?" What an ace investigator, Berry.

"Saul Samuels."

"You can't be eighty-two."

"Thank you. I have been blessed with good genes, bad luck, and a will to survive."

"Bad luck?" My old fear jumped on his statement.

"It's my euphemism. My extended family perished in the war. My family got me out early by sending me to England to study, but I stopped in Paris en route and came within a hair's breadth of not making it at all. Then in England it was almost worse for me. I was helpless, a young Jew studying in Britain, helpless to do anything about what was happening to my family, especially in Poland. Now I spend my time . . . what time I have left . . . to try and . . . assist justice."

Saul Samuels incensed me with his plummy accent and lofty phrasing. At the same time, the old warrior sounded true. But he had twigged something else on my mind. I'd been wanting to find this out for days. How could I ask him? This man had just told me he had lost his whole family in the war. But I had to know.

"One question. Off-topic." Samuels looked at me and waited.

"What's the difference between a schlemiel, a schnook, and a schmuck?"

Now it was his turn. Between bouts of high-pitched laughter, his sleeve wiping away a few tears, he managed to rasp, "I'm glad you said this was off-topic."

"I'm serious!" I persisted. "I need to know."

"Yes. Of course, Ms.Cates. For your education, a schlemiel is a 'can't get it right,' a schnook isn't much different but is the kind of lad who's an easy mark, and a schmuck is a, and I'm terribly sorry to have to say this in front of you but, for educational purposes only, a, excuse me, a stupid, no good fuck-up. A complete jerk. There, that's better."

He wiped away more tears. "Please, now. I was simply told to tell you about the Bells painting."

"Mama told you this?" I moved to it quickly. "How do you know Mama? She tells you what to do? What's your real name, anyway? 'Samuels' isn't Polish." I shut up before I got in deeper.

"No, not quite. It's my English name, the name I've had for almost sixty years." Samuels eyed me steadily as he continued. "And yes, I've known Mama for half as long, and it is my pleasure to do for her, when her blasted independence lapses for an instant once a decade and she actually asks a favour. How did I meet Mrs. M.? I came to Canada and found myself, beginning in the late sixties, as a lawyer working in Alert Bay for a Native association, helping out with their legal matters, trying to get artifacts back for them that had been seized illegally in the 1920s at a potlatch. You probably know about this from your work in the museum; the potlatch regalia had been distributed by the Indian agent of the day to several museums across Canada and in the States.

The sixties were early for repatriation, but we were beginning to have some success. I met Rose Mam at that time. I was also doing personal legal matters, adoptions, inheritance, that sort of thing. Mrs. M is quite an incredible survivor of some hard knocks. I've always admired her spirit. I help her out if I can. I wish she'd ask more often."

"I don't really know her. What's her story?" With my insatiable curiosity I should shorten my last name to Cat.

"Her story is her own. Why I'm here is to tell you about the painting. Which I will do if you would be so kind as to tell me if there is any tea left."

I had finished the small pot with my own cup so I got up to put more water on. My body felt painful and decrepit, and I hobbled off-balance back to the sink and stove. He was watching me. So what. He looked more like a lean wolf than a grizzly, but after my first panic he had proven he wasn't there to attack the weak and vulnerable of my species. I could hobble all I wanted. He made good tea, after all. He was actually in my herd.

I avoided looking at the kitchen clock. I also avoided taking more painkillers, much as I wanted them. Not after last night. Saul Samuels was human, not wolf, but more than ever I needed to keep my wits about me. As soon as I sat down, he began recounting his story about the painting, basically what I'd heard from Max Turpin, about Mama seeing the laundry blueing on the picture and thinking the picture was by Graham Bells.

"Mrs. M called me to get my opinion on what she should do. To make a long story short," he continued, and I tried to keep the surge of pleasure off my face, "I advised her to tell everything to Sally Luykes. I've known Sally for many years, beginning with my time in Alert Bay, and in the last decade I've been with the Friends of the Museum and attend all their functions whenever I'm in town. Sally's made the museum her life. She absolutely needed to know if there was any ethical conflict."

I wanted to say, "She acts like she knows, and she makes sure people come and tell her everything." I poured myself more tea. I'd had enough of back-slapping paeans to the Director. Back-stabbing interested me more.

"Now, I don't know what part of my story is going to mean anything to you." Nor I, my mind echoed. "Mrs. M didn't indicate. But since she said your friend Reiko Smithson had asked her to get ahold of me to tell you about the painting, I don't want to leave any detail out, especially about how Reiko Smithson was involved."

I involuntarily looked over at the clock in the kitchen. It was past five-thirty.

"Don't worry," said the smooth voice. "They'll hold the plane for me." To my wide eyes he added, "It's not a commercial flight," and said, as I continued to stare, "Ms. Cates, I'm not so very important. It's only to make a short connection. There's leeway in the timing." He continued with only a slight increase in pace. "Sally did the right thing, of course."

Oh, yawn. Then came more of what I knew, that Reiko had been brought in, that a technical analysis hadn't been done because it was too expensive, and that the painting was refused by the museum and returned to its owner. When I heard, "But that's not the end of the story", I had to pull myself back from looking out the window. Samuels said, "Some time later the owner . . ."

That caught my attention. "Who was?" I wanted him to confirm this detail.

"Max Turpin, I'm sorry to have to tell you. I'm sure you know him at the museum."

"Yes, well . . . you have a great memory," and I added, "better than mine" before the words "for your age" escaped.

The pat phrases, insinuating insult. Thirty years my senior. I would have no worries about aging if I turned out like him.

"The genes. Max Turpin put the painting up for auction through an art dealer. Turpin wanted an arms-length appraisal of its fair market value. But before Turpin sold the painting, he had the full technical analysis done. I don't know why or what it cost, but I guess the whole matter had been bothering him all that time. And indeed, the artist was Graham Bells. But nobody knew except a handful of people at the museum and whoever did the analysis. Reiko Smithson found out that the painting, even after analysis, even after Turpin knew the results, was being sold under the name of the artist that he, Turpin, originally thought had done it. It wasn't being sold as a Bells. She told the auction house and the sale was off. There. Have you learned anything?"

"This doesn't make sense," I said slowly. As I tried to grasp the difference between what Samuels had just told me and what I had learned from Max himself at lunch, Saul Samuels got up and put the kettle back on the boil again. I turned the affair over in my mind while the tea brewed.

"May I change topics?" he said.

No. But he was pouring me a fresh cup.

"Mrs. M. said you might be able to advise me about 'something in conservation.'"

"Of course." Flattery worked on me like a ringing phone.

"She said one of the guards took some solvent from your chemical storage a while ago. The usual to clean some electronics, I gather. Didn't ask permission, but did tell Mama. She forgot to tell you. Is she in a spot of bother? Do you register each chemical?"

No, we operated on trust. Look where that had gotten us. Since the Conservation lab storage served the whole staff for high-end cleaning solvents, I made a mental note to start record-keeping, ASAP. Even for cleaning a computer mouse or tape deck. Solvents were not the only problem chemicals in the cupboard, as I and the police had found out.

"We've relied on being asked first," I replied, "But it's obviously problematic. We've just begun a register." As of now. "Do you know what was taken and which guard?"

"You'll have to ask Mrs. M. So her lapse in reporting was not terribly significant? I'll tell her, and about the new register."

"I will ask," I muttered. Another loose end I might be able to knit into the pattern.

Samuels nodded, and sat and looked at me with patient interest. He could probably hear the gears grinding. I'd shifted into reverse, scrolling back over the story of the painting.

"The arms-length appraisal!" I squawked. "Who did it?" I smiled to myself when I heard the answer: Cuyler Foley.

"Okay, so now we know that Max Turpin had business dealings with the man who was murdered at the museum."

"Murdered? Cuyler Foley?" Samuel's face went white. His hand reached for his cup and spilled it instead. "I didn't know it was murder."

"I'm so sorry. I don't know how much is public knowledge yet. They're still saying—maybe hoping—it was a heart attack, but it looks more deliberate. Was he a friend of yours?" I watched him in alarm, my hands wiping the table surface with the tea towel. Neither Mama nor Sally had put him in that loop.

"No, an acquaintance, but one I've known for, what, thirty, forty years? Poor Cuyler."

I felt bad for skirting around the subject, but there couldn't be much time left before he'd have to go. A man like Samuels could get the information from any number of sources. I asked instead, "Was Cuyler Foley a reputable or disreputable art dealer? I've heard both."

Samuels pierced me with a stone-cold look and said, "Neither. He was a survivor in a particular business. You tell me if making a profit in business is reputable or disreputable."

"Well . . ." I left it hanging because I didn't know how to finish the thought. Too big, too fraught, and the man opposite me was still too unknown. Then, thinking back on my conservation schooling, I said, "What is this technical analysis they did? Pigment analysis? Indecipherable signature? Did they analyze its remnants with infra-red? The documentation," I was talking out loud to myself now, "I could find out which conservator did the analysis and look at the documentation."

Samuels said, "I don't know who the practitioner was. There were two signatures on the painting, though. The signature on the front said 'Morrisey' or 'Morrisseau,' if I'm remembering correctly, and another on the back of the canvas was 'Bells'."

"On the back and the front? Two different signatures? But then it was obvious there was a problem."

"No, the back signature was uncovered during the analysis. The painting had had a second canvas laid on the back of the original one—you probably know about this kind of preservation to strengthen a worn painting—and when they took the second canvas off, the signature was revealed."

I did know, and I didn't want to explain it to Saul Samuels. Taking a canvas off another? This wasn't an analysis. This was a conservation treatment. Max Turpin must have gone to a private fine art conservator to have his painting put into good shape for auction so he would get the best price. It was not uncommon for paintings to be relined. If the original canvas had deteriorated, it was standard practice to add a new one to the back to keep the paint layer well supported. Max had run into an ethical conservator who had found a signature on the back of the original canvas. The original signature, too, or else why would it be there? The obvious place for a fake signature was on the front, where it was visible. There weren't many conservators in Vancouver. It was certainly possible to imagine Reiko hearing about this. How could I talk to her? That wouldn't be easy in the present circumstances. But I could talk to Max.

Saul Samuels had gone into the kitchen. This hand-combat eighty-two-year-old "they'll hold the plane for me" had not only made tea but cleared up his cup and saucer afterwards. Does one hug a gentleman?

"Mind if I put on my coat?" he asked, looking at the crumpled elegance still on the floor. "I really must be going."

In the hallway Samuels said, "I'm going to bend down now to pick up my hat. Not the bear spray." Then came a real glimpse of his age, his frame descending in ratcheted stages to retrieve the black homburg. I still had a lot to learn about aging. As we reached the front door, he put a hand in his coat, and I shuddered involuntarily. "My card," he said. "The office has a toll-free number if you need to reach me. I'd be interested to know what conclusions you come to, and I'd like to call you, if I may, about poor Cuyler."

I took the card with a smile, informed him that I was going to wish him bon voyage *à la française,* and kissed him lightly on both cheeks. I closed the door on a gaunt figure, hat in hand, heading down the steps to a black chauffeured car.

My whole body felt stiff and sore. I could deal with today, though. It was still early yet, just past 6:30. I would find Max this morning, and Luykes, if she were back. But first of all, I would call Daniel. Even if he wouldn't get this 1-800 number for his routines.

# Chapter
## 17

## Friday Morning

I had time for a shower. Washing my bruised body made me proud; like going swimming in cold water, you forced yourself to do it, and it felt awful in the beginning, numb after a while, and great when you were out. Steam from fresh Irish Breakfast rose from the pot, and I sat down in my bathrobe to phone.

I got Daniel's recorded message and said. "Hallo, D; *me voil–À,* . . . B.C."

"Are you there?" I continued, knowing he was able to juggle his hours so he could do quiet research from home. Sure enough, he picked up the phone. Daniel screened his calls. He assumed there was an adoring public who heard his brilliant work on radio and somehow found out his home number. Daniel Tremblay? In Quebec? I don't think so. Daniel Tremblay was a French equivalent of John Smith. There must be tens of thousands of them. If I said no one would find his home number, he would take it to mean that I didn't think he was brilliant. Didn't want to go there.

*"Bonjour la restauratrice!"* came his happy voice. Could I ever live with such cheer first thing in the morning? Then I remembered it was three hours later in Quebec; Daniel had been up for hours. Could I even live with such cheer at noon?

I launched into my adventures, dramatizing my intrepidness and gesticulating into the phone, but worming my way around details of the forgery in deference to Theo's threats. Daniel didn't interrupt. I caught my breath at one point and said, out of politeness, "Am I going on and on?" An explosion of laughter came through the line.

"All right, don't rub it in," I said.

"On your sore body?" came the reply. "Good God, would you let me?"

We were back on that delicious, dangerous territory.

Then he did a sidestep. As usual. This time by not waiting for me to reply. "Now you have to hear my story," he said.

"In just a minute." If he was going to change the subject, I was going to finish my tale. "Let me tell you what Theo said when I confronted him about where the lost report was." And I was off again.

Glancing at the clock, my cheap long-distance phone plan was a pleasure. Daniel didn't seem to want to hang up and neither did I. Once more I was going to be late for work, and Daniel hadn't even had a chance to tell me what he was up to. If I ever saw him again, I would practise hanging my head like Theo did. I tried it out right away and it helped, me at least, when I said there wasn't much time before work.

Daniel sounded put out. I apologized several times, imitating Theo. Daniel announced he had two important things he wanted to make sure he told me before we hung up. Then he talked about being at the airport waiting for a baseball team, and interviewing a guy who made and repaired folk art.

"Nice," I said.

"You understand?" His voice was anxious.

"Sure."

"You don't understand."

"Maybe you're right," I conceded. "What's to understand?"

There was a pause at the other end of the line. "Where did I say I was Wednesday night?"

"At the airport. Meeting a baseball team."

"What time was that?"

"Around three in the morning," I quoted.

I hate exams. Was I being patronized, or did he just want to make his words clear?

Daniel continued, "And who did I see?"

"Someone who looked like Dr. Luykes."

"And where was I last night?"

"Interviewing the folk artist."

"A famous folk artist," Daniel corrected. "Everything beautiful and perfect, just like the old pieces; he is very, how do you say, *poigné?*"

"A tight-ass."

"He is so tight-ass that when the guys in his workshop do repairs, he checks each one after. Old *girouettes,* for instance, what is it in English? For on top of the roof?"

"Weathervanes. Are you insinuating that paying attention to detail means . . ."

Daniel broke in on the question, hurrying to say, "And what time was I there?"

We were back to infuriating.

"Seven."

"And who did I see?"

"Sally Luykes."

"Doing?"

"Coming out of the artist's studio." Long silence. "Daniel, so what? I know Luykes went to Quebec."

"You do not."

"What do you mean? She spoke at a museum there!"

"Did she? Berry! Think!" Another long silence. "Berry!" Daniel was almost laughing. "Where is the museum she went to?"

"In Montreal."

"And where am I?"

"In Quebec."

"Yes!" came the jubilant reply. "*Québec* City, not just *Québec* province."

Daniel continued, "And where then was your Dr. Luykes?"

I was shocked into silence.

Daniel announced happily, "A big insinuendo, *n'est-ce pas?*"

"A very telling insinuendo. I hope I am told of what. Daniel, you're terrific."

"I have more," he purred. "Turn on *Radio-Canada* at 8:52 BC time. My interview from yesterday. Bye bye!"

---

I had to grab my clothes and dress fast. I needed to look good today, business-like; Constable Frick must believe me about Theo selling the forgeries. For Max who I wanted to see about a certain painting, I wanted to look somewhat "with it". Pulling off both would be impossible. Opening the small closet, I saw my good blouses had all become wrinkled. My nylons had runs. I found my light wool seeing-the-bank-manager suit and matching shoes. It might be summer, but Vancouver has a cool maritime climate. The creases in the wool would hang out in the humidity, and the jacket would hide enough of the blouse. The longish skirt would hide the nylons. So I was doing business-like and not with-it. No one at MOA except Max and the young staff dressed in current fashion anyway. It was a university museum, after all, not a downtown office. I'd fit in fine, and flew out the door.

The wool didn't disappoint. The morning was cool and grey. The definition of good weather in Vancouver is when it is not overall grey, but you can see the outlines of individual clouds. Today was a good day. Parking in the back lot, I was just in time to hear Daniel's voice on the radio enthuse about Quebec weathervanes.

Why were they playing this piece in British Columbia? As soon as I heard the woman's voice, I knew. Daniel was interviewing Sally Luykes as she came out of the artist's studio. I bent over the dashboard.

"I did purchase a piece from M. Benoit," she was saying, "but no, not a weathervane."

"Can you share what you bought with our listeners?"

"Ah, well, it's a gift, you see. I can't tell."

"Can you whisper it?" Said in a stage whisper. The charming voice, compelling in the same way as it had been at the comedy club, Daniel working his craft, building up so he had his audience in the palm of his hand.

"No, really . . ."

"A hint?"

"I don't think . . ."

"One tiny hint?" Only too well could I picture Daniel's handsome dark face, imploring blue eyes. "You're smiling, eh?"

"Let's just say it is both from Quebec and BC."

"Well, my listeners, figure that one out. Dr Luykes, also from BC, enjoy your souvenir."

I couldn't figure it out. Why go all the way to Quebec, except for the lecture? She could get a Pan here, if that was it. British Columbia was BC. I was BC, for that matter: the same initials. I'd better not be involved in this episode.

Since I was late anyway, I walked the long way around to the museum's front door, getting some exercise and stretching the traffic annoyance out of my system. The air was crisp out here on the wooded peninsula, high on the cliffs rising above the sea. Today the water below was two-toned; closest to me it was brown, and farther out was a clean line where it met blue water beyond. The brown was the muddy outflow of the huge Fraser River, and the blue was the incoming Georgia Strait ocean water. All water, but so clearly demarcated. Gazing down, I itched to find that line for the murder and for Reiko: to go beyond the mud to clarity.

———— ❧ ————

The museum was bustling. School groups were already arriving, squirming around the knapsack bins as the museum educators tried to give everyone their turn. The groups divided and subdivided and flowed around each other in the small space like amoebas under a microscope. I wormed my way through, glad, despite the week I'd had, to be in Conservation and not Education.

Someone else emerged from the crowd. Sally Luykes. Back already? A quick trip. Wait. It could make sense. She went to deliver a lecture, supposedly, but her concern would be the death at MOA. If she flew out Wednesday just after Theo and I were in her office, she would have arrived in the east at two or three in the morning, with the time difference. She could have come back late last night or on an early plane today; you arrived on the coast just hours after you left Quebec because the time difference now worked to your advantage.

Luykes looked visibly tired, her face lined, and big dark bags hung under her eyes. Even from where I stood Luykes looked like she had applied too much make-up. Was her suit wrinkled? Food-stained? What would that prove, anyway? She was undeniably here, and it was a fairly quick trip. Luykes waved a limp greeting as she caught me watching. I headed towards her to ask for an urgent appointment. She'd turned towards someone else though.

Mama was talking to her. I moved through the crowd and, back in proper intern mode, waited behind Mama for an opportunity to interrupt. But Luykes and Mama didn't stop talking. I couldn't tell what they were saying; there was too much ambient noise. Luykes was doing most of the talking and she seemed to be making a lot of "sh" sounds. I hoped she was okay. Sometimes when you were tired it was almost as if your mouth has had a stroke. I waited.

No good. Irene, the office manager and Director's secretary in the main office, waded right up to Luykes, touched her arm, showed her a paper, and the two of them were off with a one-word good-bye to Mama. I was ignored, not for the first time. I preferred the memory of my first week in Vancouver, walking into a store to get my watch repaired and seeing a small Chinese boy peer out from behind the counter and exult to his father, "Oh, it's grandmother!" I've found out that grey hair either brings you respect or oblivion. I trailed after Luykes.

"You won't make it," said an energetic voice on my left. How had I missed a burnt rose shirt and Kandinsky-abstract tie, even in this crowd? Max continued, "I saw you waiting.

I've got to report to the office, fill Sally in on my career as Acting Director. Otherwise Id give my appointment to you." I expected him to brush past, but he muttered, "Two more minutes." I hadn't said a thing, and I was curious why he was pressed-shirt-and-tied, but Max was carrying on both ends of the conversation.

"When Sally's busy, she doesn't like to be interrupted. It's like you're pestering her. Do you think she's up for business this A.M.?" Max fingered his tie. "Do I look directorial enough? Correction: acting-directorial?" Rhetorical questions, since he just kept on. "Our Leader looks dishevelled, doesn't she? Her face is actually grey, like she's got 5 o'clock shadow." A huge grin lit up his face. "Of all the people here, you'll like this. As we naughty kids used to sing, 'God shave our gracious Queen!'" Max grinned as he checked his watch, waved goodbye, and ran.

"Shave her with shaving cream." I chanted the second line and followed his back as far as the main office.

⌁⌁⌁

I spent five minutes making my case to Irene why I needed to see Luykes today. "Next week won't do."

"Well why not?"

"I can't tell you."

"What shall I mark down that the appointment's about?"

"It's about the bronze of Pan."

"Can't that wait?"

"No."

"Well, I can't promise anything until I talk to her. She's pretty well booked up for today. She would have to cancel something. If it's that important."

"It's important."

"Well, I guess, check back later."

Gatekeepers! A museum is full of locked-up exhibits and locked-up storage and locked-up work areas, including staff securing their little domains. Collecting knowledge, keeping it under wraps until it would be useful. But then, was Berry Gumshoe being any different? Why hadn't Reiko locked that hazardous chemical cabinet? No one would have minded, and then there would have been no murder.

A familiar deep voice started humming behind me in Irene's office, and I heard the paper scrape of mail being scrutinized. "She was preoccupied," said Max.

I replied without hesitation, "I need to talk to you. Now."

"Sure. Coffee?"

"Let's go for a walk. Fresh air."

He raised his eyebrows but followed. "Anytime you want fresh, Berry Cates, I'm your man. You know that." He looked to see if his joke was appreciated but I wasn't in the mood for "insinuendo". I had to get the truth out of him.

We had barely gone a hundred steps on the forested path that curves around MOA when I said, "Max, who treated your Bells painting?"

"What? Why?"

"Who, Max, who?"

"Jesus Christ!"

"I don't think so."

Max doubled over. He was still laughing when he stood up. "All right! You're too much. I confess! It was Barbara Hodges. Is this a problem?"

I didn't know a Barbara Hodges. Maybe she had retired by now. I would ask around.

"Did you sell that painting through Cuyler Foley?"

"What's put you on to all this? Yes, I did. I needed a proper evaluation of its worth. Only a gallery or dealer can do that."

"Tell me about the conservation treatment you got done."

"The analysis I told you about?"

"Treatment, Max. The relining. The uncovering of the signature on the back."

Max didn't even pretend to be shocked that I knew about the existence of Bells' signature. Instead, he grinned. "Can you research or what? Want to be a curator?" At a big log in front of the Haida houses on the museum grounds, I stopped and sat down and gestured to Max to sit too. At this hour we were alone.

"The relining," I said. "The painting had been lined before, and that hid Bells' signature. When you found out from Barbara Hodges about the signature on the back of the original canvas when she took the old relining off, you asked her to put a new relining on. So the signature was re-hidden. So you could sell it as a Morrisseau, the fake signature on the front."

A cranky voice replied, "I'd bought it as a Morrisseau. I took it in to Barbara because the canvas on the back was sagging. She recommended a new relining. I agreed. I am, whether you believe it or not, ultimately concerned about the preservation of the art I'm entrusted with."

He was sounding precious and I wasn't going to compliment him for his righteous concern. "Then she discovered the signature on the back."

"Yes, then she discovered the signature on the back."

"And?"

"Well," Max beside me was sitting a little too close. "She documented everything. She was a very ethical conservator. As are all you professional preservation zealots."

Was he teasing or trying to get me to bite? His eyes betrayed the hunter, licking his lips as he waited to see if his quarry would take the bait. He wanted me angry, off-track.

I kept my voice pleasantly steady and gave him my "female listening to such an interesting male" gaze.

He looked back. A long silence. "She gave me a couple of choices," Max admitted, opening and closing his hands as if punctuating each word. "Barbara told me she could do the new lining using canvas, or a synthetic. No difference, she emphasized, conservation-wise. Both were equally as good. As you would say, meets ANSI standards. The choice was up to me, as the owner."

"So you chose the canvas."

"Well, yes, it's traditional. It's what was on before, anyway."

"No, Max, you chose it because it's opaque." My eyes bored into his now reddening face. "Opacity would hide the signature on the back again. The synthetic would have been translucent."

Another long pause.

"Yes, I did," said Max. "And I make no apologies for it. Barbara put a label on the back of her relining to show her studio had worked on the piece. Whoever bought the painting could easily have called her up to look at the full documentation. Nothing was hidden."

"Bells' signature was hidden, Max. And you know as well as I do that to have proof of professional conservation done to a painting just increases its value, gives it a well-cared-for pedigree. I can't imagine a buyer bothering to rustle up the original documentation when the label validates that a conservation treatment was done, 'Relined with canvas using X adhesive on such and such a date by my studio.'"

Max glared at me. I glared back. One more important question. "Did you make the decision about which material you wanted the painting relined with? Or did Foley put you up to it?"

"Foley? Are you kidding? No. Sally."

"Luykes?"

"Yes indeed." Max was watching for a reaction, and got full satisfaction as my mouth fell open. He smiled. "I went to her. I didn't trust Foley to give me advice that wouldn't also be in his own best interest. I was curious, too, to know what Sally would have done in the same situation."

"Sally Luykes told you to cover up the signature?"

"She advised me that it was my decision, but she is very savvy, our Director. She knows the art market. She knew I wasn't doing anything that hadn't been done before a thousand times." Max was enjoying my attention. "Public museums, now, are a different kettle of fish, which is precisely why she's here and not at a private gallery. But the label from Barbara's studio was an important element. It made the whole thing on the up and up, because in my professional opinion, Ms. Berry Cates, any sensible art buyer knows that a conservator will do full documentation. A buyer does want that added value."

"So you're saying Sally Luykes has one set of ethics for museums, and another for the art market?"

"No, I'm not." Max slapped his hand on the log. "Sally is simply very pragmatic. She felt that the information was available to the buyer since the label was there, and besides," Max paused, "I've always suspected she discussed it with Reiko: 'By-the-by, I've heard of an interesting conservation treatment.' I think she put Saint Reiko up to warning the auction house. Ruining my sale, ruining Foley's commission. Sally may have discussed with me why it wasn't such an awful thing for the new canvas to cover up Bells' signature, but she also had an ethical failsafe. She knew Reiko well enough to guess that if she let slip about the signature, the painting didn't have a chance of getting sold as a Morrisseau."

"Why would she do that to you?"

"She didn't. It wasn't like that. She knew I loved the painting, probably didn't think it would be a hardship if I had to keep it. Sally did it to screw Foley."

"Foley?"

"Yup. She hated him. Didn't you know?"

"No." I didn't dare say anything else. Nothing to distract him. Max had centre stage and he warmed to the occasion.

"Remember I told you about being up in Alert Bay together, and seeing Foley too? We weren't competing: I was buying contemporary and he was buying the old stuff. But Sally had a big run-in with him. Or should I say, he with her. A tragic run-in, you might say. It's not for me to tell you her personal secrets, though. Let's just say that in public Sally goes on about admiring Foley, but every time he came in to evaluate something for MOA, her blood pressure would rise volcanically. She rehearsed like an actor to keep it in control. Years ago Sally told me she'd love to get Foley. She was plotting."

"Plotting as in poison arrows on a worktable?"

"No, Sally would be much more hidden, subtler."

"In coffee," I whispered. Silence.

"No, not murder," Max shook his head. "Not Sally. I think she was just going to ruin him somehow, expose him professionally. Listen, Berry, this conversation has been between you and me only. You asked, I gave you my opinion." He latched onto my hand and shook it up and down, probably not even aware he had gripped me. "Nothing's proven at all, against anyone. One thing we don't need is more rumours." With that Max rose from the log. "Anything else?" he asked, "The 'New Exhibits' meeting has started." I shook my head.

Max might not want gossip, but like the rest of us, he couldn't let go of thinking about the murder. As we walked back, he talked as much to himself as me. "Now, Theo, that's another story," he mused. "Arrows. He's a bit of a buff on ancient technology of any kind. But he admired Foley, or at least said so. If there was any crap between them, Theo would have defended himself in an academic journal, a battle he knew how to win." I nodded and walked at my own pace, dropping a bit behind him. "The police have discounted the arrow theory anyway," continued Max, but I wasn't listening anymore. What was I going to do with what I'd already heard?

---

Heather, the Collections Assistant, was just coming out of the workroom as I went past. Her "business clothes" didn't cover her midriff even when she was standing. We stopped in the hallway.

"How's Georgina?" I asked. "Apart from never wanting to make coffee again for the Director."

"She's good!" Heather seemed in a much better mood than I was.

"She saw the doctor?"

"And Constable Frick phoned her at home! I'd told the cop what you'd said. I hope you don't mind. About Georgina having no motive, that even if she'd made the coffee there was no reason for her to want to harm anyone. I asked if the police really thought that, because Georgina didn't, like, really believe you. I mean, it was great of you to say everything you did, it helped a lot."

"Of course Georgina needed to hear it directly from the police."

"And she did. And you know what? The cop said that the poison didn't come from Luykes' coffee tray anyway. It wasn't in those cups or the sugar or the pot. They tested everything. Even the stuff in the fridge, like the milk."

In my blandest voice I asked, "Did Constable Frick say where the poison was from?"

"Yeah! Another cup in the Director's office. A cup that'd had coffee but it wasn't from the tray set. So Georgina isn't suspected at all!"

"Great news." We smiled good-bye and I beetled into the Conservation lab.

Whose coffee cup? Permanent staff marked their own so the cups wouldn't get used by others or journey into the abyss. MOA had an abyss just like a washing-machine or dryer, except it wasn't socks that could never be found again, it was coffee cups and cutlery. Staff joked that Collections Management's job was to fight the good fight so the museum's collections wouldn't end up in the abyss too. Apart from staff, the coffee lounge was used by probably a hundred people: students, museum volunteers, even caterers. What did the cup look like, and what was its provenance?

# Chapter

# 18

## Friday Continues

I was hoping to spend as much time as I could today in catch-up; emails, phone, straightening and cleaning, and then the lab would be ready for Monday and a new week. The consummate intern. I would listen to the phone messages while the emails were downloading, and then go back upstairs and see if Constable Frick was there. I could check back with Irene at the same time about my appointment with Luykes. Very efficient, I commended myself. These were things I needed to do, and only one was strictly from the "want to do" side. What an employee! I punched the numbers for Conservation's voice mail.

Following four inquiries from members of the public—insects in a wooden statue from Africa, removal of dirt from the train of a wedding dress, and two further messages in rising panic and annoyance about the insects—I heard Reiko's voice. Her message was noncommittal; hoped everything was okay. Had an older man contacted me about treating a painting? If there was any emergency, she was home for the next half hour, as long as no one else could hear. I wheeled around to check her phone number on the staff list posted on the wall.

The receiver was in my hand when the door to the Conservation lab slammed and Theo came sweating in. I figured he had brought the Haida-decorated gun from his office, quickly, to keep it from prying eyes and the inevitable, "Theo, what're you doing with that? It's not from the Classics collection." I turned around. His face had no hue. I banged the phone down.

"Here," he said, holding out a crumpled package, "Look," he commanded.

"Fetch," I heard. But I wasn't being a good dog today either. Peter Pan wasn't ready to grow up. "Theo, hang on a sec. Someone's in a panic about insects in a statue. I was just phoning back. Sit," I smiled, gesturing to one of the stools at the lab table. Turning my back on Theo, I dialled, giving him a chance to get some colour back in his face, and had a pleasant five-minute conversation with a grateful woman about how to check if the insects were alive and how to freeze them to death if they were.

Theo looked no better when I turned to face him.

"What's happened?" I walked over and sat beside him. "Have you finished going over the objects that were on the table Monday night? Are there some that don't belong to MOA?"

"Forget them! This," and he held out a small bundle. "I found this when I came to work."

He tore at the loose brown wrapping and a chunk of metal rolled onto the lab table's padded surface. Theo's hands were trembling. I put on gloves, turned the object over, and shivered. I used to say, "I've never met a museum object I didn't like." I'd be lying now. This thing was dark grey, about three inches long, sharply cut out of a crude piece of metal. The metal had been rolled up like a jelly roll so it was about an inch thick. A primitive spike had been driven through its heart.

I hesitated. "What is it?"

"Tabella defixionis or, in the vernacular, a curse tablet. This is a fine example."

"What are curse tablets?" I said, backing away from the table.

"Just what they say. You're a Roman and have negative intentions towards another person, you dispatch a curse tablet. Anonymously, of course. One might even roll up some of the victim's hairs or a personal memento inside to make the curse more effective."

"Where did it come from?"

"My mailbox this morning. Sometimes people do leave donations and such like at the front desk, even though they're not supposed to. There was no note, nothing with this."

"Is it old?"

Theo squinted at me. "What do you think?"

"Let's look at it under the microscope." Cates' worst and best friend.

The object really was awful, the edges of the metal where it had been cut from a larger sheet still sharp even though they were curled and corroded. My gloves ripped as I turned it over and back to see the different areas under magnification. There was white corrosion on the roll and blotchy rust on the spike. Not a lot to go on.

"Are curse tablets made with lead?" I asked, putting a freshly gloved finger on the powdery white of the rolled surface.

"Yes," said Theo. "Is it . . .?" His voice faded.

"Do you want to look?"

"No!" Theo shuddered. "Is it real?"

"I don't know. Nothing I can see right away says it is, and nothing says it isn't."

Theo remained silent.

"We could send it to a scientist I know," I suggested, "and have them test the alloys. There may be some chemicals present that would tell us. You know, if the iron or lead have trace elements from modern metals."

Theo was beginning to sweat heavily. "I'm not sure I have time. I want you to unroll it."

"Unroll it? I can't, Theo, it would ruin the object as it is now. Besides, it has to go through Acquisitions first."

"The object is nothing now, all rolled up. That's just how they're sent." Theo's jaws locked on the words. "There's a message inside the tabellae defixionum. Inscribed in the lead. I need to see it."

"But . . ." Eloquent as ever.

"Please. This was sent to me, not the museum. It's probably a fake." Theo wiped his face. "The message will tell me if it's a fake."

Was there some other quick way to see the message, something that would mean not having to unroll the lead? Lead is a soft metal and could be easy enough to manipulate, but once unrolled, it would not be the original object anymore. I would have altered it, left my mark. The mantra ran through my mind again: conservators preserve objects. They don't ruin them. I thought about using X-rays to look into the roll but lead of course was impregnable.

"How do you know it was sent to you and not the museum?" I was being dogged.

"Because! It's a curse tablet. If someone had wanted to curse the museum, it would have ended up in the Director's office."

"Maybe someone left it as a donation."

"No! Donations always come with notes. Notes from people about their great uncle Arthur who travelled to Egypt in 1905, or notes from our receptionist or the guard the parcel was left with. This was in my mailbox, with my name on it, not abandoned at the back door."

Theo was right. The tablet wasn't official museum property. As a discard with no documentation, it might never be. Its importance was to Theo. Against my better professional judgment, I said I would try to unroll the curse tablet. How easy it is to slide, to take the first steps away from high standards and ideals, and down the slippery slope. Like a board game; what would happen? Chutes and Ladders in Seattle, Snakes and Ladders in Vancouver. Would I end up like Theo, sliding down so far that he could rationalize selling forgeries? Or would I take a ladder up? If he wasn't going to tell Acquisitions of this new arrival, should I? Blow the whistle on him for this as well as the fake bronzes? Or would I accept his argument that this object was meant for him, not MOA? It wasn't as if I could trust him, after yesterday.

⁘⊙⊙⁘

Theo paced. We made a bargain: I would spend whatever time was needed to take pictures and document the piece as it was now. Then I would call him back to the lab and try to unroll it. He would follow through and present the tablet to Acquisitions, but only after it was unrolled. If he practised proper museum procedure and sent it in its present rolled state through the "Consideration for Acquisition" process, we both knew he wouldn't be seeing the message for weeks. Theo also promised to say that it was only under great pressure that I had unrolled the tablet. If he did all this, I promised to remain silent. That was another thing

Theo wanted to avoid. It would have greased the rumour mill to a high speed that, days after a murder, he received an ancient curse tablet.

I missed lunch and did all the documentation in an hour. When nobody was around it was so much easier to get work done, not to mention having the museum's good digital camera free. I found Radio-Canada, turned it low so the talk wouldn't interrupt my train of thought, and used the rhythm of the French language as my music.

Theo came back to stand over me as I worked the metal slowly open. The tablet could have been old; the lead wasn't soft. It took almost an hour to ease it enough towards flat so the inscription was visible. I kept asking Theo to sit down. He'd obediently go and sit, and then a minute later would be up again looking over my shoulder or pacing the narrow space behind me. Luckily I was working under magnification, using a special lamp with a three-power lens that concentrated my attention on the small field of view under its glass. As I got closer to finishing the unrolling, Theo hovered. As soon as he could see what he knew to be full sentences, his hand stopped mine. I noticed a small shred of fabric fall out of one still-bent corner. Thank God Theo was concentrating on the words and didn't see it. It was a fragment of the kind of tweed he wore. Inserted into a piece of birchbark. The curse tablet was indeed personal.

I had taken Latin in high school but I'd never tried to read an inscription. The letters were hand cut into the lead, all uneven. Theo said the curse was in demotic wording, not formal Latin or grammatically correct, just something one person wanted to say to another. Like fuck off. I stood so Theo could sit and see the inscription under better light and magnification. My empty stomach was saying something to me. Demotic, of course, but I understood.

Theo was crying. His back hunched as he looked through the magnifying lens. One hand wiped at his eyes and brow, then fell, unconsciously smudging the glass when it bumped the lens. His shoulders heaved. I moved away, back to my desk. There was something to be said for locked doors on occasion, and privacy. I couldn't achieve that standard in our wide-open lab, but I did what I could.

Theo blew his nose into a nearby paper towel. He wiped his eyes. "Oh," he said. "Oh." It was like a soft moan. I went back to where he sat.

"What does it say?"

"It says," he snuffled, then cleared his throat and slowly recited, "Iovi Optimo Maximo dono tibi negotium ut Theonem exigas per mentem per memoriam per intus per intestinum per pulmones per iecur per cor per medullas per venas neve illum patiaris bibere nec manducare nec adsellare nec meiere nec vigilare nec dormire nec ambulare nec iacere; sic non posit loqui secreta neve possit perstare in operibus secretis."

"It means," and word by word, Theo read out, "To you Jupiter Best and Greatest I am entrusting the task of hounding Theo through his guts his intestines his lungs his liver his heart his marrow his veins and of preventing him from drinking eating sitting down urinating waking sleeping walking lying; so may he not be able to utter secret matter nor to persist in his secret deeds."

"If it's old," he was pleading, "it's got my own name. It could be two thousand years old and it's for me. Imagine!"

I knew it was for him. And it wasn't old. But for Theo this tablet must have been like seeing a hand reach out from a very familiar grave and hearing your name being called.

"Well, maybe it's a fake."

"Oh, hell." Theo wiped away another tear with the rough towel. "What's the difference? I've been cursed."

# Chapter
# 19

# Friday Afternoon

My right hand reached out to give Theo a pat on his shoulder, and my left hand went to snatch it back. This was the man who'd threatened to kill me with a pistol yesterday. One wretched-looking curator sat in front of me now, though, muttering apologies. I couldn't picture him as a cold efficient murderer, even if he was up to his grey saggy tweeds in trouble. Theo was a cowardly sea lion. But then again, I was no wiz. I'd verify this latest assessment of Theo when I talked to Reiko.

"Theo, who do you think might have sent you the curse tablet?"

"I don't know."

"Theo, c'mon. You must have some inkling."

He shook his head.

"I think you do know."

Silence. He hung his head further.

"Theo," I said, keeping my voice soft, "you can tell me." Confidante to the Stellers.

"If only."

An opening. I kept quiet. After an inordinate wait, probably a minute or two, Theo spoke again. "You'll think I'm crazy."

Well, yes, but that hasn't stopped me so far. And I was tantalized by the tablet showing up.

"Promise you won't tell anyone," he said.

"I promise."

"Give me your hand."

We shook on it.

"You'll think I'm crazy," he repeated.

"Tell me." I had difficulty not shouting and jumping up and down. "Who sent you the tablet?"

"I think," Theo lifted his head for the first time and looked at me, "I think it was Cuyler."

"Foley?" I couldn't hide my surprise.

"See, you think I'm crazy."

I composed my face. I tried to pitch my voice in a gentle mid-range, but it didn't work. "Look," I squawked, "this curse tablet arrived four days after Cuyler Foley died. Did it come by mail? Some long-term delivery outfit?"

"No."

"It's impossible, then, isn't it?" This man had a Ph.D. Surely he knew sweet reason when he saw it. The look he gave me said I was wrong.

"I don't know how it arrived. I'll have to think about it."

You do that. "How do you know it's from Foley?" I said.

"Because who else would it be from?" Theo looked genuinely puzzled.

"I don't know who else," I said, and then voiced a question I couldn't believe I was asking. "Theo, were you wearing your tweed jacket the night Foley died?"

"I don't think so. Was it cold Monday?"

"Good. Then why him?"

"Because he," and then Theo hit the table so hard the tablet was flung an inch in the air. A storm raged for an instant across his face, and when it disappeared Theo looked exhausted. "Because, truth to tell, Cuyler never had colleagues. For him, everyone in some way was a rival. He had to be the king of the Classical world out here." Theo's eyes tested my reaction, and in a low, incredulous voice, as if still shocked by the event being related, he said, "Years ago when I was celebrating my new appointment as Chief Curator, Cuyler said I'd gotten the job by playing the race card. A museum like MOA took me only because I was part aboriginal."

Hesitating, I said, "So his death maybe wasn't so terrible?"

"No!" Theo's large frame shook. "I'm Chief Curator because I'm good, and my research and publications show it. My scholarly reputation is solid. Foley was only a commercial dealer. But he twisted the bully's knife one time too many on Monday night."

Almost biting my fingers, I waited for Theo to go further, but he was lost in his emotions, his face red, jaws working. "Something to do with the curse tablet?" I prompted. "Monday night?"

"The very last thing Cuyler said to me was that he would get me if I ruined him, whether he was alive or dead."

"Fill me in." My own breathing was audible now. "How would you ruin him?"

Theo's head drooped. I couldn't hear him too well but I didn't want to interrupt. The gist of it was that Foley had indeed noticed on Monday night that the bronze of Pan was a well-planned fake, not the ordinary replica he was expecting like those made for the museum giftshop, because "MOA" was not marked on the bottom. He questioned Theo about it, whether Theo had been making deliberate fakes all these years, pressured him, insinuated wrong-doing, and then guessed by Theo's reaction that something was up. Or that's what Theo thought.

In the end, Theo had felt trapped. He confessed to selling fakes over a long time; Cuyler was no innocent lamb himself, after all. Cuyler was so much the wolf, in fact, that he demanded a piece of the action. "He began blackmailing me," muttered Theo.

Theo told Cuyler a split of "the action" wasn't possible, that he had only a few pieces reproduced each year and already had too many people to pay in Greece and Italy. He offered him two unmarked old reproductions he could sell himself if Foley would keep mum. If Cuyler told, though, he, Theo, would let the world know that Cuyler Foley didn't hesitate to sell fakes. It would ruin him, too.

"I was so upset at the conversation, I excused myself to go to the washroom," Theo said, "But Foley grabbed my arm and said," Theo growled in imitation, "if you ruin me, I'll get you while you're alive so you won't know what hit you, and if I don't, I'll curse you from the grave."

I could have said, "So you lied to me about what Foley knew," but I didn't. Theo had been challenged enough for a while. Besides, I was going to start acting maturely around him. Especially if here was a professor who thought dead people were after him.

"So the tablet is the curse?"

"What else? He's telling me not to tell." Theo blanched. "And first thing I do is tell you. I hardly know you."

"I opened the tablet. I'm an accomplice. Safe."

"I'm not safe," he snorted, "I've been cursed."

"Theo," I tried to comfort him, "it's impossible for Cuyler Foley to do this. People just don't send curses from the grave. Here, well, today," I added, for good measure. But

Theo lived as much in ancient Greece and Rome as he did in the contemporary world.

"Theo," I tried again. "There has to be some other explanation. Did anyone overhear your conversation with Foley?"

"No one else was around in the Workroom. Except, well, the guard walked through at one point on her rounds."

"Her" could only be Mama. Sending an ancient Roman curse tablet to a curator? It didn't make sense. The other option I didn't want to mention. Reiko had been sitting in the next room. "Were you talking really loud?"

"No. I don't imagine so. It was more like we'd become snakes, hissing at each other. Gorgons' heads," he said absently.

"I'll find out for you. If the guard heard anything." I wanted desperately to call Reiko. I had so much to tell her, and to ask.

"Thank you." Theo began to get up, gathering the rumpled paper to wrap up the curse tablet.

"Wait, save that for Constable Frick, and I'll get some better wrapping for you. You said yesterday you'd tell her about the bronzes."

"I suppose." Theo had more to tell now than he had yesterday. "But I promised Cuyler I wouldn't."

I put off my phone call to Reiko to guide Theo and his package out the door, upstairs, and to Alice Frick. I said directly to her that Theo had information about reproductions that he wanted to share with the police, and that I'd like to speak to her today, too.

I had made sure Theo would tell the police about his fakes, and gasped as he deftly dissembled and extricated himself. He hid the curse tablet with his big hands behind his back, and instead of mentioning the reproduction Pan, said, "I'd like to speak to Sergeant Daley, please. He's not here? Is he coming, or perhaps one should go to the station? I've been through all the artifacts and the Roman cloak pin is the only one that doesn't belong to MOA. I imagine Cuyler must have brought it in with him. Probably to show me later. He liked to tease. It might be a fraud, too, it's in such good condition." When Constable Frick said she'd set up an appointment for him with Daley, Theo thanked her, gave me a smug smile, and left the room. What an accomplished wordsmith. Twister of truths. Liar, liar, toga's on fire.

I glanced at Constable Frick and found she was observing me. I must have had some look on my face, disbelief or annoyance or plain anger. She waited. Fatigue crept up my legs, my stomach told me again it had no energy, and I wilted. "I need food." I said, "Can I bring a sandwich in here?"

"You take tea, don't you?" Alice responded.

Yes! I hustled to the museum's café. The nearest package was an unfortunate egg and cheese slice sandwich, but I was past caring. I spent the next half hour with Constable Alice Frick, describing all that Theo had not mentioned about his fakes. I told her about the arrival of the curse tablet, too, but less about my role and nothing about Theo's suspicions of who had sent it. I didn't tell her what Max had said, about Sally Luykes hating Foley. That would be third-hand information; the police could find it out for themselves, and I didn't want even peripheral involvement in this knowledge. I felt more tired when I was through. Alice told me that the coroner's report had confirmed that no pointed objects had caused Foley's death, neither the Roman pin nor the arrows. She wouldn't say what determination had been made for the cause of death. That was still "classified", so I asked in a roundabout way about the coffee cup with the arsenic. Alice Frick wanted to know how I'd heard it wasn't from Luykes' coffee set, but that was okay.

She told me only that the cup was a generic one, kept in the lounge for use by anybody. The kind we were drinking out of right now.

───────── ✦❦✦ ─────────

It was almost three. I had to go. What if I'd missed my chance for an appointment with Luykes? I gave the tea things a scrub and actually sprinted into Irene's office. She was typing away and ignored me, all efficiency. I stood in the area between her desk and the mailboxes, obvious but, by giving her a few minutes, meeting the image she took pains to project. She pressed "print" and had to turn towards me as she reached for the paper.

"I've been calling you all day," she said.

"Sorry, I was out in the galleries." A good standard museum excuse for not answering the phone. MOA's concrete walls blocked out cell signals.

"I thought you were going to check in with me. If your appointment's so important."

"Sorry," I repeated. "I wanted to but I got hung up."

"I almost cancelled it."

"Oh, I hope I haven't missed it." How much scraping was I going to have to do?

"It's at five," Irene smiled. "Okay?"

"Sure, Irene." So you almost cancelled it? Who else would stick around for an appointment on a Friday at five? The answer was probably only the Director herself. If Luykes had flown in late last night or this morning, she must be tired, and she'd certainly looked it earlier. But she always had work waiting on her desk. I wondered what mood she'd be in, having to meet me at the end of her long day.

After leaving, I stood for a moment at the top of the stairs to the labs and workrooms. What next? I would call Reiko, and the museum in Montreal to see if a Dr. Sally Luykes had lectured there on Thursday. Making my way rapidly to the lab I was desperate to try Reiko first, but there was another person in the room, Zoe. The earringed Collections Assistant was working against a deadline on the inventory of objects currently housed in Conservation; nothing she could be moved into another area for. Private conversations would have to wait. I could still call the Montreal conservator, though. No I couldn't, it would be going on six-thirty there. I'm calling Reiko anyway.

I had to talk to her before seeing Luykes. Composing what I hoped was a coded message, I let the phone ring.

When I got Reiko on the line I apologized for calling, said I knew I shouldn't, but there'd been an urgent question from an older gentleman who had visited—here I paused to emphasize the information—and did she have a minute now, while I was supervising one of the Collections Assistants? All very formal.

"Reiko, do you know anything about cursing or curse tablets?"

"Do I know something about cursing? Well, yes, Berry, I'm not exactly young."

"That Theo or Mr. Foley might have spoken about at any time?"

"No. But I can teach you swear words. When I get back to work."

"Did you say no? Sure? No conversations when you might have been within earshot, about cursing?"

"I never heard anything about cursing or tablets." Reiko was making it clear, as if she knew something else was being communicated but had no idea what.

"Cursing or killing? Did Theo or Mr. Foley ever have an interest in these, write papers on ancient practices?"

"I have no idea about Foley. Theo wrote about household artifacts and some temple stuff too, but not Greek and Roman military. I think there's something in him that wishes he was a warrior, but he knows himself too well. For him it would all be acting." She rambled on about conflict, hoping it related enough to cursing and killing to feed me whatever I was after. "That's why he can yell about wearing gloves. It's safe, a normal museum argument. He backs away from really significant conflicts. Especially if he's going to feel powerless. Especially in situations where he's the target."

"Thanks, Reiko. This has made things clearer. Take care."

Theo dropped to the bottom of my suspect list for Foley's death.

I turned my attention to figuring out Luykes' trip. Quebec City was only two hours by fast car or a short hop by plane from Montreal. Someone could be in one city, then the other, then back to the first in the space of 24 hours. Daniel had seen Luykes. Even though she was speaking in Montreal, she must have flown in and out of Quebec City, then gone in to Montreal for her noon lecture. Problem solved. I doubted if I could figure out a way to ask Luykes about this at my appointment, but I would try.

Now to find Mama. She had the information about what the guard took from our chemical cupboard, and as well she knew the state Luykes was in after her quick trip. This would be useful before I walked into the Director's office.

Back to hanging around at the guards' station. Back to smiling and light chit-chat, this time with a young guard whom I couldn't remember seeing before. The talk lifted my mood, though, and I would need it for my 5 o'clock with Luykes. The guard said Mama was somewhere on her rounds. I quickly toured the museum. On my second fly past of the security desk, the young guard stopped me to say he'd made a mistake; Mama was at her regular appointment with Dr. Luykes.

Regular appointment? Maybe that's what they were talking about this morning. But if it was so regular, why couldn't it be broken just this once, for something I said was urgent? Had Irene even tried? Or was I just a lowly intern? Maybe to Irene, who chose to exercise what limited power she had in her job at MOA. But not to Sally Luykes, I hoped. Then I thought about how the Director had ignored me when I was cleaning the sherds in the workroom, and how genuine she had been with the students in the lounge. But she was genuine with me in her office, wasn't she, when she explained the cleaning she wanted me to do? Not if it was true what Max had said about her real feelings for Cuyler Foley.

Down to the lab again. Zoe was still there. I groused at the emails and two new phone messages. My brain flitted to Daniel. That was a better diversion. First I enjoyed his voice, then I caressed the image of his face kept in the back of my mind. Finally his news. No, dammit, it was not normal to fly into Quebec City from the west coast when you were speaking in Montreal at noon. Nor to be back in Quebec City that evening. Damn, wasn't it 4:30 by now when Zoe would be gone? I could phone Reiko and talk openly. But Zoe was still over there at the lab table.

What was Sally Luykes up to in Quebec City? On the radio she said she hadn't bought a weathervane. Sally Luykes was in my age range, and we missed enough of our sleep with the hot flashes without having to work all day and then jet-set to the east for a three in the morning arrival. Something was up. Damn damn damn. I felt Zoe's eyes on my back, and, sure enough, when I turned around I knew I'd been swearing out loud.

"It's nothing," I said, "just stuff I should have done."

Zoe smiled back. Anyone at any job understood.

"Aren't you supposed to be gone at four-thirty?" I added. I hoped she took it as a concern for her health and welfare.

"I got in late. Those buses, you know, they don't run the same in summer when classes aren't on."

"Damn nuisance," I said, and Zoe took it I meant the buses.

I said out loud, "Well, I'm going to the coffee room. I can't do any more work anyway, I'm exhausted."

"More work?" said a voice in my ear that sounded like Daniel's.

I cursed back in French.

And then, finally, I got it. I deciphered the riddle of Sally Luykes. A large grey Roman tablet unrolled before my eyes. I thought it was going to say, "took you long enough". On it was inscribed simply, "FOOLED YOV!"

"That's not so bad for a curse." And I hauled my body, my brain, and its big grey lead tablet upstairs and made tea.

---

As I sipped the amber nectar, I contemplated the origin of the curse. Sally Luykes, whom I was going to see in a little more than fifteen minutes, had obtained a curse tablet or reasonable facsimile in Quebec City. A replica of an antiquity made before Christ: B.C. From a perfectionist artist who worked in metals. Said curse tablet found its way directly into Theo's mailbox on her return. Why? Don't know. But maybe it had to do with the fakes; maybe she already knew that Theo was selling them. Or it went back to that conversation between her and Theo just before she left. I was going to be seeing her about the fakes. If she looked like she already knew . . . how would she know about curse tablets? Maybe she learned about them in school, or from Theo, or from the museum's collections. The point was, though, she knew a curse tablet would really get to Theo. How? Because Mama did overhear those guys when they were talking in the workroom. Mama heard Foley curse Theo. And when Foley died, Luykes put her knowledge together and knew what to do.

"*Mama has a regular appointment with Luykes every Friday*," I thought. "*Mama is Luykes' eyes and ears at MOA. She's a goddamn spy. She's sitting in there right now, telling Luykes everything she hears and sees.*" I got up, hurting myself on the corner of the lounge table, crossed over to the main office, and went righteously to eavesdropping.

Irene had gone for the day. I sat in the secretary's empty chair, thinking I could say I was just waiting for my appointment if anyone came in. To no-one's surprise, the museum's temperature and humidity system controlling the artifact environment still wasn't working properly, and with the sun beaming in all afternoon wherever there were skylights or windows, the heat inside had ramped up. Many office doors were open, including Luykes'.

Lorna stepped out of Luykes' office. Was she always in on the regular appointment with Mama and Luykes? The single silver feather on her necklace rocked as she concentrated on not rattling the Director's teapot and the three cups.

"I'm here for an appointment," my cover story said to her retreating back. Lorna was heading straight for the lounge. "I've got some more bags in my office," she was saying, "this stuff's too cold." Luykes' door stayed open. No curse operating here.

I wheeled myself as far forward as I could towards that door while still looking like I was occupying the chair at the secretary's desk until my appointment. Mama was coughing. She'd probably been a smoker if she wasn't one now. Luykes said a few words with an accent I'd never heard. Mama replied with something very gutteral, between coughs. They spoke for another minute like this. I didn't catch a word. Maybe eavesdropping isn't like eye focus: the organ does not improve with exercise. I heard a burst of laughter. Luykes said in an English I understood, "You're getting a good vocabulary, Mama."

And Mama answered, "Thanks. I have a lot to thank you for."

"Oh, Mama, stop that. You give back. You're my oldest friend here."

"Feel that old, too."

There was a chuckle. "Hey, look," Mama said. "That raven on the roof's rolling a soda pop can. Raven the Trickster. Loves the shiny stuff. Like that trickster Foley, eh. Never could keep his beak away from the gold or silver."

There was complete silence. Then Luykes spoke, and her voice was different. Choked or something. And spitting. I could barely hear her words now, she was probably looking out the window or her voice had dropped. But, unmistakably, I heard, ". . . did it . . . gave . . . little bit each time . . . creature made me sick . . . turn the tables . . . suffer."

A cold clamminess penetrated my skin

There was no answer from Mama. She probably made some movement.

Luykes tried to control a sob. Then another. Then, " . . .never meant to kill . . ."

As I heard a chair inside the office creak back, Lorna returned balancing tea-tray paraphernalia and a large glass of water. I saw her coming and bent down towards the garbage pail as if I was looking for something. Or to throw up in it. I didn't think Lorna even noticed me, she was too intent on not spilling the water.

"The kettle's on. Oh! Dr Luykes? Is everything okay?"

"Thanks for the water, Lorn," said Mama, "Everything's fine. Sally's just upset about this week, and she hasn't had much sleep either." It sounded like Mama had moved near Luykes.

"Sorry," I heard Sally Luykes say, and blow her nose. "It's nothing, Lorna. Like Mama said, I'm just overtired, and it's been such a long and terrible week. Please sit down." A chair creaked again. "We only have a few minutes before someone else is coming in to see me."

And a uniformed Alice Frick walked into the main office. She went right up to Luykes' door and knocked, acknowledging me with a nod.

"Is that you, Berenice?" came Luykes' voice.

"No, she's waiting," said Constable Frick. "But I need to see you first."

"Come in," said Luykes.

"May I see you privately?" said Frick.

"Privately? I'm not feeling very well." I could picture Sally Luykes wanting to explain red eyes and nose.

"Please."

"Lorna, would you mind?" said Luykes. "Thanks. Mama, could you pour me some of your water?" She addressed Frick. "I don't mind if Mama is here, if it's all the same to you."

Lorna came out of the Director's office and saw me. She hesitated and slowly let go of the door handle she was closing so it didn't shut all the way. Quietly she propped herself on Irene's desk. Luykes would know the door was still open, but the other two would have their backs to it. We were rewarded when the door stayed open. Maybe Luykes thought she might need us.

My legitimate excuse to stay was my appointment. I would wait Frick out. The office clock showed 5:05. Out of the corner of my eye I saw a man in full tennis outfit striding down the hallway. Max glanced towards the office as he passed, and hesitated when he saw our two tense figures. Curiosity rising on his face, he stuck his head in. Lorna put a finger to her lips, and Max placed his tennis racquet silently on the floor. He leaned against the doorframe, eyeing first Lorna then me, trying to figure out what was going on.

Constable Frick began to tell Sally Luykes about the fakes. I let out my breath. I knew this part of the story; I had told Frick. Lorna hadn't heard it, though, and her face grew paler and paler. What did Mama look like? She had probably withdrawn into her mask.

Frick laid out the details in a few words. Max made his eyes and mouth pop wide open at me and Lorna. Somebody inside the Director's office sighed. Luykes said, "I knew Theo was into something. I knew he had a hand in the Shop replicas, but I didn't know he was masterminding fakes like this. He told me he was making extras for teaching."

"If you thought he was into something, why didn't you stop him? Or ask us to investigate?"

"You know, I almost asked you to investigate our other senior curator. Max Turpin."

The white tennis body jerked and Max was all concentration now. Luykes was saying, "There's been some rumours of sexual harassment. And then Cuyler Foley dies, and I know Max and Cuyler used to go out tomcatting together, gallery openings and artists' parties. Maybe Cuyler knew something that Max didn't want let out, and there was some blackmail that ended badly. Poor Cuyler never was the equal of Max, in any sense; he never understood that beside Max, he was a fat and declawed alley cat." The hard, angry creases around Max's jaw dissolved into a smile.

"But Max," Luykes was thinking out loud. "I don't believe he was in the museum on Monday night when Cuyler died."

"No," Frick corroborated. "We have that list. Max wasn't on it."

Luykes's voice cracked as she exclaimed, "Theo! Making and selling fakes! I had some suspicions, but . . ." Her voice trailed off, then picked up again. "Well, my suspicions only became more pronounced recently. Especially after Cuyler Foley died. I honestly thought Theo might have done, well, that. I had to leave for Montreal, and I came back as soon as I could, this morning. Theo is a senior curator, you know. I guess I didn't want to let my suspicions be known right away and influence your investigation. But I did try to stop Theo when I got back. I had words with him."

That was a neat way of saying "Roman curse tablet". Luykes had tailor-made a stop to Theo's forgeries that could not have been more effective in reaching him.

---

Constable Frick said, "I have another matter."

"Yes?"

"Mr. Foley has been known to you for a long time, hasn't he?"

"He's been an art buyer and seller for as long as I've been a linguist. Even before, when I was in graduate school."

"Dr. Luykes, Mr. Foley had a personal association with your family, didn't he?"

"I'm not sure I understand what you mean."

"Dr. Luykes, forgive me for bringing this up, but was it not Cuyler Foley who ran over your little daughter in 1972? At Alert Bay?"

No voice or breath answered.

Frick broke the silence. "We've been doing some investigation."

"Yes," said Luykes quietly. "Yes." She coughed. "My little girl, broken and bleeding. Her legs like a bent puppet and her face . . ." Her voice broke into the sounds of soft crying. We heard Mama's croak as she offered Luykes a tissue.

"Constable Frick," Luykes began again, her voice less weepy, choked instead with anger. "I hope you never go through something like this, personally or professionally. When that murdering driver got out and saw Nathalie, he just had this annoyed expression. I was screaming and running towards my daughter. All Cuyler Foley said was, 'Sorry. She ran right out on the road.' He offered to pay for the funeral. Everything was a dollar transaction to him."

I could hear a chair shift back. Constable Frick said softly, "Dr. Luykes, I'm sorry to have to ask you to come to the station. To answer a few questions."

Lorna and I gaped at each other.

"Do I need a lawyer?" Luykes weary voice answered.

"I can't advise you, but I suggest that you do what makes you feel most comfortable, Dr. Luykes. And it is easier to do it from here than there."

I heard keys being punched, and a short conversation with not much detail except for the station address. Then came slow, low shuffling sounds from inside the office. A computer fan stopped. A desk lamp was turned off. A voice said, "You've got the wrong woman."

# Chapter
# 20

## Friday Ends

Lorna jumped up from the secretary's desk, her hand stifling her mouth. My arms were wrapped tight around my chest.

A small wail from the Director's office. Then louder. Luykes, shrieking "Mama!"

Constable Frick said, "Please." Her voice was scratchy. "Sit down. Mama, what are you saying?"

"You've got the wrong woman. I gave him the poison, but I didn't know he had a bad heart," came Mama's clear reply.

I don't think anyone heard our gasps of shock, there was noise enough from inside Luykes' office.

"You killed Cuyler Foley?" said Frick.

"I guess so."

"Why?"

"Because," said Mama, "He killed my granddaughter."

"Your granddaughter?

"Yes."

"What was her name?"

"Nathalie Luykes."

265

"Nathalie Luykes was your grand-daughter?"

"That's what I said."

"Mama, Dr. Luykes," said Constable Frick, "Please explain. How Nathalie Luykes is your granddaughter, and, Dr. Luykes, your daughter."

"She was," said Mama, "my daughter's daughter." Mama spaced out every word so that if Frick didn't understand the definition of grand-daughter, she understood it now.

"I adopted her," murmured Luykes. "My husband and I. The mother left Nathalie with her own mother, Mama here, Rose Mam, and when Nathalie was eight months old, Rose asked if I would take her. After a year, I adopted her formally, with Rose's blessing."

"You let a white woman adopt your child?" screamed a voice beside me. Lorna was shaking. Not from anger. Fear. This woman who had been important in her life since she was ten had just confessed to giving away a granddaughter and to a murder, and Lorna had burst.

"I did good for her," shouted Mama through the door. Constable Frick was out of her seat and opening the door wide, glaring at us.

"Let them stay," said Luykes. Nobody moved, except eventually Constable Frick who returned to her seat. We all stared at each other.

"Did your daughter consent to this adoption? The child's mother?" Frick's back turned on us again as she faced Mama.

"My daughter was run by a pimp. She couldn't consent to nothing. She left Nathalie to me. I tried to find my girl here, downtown. She was seventeen and gone to hell. Three years later she was dead."

"You didn't want to raise Nathalie yourself?"

"Of course I did!" Mama glowered at Constable Frick. "But you don't understand what happens when you lose.

Everything goes. You'll never know." An edge of bitter anger vibrated in Mama's voice. Then she said evenly, "I was a mess. My husband beat up on me. You know he was mean." She looked out at Lorna, who nodded back through tears. "I came to Vancouver to get my daughter. Didn't have money. Didn't have work. But at least I had a friend. A good friend who coached me for a job. I got to be a guard here. Full-time." She turned to Sally. "It would've been a lot different for Nathalie and her mom if I'd been where I'm at today. I've turned things around. Recycled my life."

Sally Luykes opened her mouth to say something, but no words came out. I wanted to close my eyes; my image of Mama couldn't bear much more of this.

Luykes started to stutter and stared at a piece of paper on her desk. "I owe you, Rose. I have for a long time." She lifted her head from her desktop to look Mama in the eyes. "It's me who owes. The precious time with Nathalie." She swallowed. "And you still don't get that I owe you in this job, too. Directing a museum is about people, not just artifacts. My head's in my books, and you keep me in the real world."

Then we all heard Lorna say, "Mama, what about your own family?" Lorna couldn't let go of the fact that Mama had let Luykes adopt her grand-daughter. It was easier than thinking Mama was a murderer.

Mama turned to face Lorna. Her voice was quiet, composed. "Don't have none now, no family," she said. "That's why I'm learning my language from Sally. Getting in touch with my inner ancestor." Mama's lips twitched. "Every Friday here in Sally's office, but too much homework!" There was a coughing chuckle. "That summer, when Sally was learning the Kwakwala language in Alert Bay, she began to teach me Delaware, my language, because she found out I was born in Ontario, near Sarnia. Right near Michigan in the States. She'd studied Delaware way back, tried to put down on paper what the couple of elders who still spoke it remembered. I'll at least have my ancestors."

Mama laughed out loud. We all stared. "Or," she said, "at least the ones that spoke Delaware. And then there were the ones that spoke French, and the German farmer. I'm making real progress with my English too, you know."

Constable Frick laughed softly. We did too, but it all sounded very hollow.

Then suddenly Mama stood up and leaned on the desk so she could see us as well as Frick and Luykes in the office. She waited, open-mouthed, and then finally spoke.

"I ain't going to be nobody's victim," she said. "I decided that for sure when I saw my dead daughter. I made hard decisions. I maybe didn't have choices, Lorna, only hard decisions." Mama stopped talking and looked at the desk. We all waited. "I'm sorry I disappointed you," she muttered. "I'm sorry I didn't think things through this time."

Lorna was crying openly. I was in one big knot, cold to the bone, hugging my arms. Max remained impassive, but his fingers drummed against the doorframe. After her speech, Mama sat down. A few more minutes passed in silence, then Constable Frick picked up her questioning.

"How did you kill Cuyler Foley?"

Mama explained, "With arsenic. You know that."

"That was your cup, then? Here in Dr. Luykes's office?"

"Not mine. I got it from the lounge."

"When?"

"When he got here."

"When did Foley get here? Describe it to me."

"This big guy got here around four-thirty. I was on at the guards' station, so I knew Sally and Theo were both over at the next building because I'd seen them leave. The man asked for them, said he was early. I signed him in anyway and, when I saw his name printed out like that, it just burned across me. I saw him like I'd seen him thirty years ago. Like Sally told you. Stepping out of his big car, irritated at the ugliness under his wheel. Here he was now, the first time I guess I'd really put two and two together, and he was smiling. Then Max," she gave a nod towards the door, "came by, and started talking to him."

"And?"

"And I went down to Conservation, I got the arsenic out of the chemical cupboard, and I made him a cup of strong coffee. Max had put him outside Sally's office to wait. I gave him the coffee even though he'd already been given a cup. Told him this cup would taste better and took the other out of his hands. He'd drained it anyway."

"Wasn't Reiko in the lab when you went down?" I interjected.

"Sure, but she was working on those files. She asked if there was anything I needed. I said just some alcohol to clean the tape player the guards have, so she said take the ice-o-pro-pill alcohol in the chemical cupboard. I'd done it before, and she was very busy." Mama was watching my face. She anticipated my next question.

"I had to make up something for those files afterwards. I didn't know if you'd miss the arsenic I took. You probably measure every little teaspoon." She was still looking at me. "I told a story about a guard using your solvents, to see if you knew stuff was gone from your chemicals. Found out too late you didn't know. I'd already gone back down late that shift and moved some numbers around after Reiko'd left the room. I was pretty scattered by then."

Constable Frick picked up her line of questioning with, "So you decided to kill him."

"No. I wasn't thinking at all. I don't think I knew what I was doing. I just wanted to give him something back for what he'd given me. Maybe it was sitting in my gut. Years of hearing about his dealings, him cheating people when he bought stuff, knowing he'd robbed me, too, of Nathalie, and her of her only life on this earth, and then seeing him right there in front of me."

My chest collapsed and I couldn't rise from my seat. Nobody could move. Not Max or Lorna either. Constable Frick stood to leave, and gestured for Mama now to do the same. Sally Luykes stared from her chair, and when Mama said "Bye for now," she started and said, "I'm coming with you."

"Nope," said Mama. "A big-shot lawyer'll come, that's good enough. You get some sleep. You're running on empty. Drop by tomorrow."

Mama walked straight towards Lorna and grasped her in a tight hug. She held on while Lorna cried. "Don't worry, girl, I've come through worse than this. Much worse. Hey, you know me, we're survivors, girl. You and me both." Lorna had to nod.

"Lorna," Mama continued, "there's a Friday late afternoon spot that's just opened up on Sally's calendar. You don't need Delaware practice, so you're going to sit in this office and Sally, you're going to tell her everything you can about management. Don't look at me like that, Lorna! I'm not going to be the next Director of the museum." Mama grinned. "See, my teeth aren't good enough." Lorna laughed despite her tears.

Mama let go and turned and looked at me. The corners of her lips twitched. "Berry, I'm thinking of you for a place on the Board of a recycling depot downtown. Only temporary, mind you, don't get any ideas." Her eyes shone and then she started to walk straight out ahead of Constable Frick.

"Mama!" My voice scraped. "Wait! I've got to ask her one more thing, please, Alice!" Curious stares greeted this use of Frick's first name. The procession stopped.

"Mama, the arsenic you took, what kind of a bottle was it in?"

"Glass bottle."

"I mean, was it brown or white?"

"The colour? Did it have a colour?"

"Did it look clear like a mayonnaise jar, or did it look dark?"

"Mayo."

"Are you sure?"

"No."

"Did it have anything written on it?"

"A label?"

"Yes."

"Sure."

"Well?"

"I don't know exactly. Find it for yourself."

"Can you picture it, Mama?" I pleaded.

Mama snorted. She lowered her head and laughed. Keeping her gaze down, she said, "Berry, I didn't want to say this here, but what I saw was 'arse' written on that jar of yours."

I heard scuffling as people shifted in place.

"Arse?" I said. "Really?" More shifting, hemming and hawing. "Like this? I reached back to Irene's desk, grabbed a pen and some paper and wrote. I showed it to Mama.

"Yeah, that's it."

"Are you sure?"

"That's it exactly. This time I'm sure."

I just let go, whooping and jumping. Even Alice Frick looked shocked. I yelled, "It's okay" and hugged Mama hard. Her mask of courage momentarily slipped, and I saw for the first time an agitated anxiety. I repeated, "It's okay! It's okay!" Mama's face transformed back to neutral, she heaved her arms and broke my grip and said something guttural.

And I burst into tears. "It wasn't arsenic!" I wiped a childish runny nose on my sleeve. Everyone was staring at me, Frick moved to get me away from Mama, and even Max had his feet planted, arms poised for action.

"You didn't give him arsenic!" I exulted.

"I didn't? I meant to."

"Shut up! You didn't. *Arrête!*"

"What?"

Constable Frick took over. "Give me that paper, please, Berry. What you showed Mama." She had solidified back into one hundred percent policewoman.

I showed her. Lorna and Max craned their necks. Sally watched from behind her desk, her face rigid. Mama glanced at Sally.

"Look," I said, and jabbed the paper. "Mama took the wrong bottle. She saw 'arsi' like it could be 'arsinic'. The bottle was marked 'Ar.Si'. But arsenic is just 'As', that's the chemical standard. The police've got everything from our cabinet. You can check."

"What's Ar.Si?" Max said, pronouncing it "Arseye."

"Aerated silica. Aerogel silica. That's not the chemical formula, just a short form Reiko and I use for ourselves. We put it in the solvent cabinet to hide it from the students because, well, it's tiny particles that fly into your lungs when you open it and could give you silicosis. But actually it was in the cabinet because our new order hasn't come in, and we needed every bit for 'Beads and Seeds'. For the infills and paint, to matte the colours. So we hid it." As I rattled on my face beamed like a lighthouse.

"You fool," muttered Mama under her breath. She snatched a look at Sally Luykes, then faced me again. "So

I might have killed myself by opening that jar, eh?" she declared.

I didn't answer. My lousy hearing had still picked up, "You fool". Was she referring to herself or me? My jaw dropped as I remembered what I'd overheard earlier, when Sally Luykes broke down crying. When Constable Frick was about to take her down to the station for questioning. Now they'd get Luykes. I'd left my mark again, infinitely worse than a scratch on a sherd of old pottery. Crumpling backwards, I slumped into Irene's chair. Lorna and Alice Frick were all over me, thinking I'd fainted. Pushing down into the chair, I took my time, unaware of how many minutes passed.

My closed eyes saw a large three-panelled painting, a triptych of "Means", "Motive", and "Opportunity" hung as if on exhibition. Hung with gallery lighting on a cold white wall. The left hand panel showed "Means", painted an unusual brilliant yellow: orpiment, the ancient arsenic-based pigment. The right hand panel, "Opportunity", displayed a long calligraphy of names. I saw familiar ones who were in the museum Monday night, and museum staff who knew about the pesticide research project. Reiko was near the top of the list, and I was not far behind; other names were hardly decipherable. The central panel, the largest, was labelled "Motive". A faded photograph of Cuyler Foley was pinned at its centre. My aging eyes were jerking the photo to the left and back again. The eyes and the brain are not separate, and I knew the face of the murderer.

All along I had been asking the wrong question: who had it in for Cuyler Foley. Now I understood. Foley was on the Means panel, not the Motive. Cuyler Foley was the victim, the means to an end, not the end in itself. The triptych displaying photograph and text was a contemporary work of art. A second clue. It all hung together.

"If Mama didn't put poison in the coffee, who did?" Lorna voiced the question on everyone's mind.

From my chair, I pointed. "I don't want to say this." I turned to face the murderer. "Max. Max gave Foley the cup with the arsenic."

<hr />

All eyes turned on Max Turpin. His lips had become as colourless as his tennis clothes. His eyes had filmed over. I knew where we stood. The place in life he'd described to me during our lunch, when he'd shared the sorrow of his brother's leukemia. "We spend our lives trying to keep control, make our world a certain way. Sometimes we just can't."

A spreading snarl meant he was going to try this time, though. It was as if every collapsed cell of his body had been flooded and then burst. Max shuddered, and his fists pounded against the doorframe. His voice spit "Fuck!" and "Jesus H. Christ!" and "Can you believe this?" His eyes darted like the knife I'd thought Saul Samuels had in his coat. A metallic glint, steely sharp. The same coldness, the same quick sting of a movement, just enough slim efficiency to do the job. Directed at me.

"Fuck! You nuts?" he yelled. "What the hell are you talking about?" The Curator of Contemporary Art would fight me down to the last. He was respected, intelligent, a golden boy. I was a temporary intern. Who would have the harder fight? And what real evidence did I have? Besides my own smarts, what I'd heard and figured out, and my gut feeling? I would land this fish, though, finish what I'd started. He'd launched the boat and I could see wild water coming.

"Bloody conservators. Liar! Why would I kill Foley?"

Frick's eyes riveted to me.

I rose from the chair so I stood near his level.

"To get what you wanted."

"What the hell would I want from Foley?"

But right now it was me Max wanted something from. In one white leap, the tomcat sprang. His claws sank into my chest. Alice Frick pushed between us and yanked hard to pull his arm away. Frick forced her face inches from his, and said "assault". He let go. Mama had ducked out. I prayed for reinforcements.

Pain and shock and tension almost froze me, but I wasn't going to show how much it hurt. Max would not get that satisfaction. In this arena I had enough experience. "It wasn't Foley you wanted something from, you wanted revenge."

Revenge. Hardly a word in the mission statement of most museums. But if museums have been pegged as western culture's placid backwater, where the dust floats sedately down through the decades, I had news for western culture.

Mama arrived back. Two uniforms appeared at the door. Good. More witnesses.

"Max, you killed Foley to get at Sally Luykes."

"Fuck you." He sneered. "Excuse my French."

Constable Frick intervened, "Explain your accusations, Berry. What's your evidence?"

I ignored the last half. Holding her gaze, I tried to keep an eye on Max as well. "Max has wanted the Director's job for a long time. He also knows all about Sally Luykes' history. They were friends at Alert Bay. He knew who killed her daughter."

"So you assume I knew this, that's great evidence, and so I killed Foley. This would have been a service to Sally, not fucking revenge."

"You've always had your eye on the Director's job," I repeated, watching his face. He didn't flinch, but his eyes couldn't stay still. "The only way you could get it was by competition. You lost the competition, and Luykes won it because you'd tried to sell a painting with a forged signature. Everyone thinks that's why you hate Reiko, because she made it public that the painting wasn't by who you said it was. But you told me yourself you suspected Sally Luykes behind Reiko."

There was an audible intake of breath. I continued. "She'd put the bug in Reiko's ear about the painting having Bells' signature on the back. Reiko, being honest, didn't hide what the conservation treatment had discovered. Sally Luykes knew that by telling Reiko, ethical Reiko would go to the auction house and tell them the truth. After that, no one would ever hire you as director of a public museum. Your ambitions would be over. And at any time Sally Luykes could use your tacit approval of a painting forgery against you. You hate her."

I wanted to turn and see how Luykes was taking all this, but I couldn't. I didn't trust Max not to strike.

"What are you talking about? What painting forgery? You told me a bronze," said Frick.

I didn't answer. My eyes were fixed on Max. "You had to get even. You saw your opportunity and gave the coffee laced with arsenic to Foley, laying the ground so it would look as if Sally Luykes had done it. You insinuated to me she might have plotted it."

"Sally did do it!" he bellowed. "She gave Foley arsenic. And she told me any number of times she wished him dead. She said she was going to make him sick. He sickened her; she was going to sicken him. Sally knew about the arsenic. So I tried a little test. I told her the police thought Foley might have been poisoned, and she was catatonic until I mentioned curare and didn't mention arsenic. The look of relief on her face said it all. She did it."

"Prove it," came a strangled voice from the desk area.

"At the station!" commanded Constable Frick. "Everyone here is going down to the station. Now."

---

I was conscious of something that I hadn't even guessed before. The Museum of Anthropology was a wonderful museum, but I wasn't ever going to apply for a permanent job at MOA. I knew what would happen. I would come to work every morning, put on a lab coat and feel a death scene at my back. I'd walk through Visible Storage, lose my footing on construction debris no longer there, and scream.

How often while I'd been cleaning those shattered fragments had I told myself I was asking too much to expect perfection, the ideal? How often had I chastised myself for not living up to expectations? Human fallibility was no excuse for not trying, though, striving to be the best I could. That was the other reason I couldn't work here. I'd admired people in this room too much, and I was too disappointed in them. Maybe as an eager intern I'd put them on a too-high museum plinth. Falling, they'd shattered my illusions. I couldn't take a job at MOA after all this. I'd look elsewhere to continue in conservation.

Once one of my profs in conservation school was lecturing on the factors that deteriorated objects. He showed a painting from a historic house situated by a river that flooded its banks every decade or so. The surface of the painting was cockled and broken from water damage. "What agent really caused the deterioration?" the prof had thundered. "The river water? The person who stored the painting in the basement when they knew the river habitually flooded? The funding agent that didn't give them enough money for off-site storage?" All true. No one black-and-white answer. I suspected the same with Foley's murder. Would Max's cup of coffee have had the same results if Sally Luykes hadn't been giving him other small doses of the poison, as she had as much as admitted to Mama? Who could prove which quantities happened when, anyway?

When this year's out, maybe I would go to Quebec, see if I could get a job nearer Daniel. Let the younger generation, the new bright lights take this stunning museum into the future. Let them put the sherds together.

―◦◦◦―

A low voice growled, "She's making this up!" My arms tightened. I knew that venom meant me. Max leapt and tried to slug me again. I swung and got a bit of his pretty face just as the two uniforms at the door grabbed and pulled him back. Alice Frick did not mention assault. I chilled.

"I'll give my statement at the station." My voice was hoarse.

"I'm going to sue you for assault! And libel, Berenice Cates."

"I have a lawyer," I replied. "A very good one. Mama's lawyer." I looked over at her. Lorna had her arms draped around her, and Mama stood silently accepting the embrace. She nodded slowly back at me.

"You've got no proof of anything!" Max's bark brought me back to his corner. "But I have. Sally did it!"

"This is what I've got, Max," I responded. "For you, good news and bad news. The good news is, and you can tell your tennis partner, you really are a schlemiel. What you once said you wished for. The bad news is, you are also an incredible schmuck."

Max actually laughed. A kind of choking, but this man was, for the moment, his old self again. "Maybe I am. I was afraid someone would say that one day." Then his mouth set. "Berry, I mean you no harm. But I can't let this crap happen to me. You can't prove anything . . . can you." It was a declaration, not a question.

"No, and I don't want to." I said. "I'll give my statement at the station, and that's all I know. It's just words. Some of them overheard. Someone else can try and prove whatever's inferred. All I know is insinuendo. There's no smoking gun."

"Insinuendo?" Max choked up again. "You're too much." He perused my face and said, as if no one else was present, "Have I disappointed you, Berry?"

I looked back at him. The charm in his eyes, the fun, the intelligence, the dyed black hair. The real and symbolic pain in my breast. "Yes, you sure have. More than you know. I'm sorry about all this crap too, Max. Disappointed? You can start when you told me you covered up that signature on the back of the painting." I swung around to Sally Luykes. Her jaw was open, her eyes red. "Let's just say, that's when I knew how much what I still want to do in my life is different from you. How I'm different and want to stay that way."

I turned back to face Max. "I'd like to think there's part of my youth I'm never going to lose. Like living my ideals. With you, there's too much smoke and shaving mirrors."

We were herded out of the office. Mama wheezed, and her steps faltered. She coughed, then stopped altogether, blowing her nose. I caught up and held out my arm. She gave me a quick wink and started matching my steps.

"You're a real troublemaker, Berry," she grunted. "A real good one. We need you on that Recycling Board. City Council's giving us the old, what you said, the shit de merde."

I managed a weak smile and shook my head. I had no energy for words.

"Berry, the Recycling could be gone in a year if Council makes us sort with machines. Help us out. Preserve what's alive, not just what's in this crazy museum."

"Preserve good things," I muttered my old toast.

"We need a pro like you. Okay?"

The corners of my lips worked themselves into a smile. "Sure." I took a long breath. "I don't have much on here in the evenings unless a fun tenant moves in upstairs. Reiko won't be needing her house or Hound Dog looked after. You, me and her'll be back at work Monday. Let's talk then."

---

I guess people would say the conservation intern had done good work—the mess was pretty well cleaned up. But that night, as we walked out of the museum, I'd been too tired to remember one of conservation's basic principles: the details are important. All three of us were not back at work at the beginning of the week.

Monday, Reiko had greeted me with a huge hug. The lab danced again to "Rock Around the Clock" and Buddy Holly's "Rave On". Mama wasn't there, though. She'd been booked for attempted murder. She had, after all, intended to kill Foley. Saul Samuels was flying back. He declared he'd have her free on bail and in the end exonerated; she'd done nothing criminal.

After work that day I volunteered for the recycling outfit, and began searching for a new job. Archaeological digs needed conservators, and collections stowed in the ground for centuries might remain peacefully dormant. This museum had proved far too exciting.